"A complex and engaging universe."
—*Open Book Society*

BLACK SPRING

SHE WAS AN AGENT OF DEATH. NOW SHE'S HUMANITY'S ONLY HOPE FOR SURVIVAL.

A Black Wings Novel

CHRISTINA HENRY

Author of *Black Heart*

ACE

$7.99 U.S.
$9.99 CAN

ISBN 978-0-425-26678-6

9 780425 266786

50799

PRAISE FOR

BLACK HEART

"A fast-paced, spine-tingling adventure ride that won't let you go till the end . . . Maddy is one gutsy heroine . . . A very good read . . . I can't wait to see where [Maddy] goes from here." —*Fresh Fiction*

"With this sixth entry in the heart-pumping Black Wings series, Henry delivers once again. Maddy is a strong, courageous character, and she grows with every book in the series. The supporting characters are just as engaging . . . The plot also continues to develop with steady, satisfying action." —*RT Book Reviews*

"For urban paranormal action, this is a good choice. If you like quirky mini-sidekicks, there's a gargoyle with an attitude in here that you should meet. If you want to hobnob with Lucifer, Puck, Titania and other immortals, you'll have a great time. *Black Heart* really has a heart of gold." —*Kings River Life Magazine*

"Nothing is as it seems . . . *Black Heart* is a pretty wild ride, and I firmly remain a huge fan of this series." —*My Bookish Ways*

BLACK CITY

"A complex and engaging universe. The monsters and mythological creatures encountered are dark and delightfully horrifying." —*Open Book Society*

"*Black City* is the butt-kicking continuation of the Black Wings novels. It's fast-paced with intriguing twists that keep the reader enthralled right to the last page and wanting more." —*Fresh Fiction*

continued . . .

JAN 1 5

BLACK NIGHT

"The Madeline Black series employs a blend of two great common urban fantasy tropes: the 'big reveal' (where a mundane character discovers magic exists) and an open world where magic is commonly accepted. The mix of these two story lines creates a chemistry that adds new zest to familiar concepts, an energy that I thoroughly enjoy."
—*All Things Urban Fantasy*

"Madeline Black is back and super badass in her second installment . . . If you're looking for a brilliant urban fantasy with page-turning action, witty dialogue and fun characters—this is your book." —*Rex Robot Reviews*

"The style of this book is just like the first book in the series—playful and light, yet also adventurous and dark . . . The bottom line is that if you enjoy adventure stories, you will enjoy this book, especially if you're a nonstop-action junky." —*SFRevu*

BLACK WINGS

"A fun, fast ride through the gritty streets of magical Chicago, *Black Wings* has it all: a gutsy heroine just coming into her power, badass bad guys, a sexy supernatural love interest and a scrappy gargoyle sidekick. Highly recommended." —Nancy Holzner, author of *Hellhound*

"An entertaining urban fantasy starring an intriguing heroine . . . The soul-eater-serial-killer mystery adds to an engaging Chicago joyride as courageous Madeline fears this unknown adversary but goes after the lethal beast."
—*Midwest Book Review*

"Henry shows that she is up to the challenge of debuting in a crowded genre. The extensive background of her imaginative world is well integrated with the action-packed plot, and the satisfying conclusion leaves the reader primed for the next installment." —*Publishers Weekly*

BLACK SPRING

CHRISTINA HENRY

ACE BOOKS, NEW YORK

THE BERKLEY PUBLISHING GROUP
Published by the Penguin Group
Penguin Group (USA) LLC
375 Hudson Street, New York, New York 10014

USA • Canada • UK • Ireland • Australia • New Zealand • India • South Africa • China

penguin.com

A Penguin Random House Company

BLACK SPRING

An Ace Book / published by arrangement with the author

Ace Books are published by The Berkley Publishing Group.
ACE and the "A" design are trademarks of Penguin Group (USA) LLC.

For information, address: The Berkley Publishing Group,
a division of Penguin Group (USA) LLC,
375 Hudson Street, New York, New York 10014.

ISBN: 978-0-425-26678-6

PUBLISHING HISTORY
Ace mass-market edition / November 2014

PRINTED IN THE UNITED STATES OF AMERICA

10 9 8 7 6 5 4 3 2 1

Cover art by Kris Keller.

For all the fans who have
read and loved Maddy's adventures.
This one is for you.

ACKNOWLEDGMENTS

Thanks to Danielle Stockley for shepherding this series through many ups and downs. These books are better because of you.

Much gratitude to Lucienne Diver, agent extraordinaire and part-time therapist to crazy writers.

Special thanks to Kris Keller for all the beautiful covers for this series.

I could not get through each book without the friendship and support of my running buddies, Anne Posner and Pamela Schneider.

Love to all of my family, who have supported me throughout this process.

1

I WOKE TO THE SOUND OF DOGS BARKING. MY EYES drifted open halfway, just enough to register the sun streaming through the open blinds. Nathaniel's arm was thrown around my waist, his body snuggled into my back. The child inside my belly shifted under his hand. The scent of bacon cooking drifted from the kitchen.

My three dogs, Lock, Stock and Barrel, nosed inside the bedroom door, their nails clicking across the hardwood floor. They came around to my side of the bed, their doggy faces set in mute appeal, tongues lolling.

It seemed like a pretty typical domestic scene, except that there is nothing typical about my life. The dogs weren't dogs at all, but Retrievers—powerful magical creatures who'd given me their allegiance when I'd freed them from slavery to the Agency.

The man in bed with me wasn't a man, but the son of an angel and a . . . Well, I wasn't sure exactly what Puck was, but he was definitely something old and powerful. Besides his lack of humanity, Nathaniel also wasn't the father of my child. He wasn't even my lover, or my boyfriend. I didn't know how to define our relationship status as any other way except "complicated."

The person cooking the bacon in the kitchen was my many-greats-uncle Daharan, brother of Lucifer, dragon shapeshifter, creature of fire and something older than the Earth itself.

As for me, I was the daughter of a fallen angel and an Agent of Death. Lucifer was my grandfather. My baby had the blood of a half nephilim inside his veins, a legacy from his dead father. I had more enemies than I could count. I'd spent the last several months trying to stay alive while those enemies tried to kill me and my very ancient family members plotted around me.

We were definitely not going to win any awards for normality in this family.

The dogs needed walking, but everyone pretended not to notice because no one could control them except me.

"I'm coming, I'm coming," I grumbled, sliding out from beneath Nathaniel's arm.

This was harder than it sounded. I was only three months pregnant, but it appeared that I was twice that. I'd never fully appreciated the ease and elasticity with which I'd rolled out of bed before I took on the aspect of a hippo.

"Do you want me to come with you?" Nathaniel murmured.

"No one is going to mess with me while I'm walking these three," I said. "Besides, it's been a quiet couple of weeks."

And it had been, I reflected as I got dressed. Since I'd killed Titania, the faerie queen. Since Nathaniel's half brother—and heir to the court of Titania and Oberon—Bendith had been killed by his biological father, Puck. Since Puck had tricked me into freeing him from his bondage to Titania.

Since I'd had an adventure in another space and time, and discovered the darker places in my heart, the black menace at the core of my magic. I'd worked hard to force that darkness to recede, to let my natural personality reassert itself. But it seemed that since I'd tapped into that power, it floated closer to the surface, shadows seeping into my edges.

Like so many things that I'd discovered since becoming aware of my ancestry, my new magical abilities were impossible to undo. And my darling grandfather Lucifer definitely preferred it that way. *All the better to tempt you with, my dear.*

Lucifer cherished a long-held hope that I would give up my life and become heir to his kingdom. I'd rather eat nails for breakfast than manacle myself to the first of the fallen. Besides, Lucifer's crazy lover Evangeline was pregnant with his child, and I knew very well that she was angling to put that kid on the throne. If I expressed even the smallest iota of interest in taking Lucifer's offer, she would set a thousand assassins upon me, regardless of what Lucifer might want.

No, embroiling myself further in Lucifer's machinations was definitely not at the top of my to-do list. I pulled on a pair of jeans I couldn't button. The taut roundness of my lower belly protruded over the fly. I pushed a rubber band through the buttonhole, looped it and wrapped the other end around the button to keep the pants from sliding down. A long, baggy Cubs sweatshirt completed this uber-stylish look. I shoved my slippers on and padded out of the room.

In the kitchen, my uncle Daharan was making pancakes and bacon in large quantities and placing them on covered platters I didn't even know I owned. He's not your garden-variety uncle. He's an ancient being, one of Lucifer's three brothers, and he spends at least part of his time in dragon form.

For the moment he was living in the apartment downstairs. Locks didn't keep him out, and he came and went freely between my place and his. Somehow I couldn't be irritated about this. There was some quality about Daharan that made me trust him, trust that he would do me no harm. Beezle wasn't so sure, as he tended not to trust anyone so closely related to Lucifer, but as I entered the kitchen I noticed his mistrust of Daharan did not extend to disdain of his cooking. Beezle was perched on the counter next to the platters filching as much bacon as he could while Daharan's back was turned.

The dogs trotted ahead of me, down the hall, and stopped before the front door while I paused in the kitchen.

"That's a whole lot of breakfast for three people and a gargoyle," I remarked.

"You're eating for two," Beezle said before Daharan could answer.

"And you're eating for five," I said.

Daharan ignored the byplay. "We will be having guests this morning."

"What guests?" I asked warily. The last thing I wanted was for one of Daharan's brothers to show up. Alerian terrified me. Lucifer infuriated me.

And Puck . . . Well, when I thought of the way Puck had manipulated me into destroying one of the oldest creatures in the universe for his own personal gain, those shadows on my heart threatened to overtake me. I truly thought I could beat Puck bloody with a crowbar and it wouldn't bother me in the least. Of course, when I had thoughts like that I knew that the darkness was spreading inside me like a cancer. I wasn't sure if there was anything I could do to stop it.

"You will see when they arrive," Daharan said.

I'd almost forgotten I'd asked a question, so caught up was I in thoughts of vengeance on Puck.

"Did you invite someone?" I asked.

"No," Daharan said mildly, but with a finality that let me know he wasn't going to tell me anything more.

Lucifer and all of his brothers could see aspects of the future. Daharan was able to see with the most clarity. So someone was coming. Someone whose arrival Daharan had foreseen, but he didn't want to share with me for some reason.

I shrugged and went to the waiting dogs, who panted in anticipation. As soon as I opened the front door they crowded out in a rush, jumping all over one another in their eagerness to leave. They thundered down the steps ahead of me, whining when they reached the closed door at the bottom of the stairs.

I trudged slowly after them. I might be imbued with some of the strongest magic in the universe, but I was an ungainly waddler just like every other pregnant woman there ever was. I finally made it to the bottom and opened the door.

The dogs created another bottleneck in the foyer, where a final door, this one clear glass, made the first threshold between me and mine and anything nasty that might come knocking. I managed to herd the dogs to one side so I could get the door open. They ran down the front porch steps and out to the sidewalk, terrifying a nanny walking a couple of babies in a double stroller.

The former Retrievers looked like oversized black mastiffs, and while I was pretty sure they wouldn't attack an innocent human being, they definitely looked intimidating. She gave me a look like she wanted to chastise me for defying Chicago's leash law, but then gave the dogs a second glance and obviously thought better of it. She hurried down the street with the kids, eager to get away.

I'd tried to keep Lock, Stock and Barrel on leashes. But they would weave in and out and get tangled up, and finally I threw up my hands. They would do what I said—mostly—so why bother with leashes?

The dogs ran in three different directions to do their business. They each had a preferred spot staked out. I monitored them from the sidewalk in front of my house, wondering idly why supernatural creatures made of darkness and bearing the power to destroy souls needed to crap on the neighbor's lawn in the first place. Was it because I expected dogs to do such things?

The Retrievers had become more doglike as I considered them so. They were connected to me in a way I didn't fully understand. I could feel their presence always in the back of my mind. It wasn't as disturbing as it should have been. It was comforting. It kept me secure in the knowledge that they would come to my defense if I needed it. More important, they would come to the defense of my baby.

I placed my hand over my protruding belly, secure in the knowledge that my son was safe inside me. I hardly allowed myself to consider what might happen after he was born. At night I was plagued by dreams of him being rent from my arms, stolen and kept by one of my enemies—or worse.

My own family might try to take him from me. Lucifer had made no secret of his interest in the child. Did I have the strength—and the allies—to keep Lucifer from my son? Maybe. But I didn't want to be forced to find out. I was thinking all these things, lost in my own worries, when the growling of the Retrievers brought me back to the present.

They crowded around me in a protective circle, making

horrible noises low in their throats, just waiting for me to give the signal so they could leap, rip, tear.

A figure approached cautiously, the object of the Retrievers' suspicion. The person was dressed like a college student, a slouchy gray T-shirt over loose-fitting jeans and beat-up sneakers. But the baggy clothes could not disguise the obvious strength in his body, or hide the muscles flexing in his arms. Nor did the grimy Cubs cap completely cover the gold-blond of his hair or shade the brilliance of his green eyes.

He'd veiled his wings, and his eyes were unsure as he stopped a few feet from me. The Retrievers growled more intensely, but I put my hand on Stock's neck, and they quieted instantly. They were obviously still on their guard, though.

The man before me stood silently, waiting to see what I would do.

"Samiel," I said.

Everything was knotted up inside me. I wasn't sure how to feel. There was happiness, and pain, and lots and lots of anger.

Samiel was my brother-in-law, and seeing him again reminded me of happier days, when Gabriel was alive. But I was also reminded that he had left me, left me when I was in need of help, left me after I'd taken him in and sheltered him.

He'd left even though I'd risked my life to save him from the court of the Grigori. He'd left knowing I carried his brother's child, blood of his blood, and knowing that child needed protection.

As I thought these things the anger and the darkness rose up inside me, and he took a step back, like he could feel the pulse of dark magic. The Retrievers crouched, ready to strike.

"What do you want?" I asked, and my voice did not sound like my own. The effect was lost entirely on Samiel, who was deaf. But he could see my face, and read my lips, and know he was not welcome.

His hands moved tentatively, signing out the words, *Maddy, I'm sorry.*

He meant it. I could see it in his eyes, in the pleading lines of his face. He *was* sorry.

Part of me wanted to unbend immediately, to take the apology that was freely given, to return back to the way things were before.

The other part of me knew that we could never return to who we were before, and that part wanted to hold on to the anger and the hurt, to rage in pain and make Samiel suffer, make him hurt as I had when I thought everyone had abandoned me.

An image of Samiel bent and broken, blood seeping from many wounds, flashed across my brain.

That shocked me out of my anger, made me realize it was wrong, all out of proportion to his crime.

The Retrievers would take him down if I gave the words. They were attuned to my feelings, had sensed the building inferno inside me. I willed that anger away, fought to remember who I was.

"Stand down," I told Lock, Stock and Barrel. They immediately sat back on their haunches and let their tongues loll out. I sensed their watchfulness despite their easy posture. "He's a friend."

Some of the tension seeped out of Samiel's body, but not all of it. *Am I?* he signed.

"Are you?" I asked, raising my eyebrow. "Or have you come to try and eliminate me before I give birth to this baby, who just might be a monster unleashed on the world?"

Samiel looked shocked. *I could never hurt Gabriel's child. And why would you think your own baby is a monster?*

It was a thought I allowed myself only rarely and briefly.

Mostly because I was sure I would still love and protect him, no matter what he was.

"It's always been a possibility, hasn't it?" I said. "Gabriel was Ramuell's son, and Ramuell was most definitely a monster."

But Gabriel wasn't. And neither are you.

"Are you sure about that?" I asked, thinking of all the things I had done, the dark compulsion that was becoming more difficult to control.

Samiel shook his head. *I know who you are, in your heart. I nearly killed you twice. I cut off two of your fingers. And yet you saw how my mother had twisted my love for her. You forgave me. You made me a part of your family.*

"And you left me," I said. There was no anger now, only hurt and sadness. "I trusted you. And you left."

I was confused, he signed. *It's not an excuse. I just wasn't sure what would happen after everyone in the world saw you on television destroying those vampires. And Chloe . . .*

Here he stopped signing and frowned.

"I know," I said. "You wanted to protect her from the hordes you thought would be breaking down my door at any moment. She's your girl. I get it."

No, he signed, then backtracked. *I mean, yes, I did want to protect her. But she's not my girl. At least, not anymore.*

"She kicked you out and now you're here looking for a roof over your head?" I asked, getting annoyed again.

No, Samiel signed, shaking his head. *It's not like that. We broke up because I wanted to come here, to make amends.*

"Let me guess," I said. "Chloe didn't agree."

You could say that, Samiel said, grinning.

I could imagine how that argument went. Chloe has an extremely strong personality. And once she's decided something, no force in the universe could make her change her mind.

"What's the heaviest thing she threw at your head?" I asked.

A cast-iron frying pan.

"Seriously? A little cliché, that," I said.

She had just finished cooking breakfast, he signed. *I thought it would be a safe time to raise the subject since her stomach was full.*

"According to Beezle her stomach is never full," I said.

Beezle should talk.

And just like that, it was all right. I didn't want to be angry at Samiel. I had enough legitimate enemies without spurning an apologetic friend just to soothe my pride. I stepped forward and he put his arms around me. I felt safe and warm there. He leaned back, his hands on my shoulders for a moment, and looked me up and down, shaking his head.

"Don't say anything about my weight," I warned. "Don't say it looks like I swallowed a basketball, or that it looks like I'm about to pop, or ask me if I'm having twins."

Samiel shook his head. *I was just going to say you look tired.*

"And don't say that either," I said. "When speaking to a pregnant woman, only compliments should flow from your lips. 'You look great' is an excellent fallback."

Even if it's not true?

"Especially if it's not true. I already feel like a whale on two legs. I don't need anybody to tell me I look like one." I sighed. "I have to clean up after the dogs. Why don't you stay here for a minute and get to know them?"

Samiel crouched warily before the three Retrievers, holding his hand out for them to sniff. I went away to collect the dogs' leavings, confident that Samiel would make friends with them. Everyone loved Samiel.

And if for some reason the dogs didn't like him . . . well, at least Samiel could fly if necessary.

I went down the gangway between my house and the next to drop the plastic bag in the garbage can in the alley just outside the back fence. When I reentered the backyard I noticed someone standing there, his back to me.

"No wonder Daharan made so many pancakes," I said. "Apparently it's my day for a family reunion."

Jude turned around, his shaggy red beard and piercing blue eyes as familiar and welcome as Samiel had been. He looked like he couldn't believe what he was seeing.

"They told me you were dead," he said hoarsely, taking a step toward me.

"I could say that thing about death and rumors and exaggeration, but you probably wouldn't get it," I said. Jude was very old, and very serious, and very literal-minded.

"I thought you were dead," he repeated.

I realized I'd been a little thoughtless. Jude remembered the "B" in B.C. He also had lived through the "A" in A.D., long ago, when he was called Judas Iscariot and his name became infamous. He'd lost someone he'd pledged his life to, and for more than two thousand years he hadn't made a pledge like that again. Until me. And he'd thought I died.

"Jude, I . . ." I began.

Several things happened at once. The back door flew open. Beezle, Nathaniel and Daharan streamed out onto the porch, all looking frantic.

The Retrievers came howling down the side of the house, chased by Samiel, who also appeared panicked.

Jude spun to face the new arrivals just as Beezle cried out, "Maddy, get away from him!"

And then a huge red-and-gray wolf leapt over the neighbor's fence, into my yard, and tackled Jude to the ground.

Jude transformed into a matching red-and-gray wolf. The two canids tangled with each other, biting and clawing while I—and everyone else—stood frozen in surprise. Beezle flew to my shoulder.

"That's not Jude," he said.

"I figured that out," I said. "But is the other one Jude?"

"Yes," Beezle said, squinting at the two snarling wolves. I knew he was looking through all the layers of reality to see the creatures' true essence. "It's a good thing he showed up when he did. You looked like you were about to hug the fake Jude."

"I was," I admitted. "So who's the fake?"

Beezle's answer never came, for one of the wolves suddenly yelped and then bounded over the side fence into my neighbors' yard. The other wolf growled and made to follow it.

"Wait!" I called, then glanced at Beezle. "I'm assuming that's the real Jude there?"

Beezle nodded.

"Jude, wait," I said.

He turned toward me, his muzzle streaked with blood, and growled low in his throat. He didn't want to let his quarry escape. But I hadn't seen Jude since before I destroyed the vampires infesting Chicago. He'd gone away to attend to some pack business, and he'd never come back. Until that moment, I hadn't realized just how much I'd missed him.

"Jude, stay," I said, and fell to my knees. Beezle fluttered away.

Jude took a half step toward me, then looked back in the direction of the imposter.

"We'll find him," I promised. Tears sprung to my eyes.

I wiped them away with the heel of my hand. "Only—don't leave. I can't bear any more leavings."

Everyone in the yard was silent, watching. The last time I'd fallen to my knees in this place I'd covered Gabriel's bleeding body in the snow. Jude had helped me stand again, pulled me away from the snow and the cold and blood. It was spring now, and Gabriel was gone forever, but Gabriel's heart lived on inside me, in the beating heart of his child.

The tears fell fast and thick now, and I could hardly see in front of me. Jude's cold nose pressed against my cheek, and then I buried my face in the thick ruff of fur at his neck. He whined softly in his throat.

The spell was broken by Nathaniel, who abruptly took to the air, flying into the thick leaves of the catalpa tree that grew in the corner of my yard.

I heard someone familiar say, "Ow! You can't do that!"

I came to my feet and spun toward the tree. Nathaniel emerged grim-faced, holding Jack Dabrowski by the collar of his jacket like a truculent child. He landed in front of me with Jack wriggling under his grasp like a worm on a hook. Nathaniel held a video camera in his free hand.

Daharan moved up to my left side, Samiel to my right. Beezle returned to his perch on my shoulder. The dogs crowded around our ankles, treating Jude like he was part of their pack.

Nathaniel looked at me, then at the camera.

"Break it," I said.

"Naw, you can't—Oh, man!" Jack said as Nathaniel looked at the camera and it burst into flame. A second later nothing was left but ash, which Nathaniel dumped in the grass.

"I told you to leave me alone," I said to Jack.

"And I told you that I wasn't going to stop," Jack said,

his feet dangling above the ground. "Hey, can you get your goon to let me down? It's kind of hard to breathe when I'm in this position."

"It's kind of hard to breathe when angry supernatural creatures decide to punish you for not leaving well enough alone," I said, but I nodded at Nathaniel to release Jack.

He did so, but made sure to stand close by and loom over the blogger. Nathaniel looms well. His height—well over six feet—helps with that.

Jude gave Jack a pointed look and growled. Jack gave Jude a nervous glance and backed away a few inches, which naturally caused him to bump into Nathaniel. He glanced up at Nathaniel's cold, hard face, muttered, "Sorry," and tried to find a position far from both Jude and Nathaniel.

Since we were all crowded around him in our best menacing fashion, this necessitated a lot of uncertain shuffling on his part. I watched him with a mixture of amusement and frustration. He was so far out of his depth, but he refused to be scared away.

Jack had waited his whole life to discover that all the things he believed in were real. He'd blogged about supernatural happenings in Chicago before anyone had realized there actually *were* supernatural happenings. And now that normal folk had become aware of things like vampires and angels, Jack Dabrowski had become something of a high priest among the faithful and the true believers.

Unfortunately Jack's hobby conflicted with my own personal preference to stay under the radar as much as possible. He'd decided that I needed to be an intermediary between the magical world and the regular world. I didn't want this job for numerous reasons, starting with *I had enough trouble* and ending with *I am not a people person*.

"You need to leave me alone, Jack," I said. "Every time

you meet me I break something that belongs to you. So far it's only been your electronics."

I let the threat hang in the air, hoping it would have some kind of effect.

Jack made a dismissive gesture. "You can't fool me. I've been asking around about you since the last time you threatened me. I know you don't hurt innocents."

"Not on purpose, anyway," Beezle mumbled. "But if you're in her path when the avalanche starts rolling, watch out."

I ignored Beezle. My heart had gone cold at Jack's words. "Who have you been asking about me?"

He shrugged. "Around online. You know, you have quite the reputation. Did you really kill the High Queen of Faerie?"

"Gods above and below, you're not even supposed to know that there *is* a High Queen of Faerie, much less that I killed her," I said. "I don't know how you found out about that, but you need to stop talking about me, especially online. You don't know who you're conversing with."

My mind seethed with possibilities, all of them bad news for Jack. Leaving aside all the creatures that hated my guts and could potentially use Jack to get to me, he might draw the attention of Lucifer. And if Lucifer decided that Jack's pursuit of me was attracting too much notice to his court, he would squash Jack like a bug.

"Like I don't know how to trace people online?" Jack scoffed. "Believe me, I've verified the identity of every source I've ever had."

"Are you crazy?" I shouted. "Do you want to be killed? Do you know how insanely dangerous it is to track down powerful beings who use the Internet for its anonymity?"

"Didn't I say he was too stupid to live the first time we met?" Beezle said.

This was even worse than I thought. He was actively seeking out dangerous people in the name of research. Sooner or later he would stumble into a situation that would get him killed. And I would be responsible, because I couldn't stop him.

Nathaniel looked at me. He understood a fair bit of what passed inside my mind without my saying a word. Ever since I'd released his magical legacy from Puck, there had been a powerful connection between us.

"You've warned him," Nathaniel said. "His fate is in his own hands."

Daharan nodded. "You cannot save everyone, Madeline."

Their solemnity penetrated Jack's bravado in a way my anger had not.

"Nothing's going to happen to me," he said defiantly.

"Oh, yes, it is," I said softly. I could almost see it happening—his capture, his torture, his death. A cloak of darkness seemed to settle over him, the resolute hand of the Reaper on his shoulder. We all felt it. We were attending Jack Dabrowski's funeral.

"I'm not going to die!" he said angrily, desperately, backing away from me.

Nathaniel moved aside so Jack could free himself from our circle, from the relentless certainty of his death.

He held his hands palms up in front of him, to plead, to defend. "I'm not going to die."

Jack backed into the fence, fumbled with the gate, stepped into the alley.

"I won't," he said before the gate slammed shut and we heard his footsteps running away.

"You will," I said softly behind him. "Everything dies."

2

A SHORT WHILE LATER WE WERE ALL ASSEMBLED around my dining room table eating gigantic stacks of pancakes. Jude had changed into clothes magically produced by Daharan. The wolf shoveled food into his mouth like it had been a long time since he had eaten a hot meal. Beezle was doing the same, but Beezle always ate like that.

Samiel, Daharan and Nathaniel ate more sedately. I picked at my food, my appetite gone.

"You must eat something," Nathaniel said. "The baby is using too many of your resources."

"I'm not hungry," I said.

"She's feeling distraught because she won't be able to stop that moron from committing suicide," Beezle said through a mouthful of pancake. His chest and belly were coated in butter and syrup.

"Did you get any food *in* your mouth?" Nathaniel asked, his face a mixture of fascination and repulsion.

"You ought to be used to it by now," Beezle said.

"There are some things to which I will never be accustomed," Nathaniel said.

"I couldn't care less about that fool of a blogger," Jude growled, breaking in. "What I'm concerned about, and what ought to concern you as well, was that shifter in your backyard pretending to be me. You've no idea of the trouble he's caused."

I'd nearly forgotten about the shifter in the kerfuffle over Jack. "What do you know about him?" I asked.

Jude shoveled a few more mouthfuls of pancake into his mouth before continuing. Now that I looked at him closely, it did seem that he had a lean and hungry look about him, and new lines were present around his eyes.

He leaned back and took a large gulp of coffee. "Remember when I left, before you destroyed the vampires?"

I nodded. "Beezle said you had pack business."

"I did. Wade contacted me because we urgently needed to move the pack. Someone had discovered we were werewolves and ratted us out to the townsfolk. Before the vampire lord went on television, they would have thought the very idea of werewolves a load of rot. But after everyone in the world saw the nice Chicago commuters having their faces eaten off by creatures of the night, the locals were more than ready to believe in our existence."

"And were, doubtless, gathering up their pitchforks and torches," I said.

"You're not far off," Jude growled. "We've always lived in isolated spots, staying as far from towns as possible. Even without knowing about weres, people aren't generally fond of wolves, especially in the country. Farmers and ranchers see us as varmints, and they shoot first and ask questions later, no matter what species-protection law might say."

"But you have primarily resided on your own private land, yes?" Nathaniel asked.

Jude nodded. "That's so."

If the land belongs to you, couldn't you keep people off it? Anyone who tried to attack you on your own property should be prosecuted, Samiel signed.

"'Should be' is the operative term here," Jude said. "There are some who have decided that supernatural creatures don't have any rights to speak of. And those who have decided also have the ear of the local authorities."

He paused, seeming to swallow some strong emotion.

"They attacked us, chased us off our land, killed several members of the pack, including two cubs who got lost in the confusion. They hunted us until we were too exhausted to go on, until we were forced to split up and hide where we could."

I was afraid to ask. I wasn't sure I wanted to know the answer. "Wade?"

"Is safe," Jude said, "and so is his wife and daughter. But there are many other families torn to pieces in the last week or so, and my pack is scattered to the wind."

"Isn't there a safe place that you go when the pack is threatened?" I asked, remembering a fragment of conversation with Jude from long ago.

"Yes, but that place is under surveillance," Jude said. "We were betrayed."

Daharan spoke. "Your pack was infiltrated by this shapeshifter." It was not a question.

"Yes," Jude said.

"How *did* it happen again?" I asked. Last year, members of the pack had been killed by Lucifer's shapeshifting son, Baraqiel. "After Baraqiel and the kidnapping of Wade and the cubs, I'd have thought you would be on your guard against any newcomers looking to join the pack."

"We were," Jude said. "This shifter wasn't a newcomer. He wasn't like Baraqiel, pretending to be a lone wolf looking for a pack. He was one of us."

"A member of your pack gave you up to humans?" I asked, shocked. It seemed to go against everything that I knew of the family bonds of a werewolf pack.

"No. This shifter killed one of us and took his place," Jude said. "And there was nothing to reveal the difference. His scent didn't change; his manner didn't change. The shifter became our pack member so completely that we never suspected, almost as if it had swallowed the soul of the person he took over."

"So how did you discover the traitor?" Beezle asked.

"We didn't. We didn't even realize what had happened until Wade and I came upon the body of the real pack member while hiding from the hunters. It was decomposed almost beyond recognition."

"Which means this shifter infiltrated your pack weeks ago and you never knew," I said. "What put you on his trail?"

"I wasn't on his trail," Jude said. "We had received word you were still alive, and I was planning to come here in any case. Then the harassment began. Once the pack was broken up, I thought to come here, to see if you could help us. Imagine my surprise to discover my own self standing in your backyard, and you walking blindly into the teeth of the shark."

"She does that," Beezle said. "Responds emotionally instead of thinking and gets herself into trouble. I'd say it was a pregnant thing, but she's acted like this her whole life."

"And I stopped you from going after him," I said,

pretending Beezle hadn't spoken. It was usually the best course of action with Beezle. Anything else encouraged bad behavior.

"You said we would find him and so we shall," Jude said.

He did not blame me for letting the shifter go free. He didn't even blame me for the scourge of vampires that had revealed the existence of supernatural creatures to the world, and thus opened his pack to harm. The weight of all the lost lives that could be laid at my door became heavier with each passing day.

"It seems our pack has been under a curse these last several months," Jude said. "So many strange occurrences, kidnappings, deaths."

"It's because of me," I said. "Wade's association with me opened you to all this, brought you to the attention of my enemies."

Jude shook his head. "I believe it is more than that. We are being targeted by someone, someone with a vendetta against us."

"Someone using your association with Madeline as a smoke screen?" Nathaniel asked.

"Who would hate a bunch of werewolves that much?" Beezle asked.

"Perhaps it is not the weres who are hated," Daharan said.

I gave him a sharp look. "Do you know something?"

"I have told you before that I cannot see the future clearly," Daharan said.

"But you see *something*," I persisted. "Do you know who is doing this to Wade's pack?"

"It is not the future you should look to, but the past," Daharan said with a pointed look at Jude.

The wolf appeared disconcerted. "My past?"

"You will discover the answer behind you, not ahead," Daharan repeated.

"Wow, it's like living with our own personal annoying cryptic oracle," Beezle said.

"I only tell you what I can," Daharan said.

Beezle shrugged. "You're a good cook. That makes up for a multitude of sins in my book."

"It's the only reason he's stayed with me all these years," I told Daharan.

"It's been ages since you've cooked anything," Beezle said. "It's always 'apocalypse this, apocalypse that' with you."

"You could learn to take care of your own meals, gargoyle," Nathaniel said, frowning.

"No, no," I said. "You don't want to see the state of the kitchen after Beezle's been cooking."

"She's still upset about the s'mores incident," Beezle said, sotto voce.

"The fire department was called," I said.

Beezle looked affronted. "Every time you step out the front door, a city block burns down, and you're still angry because I got a little smoke in the kitchen?"

"The microwave was destr—Never mind," I said, because the others were staring at us. "So we've got two problems. First, find the shifter. Second, find a safe haven for the pack."

"I am not certain it is a wise idea for the pack to gather together in one place," Nathaniel said slowly.

"It would make it too easy to get rid of us," Jude agreed.

It was a sign of how much things had changed that Jude and Nathaniel behaved civilly to each other. Time was they could barely stand to be in the same city, much less the same room. Nathaniel had changed, and not just physically. Jude was perceptive enough to pick up on that.

There was something else, too—a growing feeling that all

of us in this room were linked together, and that our problems were greater than any one enemy. Ever since Alerian had risen from the lake like some Cthulhu-nightmare, I'd sensed something huge was approaching, some fate I would not be able to escape. All the crises I'd averted seemed merely a prologue. There was a larger plan at work, something that had been put in motion long before I was even born.

It was no stretch of the imagination to picture Lucifer and Puck and Alerian as major players in whatever was coming. Still, there was something I was missing. Some hand moved in the shadows, making all the puppets dance to its tune.

"Are you going to join the rest of us on Earth?" Beezle asked loudly. "Or are you going to sit there with a blank look for the rest of the day?"

"I was thinking," I said.

"I could make a comment about burning, but I will withhold it. It's too easy."

"Your restraint is admirable," I said dryly.

"Look, the Avengers are assembled," Beezle said. "Don't you want to develop a plan of action? Or at least charge out the door blindly the way you usually do?"

"Yeah," I said, shaking off the lingering sense of approaching doom. "Jude, I don't suppose you can track the scent of that shifter?"

He shook his head. "He's like no shapeshifter I have ever seen. Baraqiel's powers were startling enough, but they could at least be explained away by his parentage. Anything spawned from Lucifer is bound to have unusual abilities. But this shifter . . . he doesn't just look like whoever he's pretending to be. He *is* that person. He behaves like them; he smells like them. He is whoever he pretends to be."

"How can that be?" I asked. "How can the magic leave no trace?"

"It did leave a trace," Beezle said. "I could see through it to the essence underneath."

"Until you patent those gargoyle-o-vision glasses, that doesn't do us a lot of good," I said. "Wait a second. You could see down to the shifter's essence."

Beezle had a speculative look on his face. "Gargoyle-o-vision. That has possibilities. I wonder why I didn't think of that before."

"Beezle! Focus! Did you see the shifter's real identity or not?"

"Yeah, but it won't help you," Beezle said. "The essence didn't look like anything concrete."

"What do you mean?"

Beezle looked thoughtful. "It was almost like there wasn't a real person—or a real creature—underneath the mask of Jude. The essence was kind of fuzzy and out of focus."

"Like whatever it was had no real personality or identity other than what it took on?" I said. "It would have been born from something, right? Presumably another shapeshifter."

Daharan broke in, his face angrier than I'd ever seen it. "Such things are not unheard of. There were three like this, long ago. But they were destroyed. I told him to destroy them. I watched it happen."

"Told who to destroy them?" Beezle asked.

Daharan looked at me. "Alerian."

As Daharan said his name I felt, briefly, that sense of the ocean closing over me. "So it's nothing to do with Jude's past at all, but Alerian's."

Daharan shook his head. "I can see that the pack's troubles are tied to Jude's history, although I cannot see precisely how. The shapeshifter is merely an agent working another's will."

"Working Alerian's will?" Nathaniel asked.

"Alerian was asleep for hundreds of years," I said. "The

pack's troubles are recent. Unless he left an ancient Post-it with instructions, it's unlikely he's behind this." I looked to Daharan for confirmation.

My uncle nodded. "I believe Alerian has an agenda of his own, but I don't believe it has anything to do with these wolves."

"But the shapeshifter is connected to Alerian," Jude said.

We all looked at Daharan expectantly. Having raised the subject, he now appeared reluctant to continue. I had noticed that while there was no love lost between the brothers, Daharan, in particular, was loyal to his blood.

I believe that he, as the eldest of the four, felt the burden and responsibility of their powers most, and thus was more inclined to keep family matters in the family circle. Although as I glanced around the table I realized everyone except Beezle and Jude *were* in his family circle.

Nathaniel was his brother Puck's son, and thus the most closely related. Samiel was the next closest, as the son of Ramuell, who had been Lucifer's son. I was the most distantly related, with several hundred generations separating me from Evangeline and Lucifer, my many-greats-grandparents. Really, the least likely person to belong at that table was me.

Yet Lucifer and all of his brothers sought me out. And Lucifer's blood had manifested more power in me than any child of the intervening generations. I'd stopped asking "Why me?" It was pointless.

Daharan cleared his throat, and we all looked at him.

"Many thousands of years ago, when humans were still evolving into the creatures they would become today, my brother Alerian ruled over the seas of this Earth. This planet is particularly well suited to his powers, as there is more water than land. Lucifer and Puck squabbled over other places and other dimensions, as they always have."

"Color me surprised," I muttered.

Daharan smiled briefly before continuing. "However, as humans evolved, they became more interesting to Lucifer. He began to spend more time here, to establish a base of power. And then he was made to carry the souls of the dead, which brought him into closer contact with people. He began to covet this planet, a place Alerian considered rightfully his. The oceans were ruled by his creatures, his monsters. All life on land had come from his source, from the sea. He naturally resented Lucifer's intrusion."

I desperately wanted to ask just who had been powerful enough to force Lucifer to become the agent of the dead, but I resisted. Daharan might clam up if I started asking too many questions about the origins of the universe.

Daharan continued. "Although life on land had begun in his waters, the intervening years had separated humans and animals too much from this source for Alerian to wield his will over them. He decided to experiment. He wanted to create creatures that would be fully malleable. They must be able to change form but also have no strong will of their own. He also wished, however, that these creatures have a great deal of personal charisma."

"Seems like those qualities would contradict one another," Beezle said. "How can they have no will of their own but still be snake charmers?"

I shook my head at him. I could see what Alerian had been trying to achieve. "He wanted to be able to push his will through these creatures, to use them like high priests recruiting acolytes."

"While he remained in the shadows," Daharan agreed.

"I guess we don't need to ask if he succeeded," I said.

"The creatures were born of his own blood, the power and changeability of the sea, mixed with the blood of humans and of shapeshifters, which were only in their infancy as a species then. Through it all he infused his magic, until he had created the perfect vessel. Three of them." Daharan paused, his eyes far away.

"So what happened?" Jude asked impatiently.

"The creatures worked perfectly. They could be human or animal or bird, whatever Alerian wished, and they drew others to them until Alerian had a vast army completely under his control," Daharan said heavily.

"I think I can guess what happened next," I said. "Lucifer didn't like Alerian playing with his toy—which he had stolen from Alerian in the first place—and so he decided to just smash it."

"You understand Lucifer very well," Daharan said.

"He's not complicated," I said, a little insulted. I really resent positive comparisons between me and the Prince of Darkness. "His machinations might be beyond me most of the time, but his motivations are pretty simple. If you've got it, he wants it."

"So Lucifer did what—rounded up his Grigori buddies and started raining fire on Alerian's armies?" Beezle asked.

"Yes," Daharan said. "And the carnage was terrible to behold. It soon seemed there would be nothing left of this planet except a wasteland devoid of life. So I was sent to intervene."

Nathaniel and I looked at each other, each knowing the same question was on our lips—*who sent you?* But neither of us asked.

"I negotiated an accord between the two of them. Lucifer would continue to collect the souls of the dead, and to wield influence over humanity. Alerian would maintain his superiority over the oceans. As part of the agreement,

Alerian was to destroy the shapeshifters he had created. And he did so. I watched him do it myself."

"That couldn't have endeared you to Alerian," I said.

Daharan nodded. "It was, I believe, much like destroying his own children."

"And now one of these monstrosities has appeared," Nathaniel said. "If they were destroyed, and such was witnessed by you, then there can be only three ways it could have returned. First, Alerian made more than three all those centuries ago but managed to conceal one from you."

"It is possible," Daharan acknowledged. "Alerian's powers and mine are in direct contrast with one another. When we are together it seems that both of us are . . . muted, shall we say? But even if he was able to hide the creature, then we should still have seen some evidence of it in intervening years. And I cannot believe Alerian would be so careless as to leave such a monster formless and masterless while he slept."

Unless he thought the shapeshifter was safely locked away, Samiel pointed out.

Beezle nodded. "Yeah, maybe he stashed the little devil somewhere out of this time and place, thinking he would go back later and retrieve it. There would be no chance of you accidentally detecting the presence of this shifter until it was too late."

"Again, it is possible. But my reach and breadth extend far beyond this time or this place." Daharan said this with no arrogance, only a statement of fact. "It is unlikely the creature could be concealed simply by the expedient of moving it off this Earth."

"The second, and more troubling, reason this shifter could have reappeared is that someone—Alerian himself or another person—is using Alerian's original formula to create more shifters," Nathaniel said.

We were all silent for a moment, digesting the unpleasantness of this idea. Everyone here except Daharan had been present when the last lunatic's biological experiment had been implemented. My own father, Azazel, had tortured humans and Agents until he'd found a serum to help vampires walk in the sun. How much worse would it be if a new player had discovered how to make these shifters? These were creatures who could look like anyone, be anyone so thoroughly that even their family members couldn't tell the difference.

"They could infiltrate everywhere, do anything they wanted," I said.

"Yeah, it would be like that alien in *The Thing*, except on crack," Beezle said.

"And what could anyone do until it was too late?" I said. I'd been afraid of Alerian from nearly the first moment I'd seen him, and I was beginning to get an inkling why.

And the third way? Samiel asked Nathaniel.

My baby shifted in my belly, and I knew the answer before Nathaniel spoke. "One—or all—of the shifters bred with human women while in human form, and their powers were passed through the human bloodline."

Nathaniel nodded. "But those powers would not have manifested until now, until this particular individual was born; else we would be in the aforementioned predicament of many creatures abroad, manipulating humans to their will."

"It's not exactly the 'better' option," I said. "If magic is in the gene pool, it could pop up at any time. And we have no way to determine who could have parented these children."

"Is it that important to decide where this thing came from?" Jude asked. "It brought harm on my pack. It personally killed at least one wolf. And it came here with the intent of harming Madeline. I say let's hunt it down and kill it and worry about its origins later."

I gave Jude an exasperated look. The wolf had always been partial to action, and impatient with our councils.

"It does no good to kill one if there may be more—or the threat of more—behind him," Nathaniel said patiently. "And we must discover his master if you wish to reunite your pack and live in peace."

Jude said nothing more but looked grumbly, which meant he agreed but didn't want to say so.

Daharan suddenly looked alert. "Something is happening. Turn on the television."

"You don't have to tell me twice," Beezle said, leaving the dining room table and flying under the arch into the living room.

He grabbed the remote from the fireplace mantel and flew to his favorite spot on the couch.

"Find a news channel," Daharan said.

"But *La rosa de Guadalupe* is on now," Beezle said.

"Find a news channel," Daharan repeated.

Beezle flipped through the channels, muttering to himself.

"Something urgent is obviously occurring and you're upset because you're missing an episode of a telenovela?" I asked. My stomach was knotted in fear. The last time we'd all gathered around the television, we saw hundreds of vampires eating the denizens of the city. What could it be now? A plague of zombies? An army of faerie warriors come to take vengeance for the death of their queen?

"If I miss an episode, I won't know what's going on next time," Beezle said.

"You don't know what's going on anyway. You can't speak Spanish," I said.

"I know how to order my food in Spanish at the taqueria," Beezle said loftily.

"Just find the news and stop talking before someone in this room loses their temper," I said.

" 'Someone'?" Beezle asked, making air quotes with his fingers. "Or you?"

"I could very easily lose my temper, gargoyle," Nathaniel said.

"No, you won't," Beezle said. "You're like the stepdad that can't discipline the kids because you'll make their mom angry."

Nathaniel opened his mouth to respond, but Samiel crossed to the couch, wrenched the remote from Beezle's little claws and punched in the channel number for the local morning news.

"Hey!" Beezle said. "What is this, Gang Up on Beezle Day?"

We all gathered around the television. The news anchor was announcing a surprise press conference from Chicago's mayor. The anchor talked for a few moments over the video of the press conference, but I hardly heard what she said. The mayor stood at a podium, and just a little behind his right shoulder was Alerian. He'd covered the natural color of his hair, probably with a simple fae-type glamour, so he looked like he belonged with the rest of the respectable types.

"What's he doing there?" I demanded.

Daharan shook his head. "I do not know. Let us listen."

The mayor offered no explanation for Alerian's presence. Lucifer's brother wore an expensive-looking suit and a calm expression. I suppose anyone might have assumed that he was a bodyguard for the mayor, but I knew better. Alerian was up to something. Daharan would not have been so disturbed otherwise.

I was so busy concentrating on Alerian that it took me a

while to sort out what the mayor was saying. Something about "exposed to a new world," and "changing with the changing times," and that "given recent tragic events, it only makes sense."

"He's out of his mind," Jude said. "It's illegal. He'll never get away with it."

"Get away with what?" I asked. "I missed the beginning part."

"He wants all 'creatures of supernatural origin' to come forward and be registered with the city. And then he wants to create an area of Chicago especially for such creatures to live," Nathaniel said.

"Which will be fenced in and policed, I'm sure," I said. My hands went unconsciously to my stomach, covering the baby there.

He wants to put all of us in ghettos, Samiel signed.

"Jude's right. He'll never get away with it," I said.

"That's not true," Beezle said. "The pack's experience indicates pretty clearly that there are plenty of people who have no interest in the law where supernatural creatures are concerned. And if they want to get the fence-sitters on their side, all they have to do is rerun the video of commuters having their faces chewed off by vampires in Daley Plaza."

We all sat in silence, acknowledging the truth of this. But there was another truth that none of us had spoken yet.

"There's no way he came up with this idea on his own," I said. "Alerian put this into his head somehow."

Daharan nodded. "Whatever agenda my brother has—"

"He's making his play now," I finished.

"Yeah, and who's the best-known supernatural creature in the city?" Beezle said pointedly.

They all turned to look at me.

3

"ARE YOU SAYING THEY'RE GOING TO COME FOR ME first?" I said. "Because I would think my celebrity, such as it is, would protect me. Isn't Jack Dabrowski always going on about how people think I'm a hero for getting rid of the vampires?"

"Now that the vampires are gone, you're the only person that the general public is sure has some kind of unusual powers," Beezle said. "Well, you and the rest of the Mensa cases here, since you all were dumb enough to get caught on film fighting the vampires."

"You were there, too," I said, annoyed.

"Nobody is going to put me in a camp," Beezle said. "Some nice upper-class lady who lives on the Gold Coast will adopt me and carry me around in her Kate Spade bag while she's shopping."

"Well, I'm not going to stand around and wait for my

house to be burned down again," I said. "I think it's time to have a word with my uncle."

Beezle opened his mouth, doubtless to dispute the wisdom of such a plan, but I cut him off.

"If he's got the mayor under his influence, then it won't be long before he gets control of someone more powerful. And then whatever he hopes to achieve by cordoning off supernaturals will become a national problem," I said.

It hardly seemed possible that just a couple of hours earlier I was remarking that things had been quiet lately. As usual, once one problem appeared, several others decided to join in.

"You're not going to see Alerian in your state," Nathaniel said.

"What state?" I said, narrowing my eyes.

"The last time you saw Alerian you nearly drowned just by looking into his eyes," Nathaniel said. "If something like that happens again, the shock of it could harm the baby—assuming you survive the encounter yourself."

"Besides, how do you know this isn't all a ploy to lure you to him?" Jude said.

"I'm not that much of a solipsist," I said. "I can't believe that Alerian would arrange to have every supernatural creature in the city registered and put in a camp just so I come for a visit. He could call. I'm sure he has my number. Or he could get it from Lucifer."

Daharan shook his head at me. "Do not underestimate Alerian. His magic is deep and mysterious, like the ocean from which he draws his power. His ultimate aim is certainly not the imprisonment of nonhumans. This is the means to some larger plan."

"Any ideas of what that plan might be? It would be nice to have a clue before I get screwed by one of your brothers again," I said, thinking of Puck's intricate machinations.

Daharan shook his head. "As I have told you before, my powers and Alerian's lie in direct contrast to one another. It makes his intentions difficult to read."

"I don't think any special foreseeing powers are required here," Beezle said. "He's still pissed that Lucifer took his toy, and he wants it back."

"All the more reason Madeline should stay out of the cross fire," Nathaniel said.

"Do you really think that Alerian or Lucifer will let me stay out of it if they decide to start shooting at one another?" I said.

I read the emotion that flickered across his face—acknowledgment of the truth of my statement, anger at his inability to keep me safe.

"Let's just try to be proactive about this," I said. "If we go to Alerian now, maybe we can stop whatever he's got in mind before he really gets revved up."

"We?" Nathaniel asked, and there was a lot of implication in his "we." Like he was asking if "we" were a couple.

I was not ready to answer that question, especially not with everyone and their gargoyle watching, so I sidestepped. "Of course. Alerian is your uncle, too. But I think the rest of you should stay here."

Disappointment flickered across Nathaniel's face. I felt sorry for it, but I just wasn't ready to make a public declaration. Even if he was sleeping in my bed. Which was as good as a public declaration, if you thought about it. Which I didn't want to do.

Daharan nodded. "It would not be a good idea to ask for an audience while surrounded by warriors. Alerian might take it as a sign of aggression."

"I want to look for the shapeshifter anyway," Jude said.

I'll help you. I can take Beezle with me and fly over the area, Samiel said.

"Who said I'm going?" Beezle said.

"You're going," I said, then looked at Daharan, wondering what he would do about either of these two problems. It was like we were leaving our most powerful arrow in the quiver, as it were. But Daharan seemed to prefer to stay out of the squabbling of his brothers, professing that his only purpose was to keep me safe.

"I am going to increase the levels of protection on this building," Daharan said. "It would be best if any humans that came searching for you were unable to find you."

"Including Jack Dabrowski?" I asked. Maybe the blogger would give up if he couldn't find me anymore.

Daharan shook his head. "He knows too much about you to be fooled by any illusion that I might spin."

"Too bad. That would have been an easy solution to an annoying problem," I said.

I went to shower and attempt to make myself presentable. Maternity-wear shopping hadn't been high on my priority list so I wasn't sure what I had that would actually *be* presentable, but as usual Daharan had thought of everything. When I entered the bedroom I saw a white blouse and gray pantsuit on the bed.

For a moment I was reminded of Puck, and another occasion when clothes had been left on the bed for me. I pushed that thought away, because when I thought of Puck my brain got twisted and angry. Those emotions would not be helpful in dealing with Alerian.

I dressed, and of course the suit fit perfectly. I twisted my hair up in a knot behind my head—it was down to the middle of my back now—and found some lipstick that might have been less than five years old, but I couldn't be certain.

I was just finishing up when Nathaniel entered the room. He'd dressed in a black suit with a crisp white shirt.

Despite the recent changes in his hair and eye color, he looked a lot like the old Nathaniel, the one I'd met and despised in my father's court.

But he wasn't that Nathaniel anymore. Even though he was more powerful than he'd ever been, the old arrogance was gone. And he loved me. I knew that with the certainty of a woman who knows real love, because I'd had it once before.

I'd lost that love, and so when I thought of Nathaniel, a part of me would hesitate. Thus far he had waited patiently for me to come around. How long would he be patient?

"The others have gone to look for the shapeshifter," he said.

I nodded. "Beezle, too?"

"Yes, with much grumbling." He was silent for a moment, then said, "I want you to know that I do not think this is a good idea."

In the past I might have blown him off, said something snappy like "duly noted." I would have charged forward with an arrogance of my own, a surety that I would succeed simply because I wished it to be so. But not anymore. The events of the last several months had taught me that the risks were far greater than any reward, and that winning was an illusion. The price I'd paid for success was death, whether by my hand or another's. The death of Gabriel had nearly broken me. But the deaths I'd been responsible for weighed on my heart, too.

And even though I'd tried my damndest, I'd yet to stop either Lucifer or Puck from getting what they wanted. In many cases I'd even inadvertently helped them. So there was no guarantee that I would be able to halt the progress of Alerian's scheme. It was very likely that I would fail.

So instead of dismissing Nathaniel's concern, I turned around and met his eyes. "I know."

"Why are we doing this?" Nathaniel asked. "Why must you put yourself in harm's way?"

"Do you think I could live with myself if I allowed my baby to grow up in a cage?" I said. "Or anyone else's child, for that matter."

"They cannot put us in pens," Nathaniel said. "No one will voluntarily come forward."

"I'm sure there will be motivation for normal people to turn us in," I said. "Alerian isn't stupid. This is just the first shot across the bow. Once the idea of a supernatural holding area sinks in, they'll announce that there will be benefits for creatures who turn themselves in, and rewards for anyone who helps identify a creature living in secret."

"Even if they capture us, they cannot hold us," Nathaniel said. "What human could keep you or I in a cage? Our magic is beyond their comprehension. Even an angry werewolf or faerie could massacre dozens of humans in a moment if the authorities tried to take them away unwillingly."

"Maybe that's what Alerian is counting on," I said slowly. "The more evidence of our dangerous natures, the better. Any kind of slaughter would only add fuel to his argument."

Nathaniel ran his hands through his hair in frustration. "Then we can leave. You do not need to live in this city. Why not another, far from Alerian and his designs?"

"If he succeeds here, then he'll succeed elsewhere," I said. "And it will only be a matter of time before someone catches us."

"You could go to Lord Lucifer," Nathaniel said. "He would protect you and the child."

I stared at him. "Kind of like leaving the wolves' den for the lions'. You know I don't want Lucifer's protection. I've fought against it from the start."

He crossed the room to me, put his hands on my arms.

"How can I protect you when you refuse to see reason? Alerian is laying a trap for you and you are walking into the noose."

"It's not just about me," I said. "There are others who will suffer if Alerian succeeds."

"Do not go," Nathaniel said, and his face was white and scared. "Do not sacrifice yourself needlessly just so you can go to him again."

I looked at him uncomprehendingly for a moment, and then I realized what he was saying.

"You think I'm trying to kill myself," I said slowly. "So that I can be with Gabriel."

"Are you not? Why else would an expectant mother put herself in harm's way over and over again if not to be reunited with the father of her child?" Nathaniel said, and it was like something taut had suddenly snapped inside him. "I know I mean less than nothing to you. I know that I will never be Gabriel. I know that you cannot love me as you loved him."

"Nathaniel, I—"

"Stay with me," he said, and he pulled me into his embrace, enfolding me in his wings like he could keep me there in his cocoon forever. "I do not know what I am without you. It is only you who keeps me sane, who keeps me human. If I did not love you, I would be a monster."

I pulled back a little, shocked, and looked at his face. The skin was drawn tight over his bones, and his eyes burned with fear and anger and love.

"You aren't a monster," I said.

"But I could be," he said. "I can feel it inside me, the shadow that creeps and cloaks. If I had nothing to tether me to this world, that shadow would run free, would destroy everything in its path."

"I've felt that shadow, too," I said. "This is our legacy

from Lucifer and Puck, the darkness that pulses in our blood. But I won't let it take over, and I won't let it take you, either."

He looked at me uncertainly. "You will stay?"

I took a deep breath. "I'm not trying to get back to Gabriel. I want to live. I want to live with you."

It wasn't the same as telling him I loved him back. I knew that, and he did, too. But relief washed over his face. Our bond, forged in magic, had been strengthened. I had chosen Nathaniel over death.

I kissed him gently, his face in my hands, then rested my head on his shoulder. "Maybe someday Lucifer and all of his brothers will just go away and we'll be able to live a normal life."

"Yes, a normal life with wings and the power to destroy worlds," Nathaniel said. "I do not think the American white picket fence is part of our future."

"Probably not," I said, and smiled. "But I make great apple pie. Ask Beezle."

"I try not to speak to the gargoyle unless absolutely necessary. For some reason I find I become quite enraged when I do," Nathaniel said, taking my hand and leading me from the room.

I grabbed Lucifer's sword and swung it over my shoulder. Alerian probably wouldn't try to hurt me. Probably. But it was hard for me to leave the house without it. That sword had saved me more times than I could count. And even if Alerian meant me no harm, that didn't mean some other freaky thing wouldn't pop out of the woodwork. That seemed to happen to me a lot.

"I think Beezle's cultivating that effect on you," I said. "He could be less annoying if he wanted to be."

"And I could rise to the bait less often, hmm?" he said as we went down the front stairs.

"It might discourage bad behavior," I said. "But I make no promises."

I stopped when I got to the front porch. "Umm, do you know where we're going?"

He shook his head. "No. But I do not believe it matters. Can you not feel him? It is just as it was when he was rose from the lake. We will be able to find him without trouble."

Now that Nathaniel mentioned it, I *could* feel Alerian's presence in a way that had not been there the day before.

"He must be exerting a great deal of power for it to be palpable to us," I said.

He shook his head. "I do not think so. I think we are more aware of him than the other three brothers."

"I'm not sure about that," I said. "I can feel Lucifer in the back of my mind almost always. And I know when he's approaching."

Nathaniel looked thoughtful. "I believe that is because you are bound to him through more than one line. Your child is also blood of Lucifer's blood, and that strengthens your connection to him."

I nodded. "I'll buy that. But we both have no direct tie to Alerian. You're a closer relative than I am, being the son of his brother, but neither of us is a direct descendant. So why do we sense him so strongly?"

Nathaniel looked troubled. "I do not know. But I am not certain it bodes well for either of us."

"There is something more elemental about Alerian, isn't there?" I said as we cloaked ourselves from human sight and took off flying.

"Daharan has that quality as well," Nathaniel said. "But it seems that he deliberately banks the effect, whereas Alerian makes no attempts to hide it. Still, we all feel slightly uncomfortable around Daharan. He cannot hide his true nature completely."

"I don't feel uncomfortable around him," I said, surprised. "In fact, I feel exactly the opposite."

"Yes, well, the one thing the gargoyle and I can agree upon is that Daharan has an unnatural interest in you," Nathaniel said.

"He's the only person related to Lucifer who has never asked anything of me," I said, annoyed that Beezle and Nathaniel thought Daharan was plotting behind my back.

"Yet," Nathaniel said darkly.

"He doesn't mean me any harm," I said. "I can feel it."

"But that does not mean that he has no agenda of his own," Nathaniel said. "He had not been seen or heard from by his own brothers for many long years, and then he coincidentally appeared just when Puck sent you to that strange planet."

"To protect me," I said impatiently. "He knew Puck was up to something and he wanted to keep me safe. And he was just as aware as the other two that Alerian had risen again. It's only natural that he would come here with me, since Chicago has become ground zero in the struggle between all these ancient creatures."

"Because you are here," Nathaniel said.

"You're here, too," I pointed out. "And since your legacy from Puck has been revealed, you're just as powerful as I am. Maybe more so."

"The old ones are not interested in me as they are you," Nathaniel said. "There is something special in you, and they all wish to control it."

"Daharan doesn't," I said.

Nathaniel said nothing, only looked at me from the corners of his eyes.

"He doesn't," I repeated.

I didn't care what Nathaniel or Beezle said. Daharan didn't want to control me, or take my baby, or make me his heir or anything else. Neither of them trusted my intuition (which, admittedly, had not always been super-accurate) but I knew I was right.

"Don't worry about Daharan," I said. "Worry about Alerian."

"I can multitask," Nathaniel said.

I snorted out a laugh. "Have it your way, then."

I'd been so caught up in our conversation that I barely noticed where we were headed until we were there. That was the second or third time I'd found myself focused on one thing to the exclusion of everything else. It was a dangerous habit. If I wasn't awake and aware of potential threats, I was going to get taken down by something magical and nasty.

"Trump Tower?" I said, screwing up my face at the silver needle-topped structure. "I hate this building."

"I am sure Alerian did not choose it with your sense of aesthetics in mind," Nathaniel said as we headed down the side of the building toward the sidewalk. "It is close to the river, close to the water."

"Why not Lake Point Tower?" I asked. "It's right on top of the lake."

"Do not ask me to explain his reasons," Nathaniel said.

"It would be nice if this Alerian-radar-thing we have also came with some handy illumination-of-intentions," I said as we entered the building under a veil.

There was far too much glass and white and modern-looking furniture in the lobby for my taste. The ceilings were extremely high and there had been some attempt at softening the effect of all the sharp angles by placing huge potted plants at strategic intervals.

We maneuvered easily around the bustle of people in the

lobby—guests checking into the hotel, businessmen speaking staccato into phones as they hurried to meetings.

Outside the glass the Chicago River was bluer than usual and it looked . . . "Alive" was the only word that seemed to fit. Normally the river is a muddy-looking churn. Even on sparkling summer days the water never really looks appealing the way Lake Michigan can. But now the river seemed like a powerful, electric thing, like it was giving off its own energy.

"It is because of Alerian," Nathaniel murmured quietly in my ear, his hand on my elbow.

"I know," I said, just as quietly. People tend to freak out if they hear disembodied voices. "How is it that nobody else seems to notice? Everyone seems so relentlessly normal."

"They may notice," Nathaniel said as we approached the elevators. "But not the way you or I would. They would simply remark that the river looks pretty today."

"It looks pretty, all right, but it also looks *wrong*," I said. "Don't survival instincts exist anymore?"

"There would likely be less crime if they did," Nathaniel said.

We fell silent as we entered an elevator behind an exhausted-looking family of tourists. They did not notice our presence; nor did any of them remark when Nathaniel pressed the button for Alerian's floor and the button seemed to magically light up on its own.

Of course we were invisible to mortal eyes, but you could still hear us if you listened closely, and you can always smell another person near you—their shampoo or body lotion or cologne. But the family remained oblivious, bickering about where to go for lunch.

I guess what Nathaniel said was true. Most people had no survival instincts. No flicker of awareness on the back of the neck, no sense of *wrongness*. I'd have been dead long ago without those little cues.

And yet despite seeing the evidence of vampires, angels and werewolves with their own eyes, there was no sense of concern, no frisson of alarm evident on the faces of the family who clattered out on their floor without noticing the presence of two creatures that could have killed them all in an instant.

It made me angry. I'd pushed my mind and body to the brink over and over, trying to keep oblivious cows like those people innocent and safe. They couldn't even have the courtesy to be aware of their surroundings.

My baby shifted, his wings fluttering more rapidly as my anger built. Nathaniel's arm went around my shoulders as the veil dropped away.

"Madeline, calm yourself," he murmured. "You are in no fit state to confront Alerian."

I nearly roared at him in response, then realized my anger was out of proportion. I took a deep breath, trying to push away the haze of red.

"It is the shadow," Nathaniel said. "It magnifies your emotions."

"I can't stand it," I said. "If I don't keep perfect control at all times, it looms up, tries to influence me. And it's all because of that damned Puck."

"Yes," Nathaniel said. "But do not think of him now. It will affect your ability to deal with Alerian."

The elevator doors opened and we moved into the hall. There had been no discussion where to go. The two of us moved in perfect synchronicity, Alerian's presence pulling us like a homing beacon. I'd half expected my uncle to have taken a fancy penthouse suite, but we appeared to be on a floor of regular rooms.

Of course, when we knocked on the door and Alerian

answered, I realized "regular" was relative. This wasn't a roadside motel, after all. The room behind my uncle was richly appointed, with floor-to-ceiling-window views of the Chicago River.

"Nathaniel. Madeline," Alerian said in a voice as cool as the sea. His hair was blue-green again and so were his eyes, shifting like waves. He was so clearly not of this world that I was surprised he'd been able to stand so close to the mayor without eliciting concern from the mayor's bodyguards, even with his unusual hair color covered up.

The three of us stood there for a moment, Nathaniel and I side by side, our hands clutched together, and Alerian across from us, ancient and roiling with power beneath the surface of his gaze.

I'd been a terrible student in school. I was lucky that I remembered how to add and subtract. Yet a fragment of a Tennyson poem I'd heard in some long-ago English class came back to me as I stared into the storm in Alerian's eyes. *Far, far beneath in the abysmal sea, His ancient, dreamless, uninvaded sleep . . . Until the latter fire shall heat the deep; Then once by man and angels to be seen, In roaring he shall rise . . .*

Alerian was rising. That was why Nathaniel and I could feel his presence at all times. His power was drawing up, building in a way that it had not since the ancient days. What did he intend to do once he reached his apex?

If Alerian truly was related to Lucifer and Puck, then he would have some complex machinery in place, a knotted web that I'd spend a great deal of time cutting through before I finally figured out the plot.

These thoughts passed lightning-quick behind my eyes in the moments we all stared at one another. Then Alerian smoothly moved to one side and gestured for us to enter.

4

NATHANIEL AND I SILENTLY PASSED THROUGH THE
door. The room was pristine, not a personal object in sight
save the jacket that matched Alerian's pants slung over the
chair.

He closed the door, and I felt an uncomfortable prick-
ling on my skin. With the door closed, his presence seemed
to fill up all the empty space in the room. The energy coming from the river intensified the feeling that I was surrounded on all sides by Alerian.

My uncle did not sit. Neither did we.

"To what do I owe the pleasure of your company—
finally?" Alerian said. "I have been in your city for close to
four months and neither of you have sought me out to pay
respects as you should."

"You haven't stopped by my place for a barbecue, either,
pal," I said.

Beside me, I felt rather than heard Nathaniel's nearly

inaudible sigh. I was scared out of my wits and staring down a very old and very powerful being, but my mouth shot off without any consideration for the possibility of harm at the hands of that being. I blame Beezle.

Alerian stiffened at my tone. "I did not receive an invitation."

"You didn't send us one, either," I said.

His gaze grew icier.

"See, that's your problem right there," I said. "No sense of humor. Lucifer or Puck would have been right there with me, snappy rejoinders at the ready."

"I do not play at life as my brothers do," Alerian said.

"No, but you're happy to play *with* life," I said, taking the opening. "Tell me about these shapeshifters of yours."

Alerian grew more still, if that was possible. I'd never seen anyone with such fine muscle control. He seemed not to even breathe.

"I can only assume that Daharan has betrayed my confidence," Alerian said. He said it in a way that implied, *And my brother will pay for his treachery.*

I had no doubt that Daharan could defend himself, and he'd surely had plenty of practice dealing with his own sibling. But I couldn't let the possibility of a threat against him stand.

"Leave Daharan out of it," I said. "He didn't betray you. I saw one of your shifters myself."

A flicker of surprise moved over his face before he was able to disguise it again. "That is impossible."

"Obviously it is possible," I said. "Based on your response, I'm going to assume you didn't know one of them was out running around, terrorizing innocent wolf packs."

Despite what I said, I was careful not to make any assumptions about Alerian's potential involvement. Just because he was surprised that I had encountered the shifter didn't mean that he wasn't aware of its existence. He might have thought the creature safely locked up somewhere.

I expected Alerian to think, to weigh his words before speaking, but he surprised me by responding quickly.

"If you know of the shifters, then you also know that Daharan forced me to destroy them," he said. "Whatever you saw, it was no creature of mine."

I glanced at Nathaniel, who gave a tiny shake of his head. *No.*

He didn't think I should push it. The line of inquiry hadn't revealed any new information anyway, so I was willing to let it go. For now.

"What about this plan for a supernatural ghetto?" I asked. "Did you come up with that all on your own, or did the mayor help you out?"

Alerian smiled then, a crafty, malicious smile that chilled me to the bone. "I am merely a consultant offering my services and assistance to the city. I have no power to dictate policy to the current administration."

"What a load of bullshit," I said. "The mayor doesn't have enough imagination to come up with a plan like this on his own."

Alerian moved forward suddenly, quick as a striking cobra, and before I could blink he stood less than an inch from me. Nathaniel stepped toward us, presumably to help, but I shook my head at him. Whatever happened was between Alerian and me.

"Know this, niece. My other brothers may tolerate such disrespect from you, but I shall not. You will not speak to me thus again unless you wish to suffer the consequences."

His power became more palpable, suffocating. My natural inclination was to flip him the bird, which was fallback response anytime something stronger and more powerful than me tried to tell me what to do. I recognized that this was not a wise play. Unlike everyone else I met, something about Alerian told me that he truly was not to be trifled with. However, I felt that it would set a bad precedent if I let him think he had the upper hand.

"You will not threaten me," I said, and lifted my chin.

"Do you not care for the child in your body?" Alerian said. "I could rip him squalling from your belly and strangle the life from him before you bled out on the floor. You are nothing, a mote of dust in time and space."

He had said exactly the wrong thing. *Exactly* the wrong thing. I could take any kind of insult to myself, but not to my child. Never to my child.

The shadow inside me roared up, and with it the push of magic. It pressed against Alerian's power, furious, seeking to destroy.

Alerian smiled again and grabbed my shoulders, pulling me close to him. I heard Nathaniel shout, but the sound came from far away, swallowed by the waves of the ocean. Then I was pulled beneath its depths, descending into the cool darkness. There was no light, no air, only a suffocating pressure and the blue-green swirl of Alerian's eyes.

I kicked my feet, felt the resistance of the water, but it was fruitless. I was wrapped in the embrace of the leviathan, and he would not release his quarry.

It was dark, and growing darker, and the shadow inside me smiled. It loved the dark.

Magic surged, releasing the pressure that threatened to crush me. I kicked toward the surface, and the light.

Alerian released me abruptly, staring at me. His face reflected no emotion, but I could sense his surprise. Nathaniel dragged me away from our uncle and toward the door.

Alerian stood where we left him, frozen in place, looking out the window at the river, saying nothing.

Nathaniel didn't speak to me either as he hurried me down the hall to the elevator. I could sense all the unsaid reprimands he held back. I also felt him drop a veil over our wings only. We could be seen, but we looked like a normal human couple.

We entered an elevator occupied by another couple that were either on their honeymoon or having an affair. Nobody in a tired relationship twines themselves around another person like that in a public place.

The busy twosome took zero notice of Nathaniel or me. My companion and I spoke not a word to each other. Nathaniel kept his hand at my elbow like I was a wayward child that needed guidance.

When we were outside again he turned to me, his blue eyes snapping with anger.

"Would you like to explain what the point of that little exercise was?" Nathaniel said. "We gathered no information and you nearly got yourself killed—again."

"Look at the river," I said, pointing at the water.

The river churned, waves rising abruptly. The water turned a poisonous green and steam rose from the surface. A group of kayakers appeared shocked by the sudden change in conditions and paddled quickly back toward their launch site.

"He's angry," I said, glancing up at the glass surface of the tower. I couldn't see him, but I could feel him there.

"In the event you have not noticed, so am I," Nathaniel said. "Madeline, tell me why it was necessary to confront Alerian. We gained nothing from this."

I pulled my gaze away from the river and looked at Nathaniel, who appeared to be restraining himself at great cost.

"We did gain something," I said. "I know what Alerian plans to do."

Nathaniel's eyebrows rose. "How is that possible?"

"When Alerian grabbed hold of me, he tried to push his power down in me. He was too distracted to notice the flow of magic moving both ways. In that instant when I fought back and broke away, he was surprised, and in his surprise he revealed something that he hadn't intended to show. I saw just a flash of it, but it was there."

I paused, watching the water. The waves were dying down, the color returning to normal. Alerian was drawing back, mastering his anger.

"Let's walk a little," I said. My baby turned and kicked inside me, and my encounter with Alerian had filled me with restless energy that flying wouldn't burn off.

Nathaniel fell into step beside me. "Are you planning to tell me just what it was you saw when you peeked into Alerian's mind?"

"He's going to use the city of Chicago to herd anyone out of the ordinary into his camp. Then he's going to use one of his shapeshifters to control the whole mass as an army to start killing off humans. He's breaking Lucifer's toy, wiping the slate clean," I said. "It's diabolical, really. We know about the plan but it's difficult to stop. He's got the machinery of the city in motion, so even if we remove Alerian from the equation, all the supernatural creatures would still be rounded up and fenced in. We could find some way to prevent Alerian from controlling them as an army, but all the supernaturals will still be in one place. And what do you think will happen then?"

"A leader will rise. Someone who would tell them that they need not submit to human law," Nathaniel said. "A revolution would begin."

I nodded. "And it would spread to other places and other cities, and humans would be killed. There would be total chaos, and Alerian's purpose would be served regardless."

"What if we can stop the imprisonment of supernatural creatures before it happens?" Nathaniel asked.

"I'm not sure how. Like I said earlier today, there will doubtless be motivation for ordinary humans to turn in their not-so-ordinary neighbors. The collection may have begun already. And if we encourage those creatures to resist—"

"Fighting would inevitably ensue, and deaths, and chaos," Nathaniel finished. "You are correct. It *is* diabolical. No matter how we examine the problem the ultimate outcome is the same, and Alerian obtains what he desires."

"Yes," I said. "Maybe we're just not looking at it the right way. Maybe we need the rest of the brain trust."

I wondered what J.B. would think of all this. I hadn't spoken to him in a couple of weeks. He'd taken a leave of absence from the Agency after I'd killed Titania. He needed to spend some quality time with his faerie court. He was a king by right and by blood, but since he was almost never there tending to his courtiers, there was often a lot of rebellious grumbling.

The death of the High Queen of Faerie and her only son, Bendith, caused sufficient ripples through the faerie world that J.B. deemed it prudent to spend some time acting like a king. Since I'd been the one to take out the High Queen (and a lot of faerie were angry with me about that), he had also deemed it prudent that I not try to get in touch with him while he was there. Which was too bad, because J.B.'s advice would probably be useful.

"It is some consolation that we now know the identity of the shapeshifter's master," Nathaniel said.

"No, we don't," I said with a hollow laugh.

Nathaniel looked puzzled. "You said Alerian would use his shapeshifter to control his army, as in days of old."

"Yeah, a *new* shapeshifter that he hasn't made yet. He wouldn't risk Daharan discovering and destroying the new one before he had a chance to really get his plans under way," I said. "And there was something else, another shadow working in the background, I think. There was a flash of something that I saw but couldn't latch on to."

"So there is another master for the creature that tried to attack you this morning," Nathaniel said.

"Yup," I said. "Nothing is ever easy when I'm involved. And here's the worst of it. Have you thought of how Lucifer will respond once he figures out what Alerian's up to?"

"If it appears that Alerian is raising an army for his own purpose, then Lucifer will declare war on his brother," Nathaniel said. He took my hand and held it tight.

"Boom! goes the world," I said. "No matter what story plays out, that seems to be the result."

"Perhaps you could speak to Lucifer, make him see reason. Perhaps you could even influence him to halt Alerian's plans," he said.

"I think you are vastly overestimating the effect I have on Lucifer. Plus, when has Lucifer ever done anything out of the goodness of his heart?" I said with a pointed look at my belly. "He's made it clear from the start that he wants my baby. If I ask him to help out with Alerian *or* to give up what he would view as his rightful vengeance for Alerian's behavior, then he will want something really good in exchange. Like my child. Or me as his heir.

"Daharan might be able to influence Lucifer," I continued, "but I don't think he can do much with Alerian. He keeps talking about how their powers are in opposition to one another."

"He says that, but he can influence Alerian when he so chooses," Nathaniel said. "He forced Alerian to give up the shapeshifters, do you not recall?"

"Hey, you're right," I said, wondering why I hadn't realized this before. "Why does he keep acting like he can't do anything?"

"Perhaps he believes that if he repeats it often enough, you will think it is true, and not question his motives," Nathaniel said.

For the first time I felt a flicker of doubt. Did Daharan have some sinister purpose here? Was he in fact working with Alerian? Was it his job to lead me away from Alerian's true intentions, to distract me?

I shook my head. "No. Daharan doesn't mean me any harm. If he won't go up against Alerian, it's for some reason of his own. And if I ask him, he will tell me."

Nathaniel looked doubtful. "I hope your trust in him is not misplaced."

We had walked east in an aimless manner, unconsciously putting distance between us and Alerian's wrath. I realized we had ended up on Michigan Avenue. "Let's go to the Ghirardelli shop by Water Tower."

"There is a crisis of epic proportions at hand and you are thinking about chocolate?" he asked.

"No, I'm thinking about ice cream. Ice cream with peanut butter and hot fudge and whipped cream on top," I said, heading north through the usual midday cluster of people on Michigan.

"There is a crisis of epic proportions at hand and you are thinking about ice cream?" he said.

I laughed, taking his hand. "I'm pregnant and I will not be denied. Besides, there's a crisis of epic proportions every five seconds around here."

"I love you, but I do not understand you," Nathaniel said, allowing me to tug him in the direction of the store.

We strolled along, not speaking much. I was trying to enjoy the moment, to allow myself these few moments to pretend that we were as normal as we looked. It was not the first time I had wished that my life had turned out differently, that I had a future that didn't involve blood and magic and darkness covering the world.

As a child I'd yearned for sitcom normality—a mother who packed Wonder Bread lunches and volunteered at school instead of running off to collect souls at all hours, a dad who was actually present. Even though I loved Beezle and could not imagine life without him, there were still occasions when I wished for a puppy instead of a grumpy talking gargoyle.

Over time I'd come to a kind of peace with the presence of the Agency in my life. But since I'd discovered my relationship to some of the most powerful creatures in history, I yearned for that normality more than ever. The impending birth of my son only intensified this feeling.

Parents want their children to have what they did not, and I had never had stability. I did not want my baby to enter a world that was constantly under the threat of magical destruction. I especially did not want him to grow up like I did, always waiting at the window hoping Mommy would come home to give me a kiss before bedtime.

The worst of it was that I could not see how I could change my fate, or his. Everywhere I turned there was another wall to box me in.

"Madeline?" Nathaniel said. Something in his tone told me he had tried to get my attention more than once.

I shook my head, wishing I could shake away my gloomy contemplations of the future. "Sorry."

"We have arrived," he said, pointing at the white-and-blue awning in front of us.

The intense craving that had seized me earlier had by this time faded, but ice cream would still help my mood. There is no mood that cannot be improved by a giant sundae.

Nathaniel expressed no interest in eating. He watched me enthusiastically attack my ice cream, all the while wearing what I thought of as his I-do-not-comprehend-humans expression.

"Don't you like ice cream?" I asked.

He shrugged. "Most angels do not see the appeal of sugar. It does not seem to affect us as it does humans."

I thought back and realized I'd never seen Gabriel or Nathaniel eat anything dessert-like.

"Is it because of differences in body chemistry?" I wondered aloud. "Or because angels have such long lives that simple things become boring?"

"Perhaps some of both," he said. "I have often wished I could take comfort in small pleasures, as you do."

Somehow it had never occurred to me that Nathaniel might have some of the same longings I did, a desire to be more human. Part of this was because he had expressed contempt for humanity so often that I'd assumed he would never give up any aspect of the "superiority" of angels. The changes that occurred since his magical legacy had been released still surprised me.

"Well, there's no time like the present to start learning," I said.

I scooped a big spoonful of vanilla ice cream mixed with hot fudge and peanut butter sauce and held it out to him, smiling.

He looked at me, then at the spoon, then back at me

again. The smile faded from my face. Suddenly the action seemed fraught with implication. Something shifted in his eyes. There was a light and a heat that was not there before. My hand seemed frozen in place, and everything inside me stilled. I could not take my eyes from his mouth as it moved toward the spoon.

"Ms. Madeline Black?" a voice asked from somewhere above my left shoulder.

I dropped the spoon to the table with a clatter, the spell broken. Several patrons glanced over at the noise and my face reddened. The shop seating area was small and the tables were stacked beside one another with barely enough room to maneuver through the aisles so privacy was completely nonexistent.

Nathaniel calmly wiped the ice cream from the table with a napkin as I turned to glare at the person who had interrupted us.

It was a tall man with blond hair curling over his brow and the tops of his ears. His eyes were a brilliant green, like the poisonous shade of the river, and he was dressed like an Ermenegildo Zegna ad. There was something about him that struck me as familiar. In his right hand he held a creamy white envelope with a seal I recognized on the back. The snake tattoo on my palm twitched.

"Whatever you've got, I don't want it," I said. I pushed the half-eaten sundae away from me, any pleasure I took in the moment sucked out by the presence of a messenger from my second-least-favorite relation.

"Lord Lucifer expected you to respond thus and instructed me to wait while you read his missive," the messenger said in a carrying voice.

If anyone had not been looking at us before, they certainly were now, especially after they heard the word

"Lucifer." Some people looked confused, like they thought the guy was kidding. Others looked offended, frightened or suspicious. They may not know for sure whether Lucifer existed, but everyone in Chicago knew there were bad things loose in the world.

"What's the matter with you?" I hissed at the messenger. "Go outside, for the love of Pete. I'll be out in a second."

He looked doubtful, like I was going to try to slip away from him somehow. "Lord Lucifer instructed me to—"

"Shut. Up," I said through my teeth as I came to my feet. All I wanted was for him to stop talking and everyone to stop looking. Pretty soon someone would put my face together with the video footage of me destroying the vampires at Soldier Field, and then who knew what would happen?

I didn't want to wait to find out. I waved the messenger ahead of me as I waddled my way out of the seating area and past the bar where the ice cream was prepared. The stares of everyone who had witnessed the scene pressed into my back.

Nathaniel moved up beside me as we followed the messenger out to the sidewalk. As soon as we were outdoors, Lucifer's errand boy turned to me with the envelope. I snatched it from his hand but did not open it. The Ghirardelli store was next to a Topshop and only half a block from Michigan Avenue. There were a ton of people walking back and forth, and a lot of women giving both Nathaniel and the messenger admiring glances. A little privacy was necessary.

We crossed Pearson and went into the little park next to the water tower. There were several benches with people on them, checking their phones, reading magazines, eating potato chips. I looked for a semi-secluded area where I could read what was in the envelope. Anger and embarrassment coursed through me. I was beyond tired of having every decent moment in my life ruined by Lucifer, and I was in a bad enough mood to take it out on the messenger.

"Are you one of his kids?" I asked as I tore the seal from the envelope.

I really did not want to see what was inside. Every time I received a letter from Lucifer he asked (read: ordered) me to perform some crappy task that would endanger my life and create more enemies.

"One of whom's?" the messenger asked.

"Lucifer's, of course," I said. "You've got that look. What's your name?"

He seemed surprised. "My name is Zaniel, and yes, Lord Lucifer is my father."

"Who's your mother?"

"Ariell," he said with a trace of stiffness in his voice.

I'd started to unfold the paper but stopped at the name, staring at Zaniel in surprise.

"Ariell the psycho? Ariell who I—" I stopped, realizing what I was about to say.

Zaniel finished for me, his green eyes stony. "Killed. Yes."

That meant this character was Samiel's half brother. They shared the same mother. And while Samiel had come around pretty quickly to the idea that the world was better off without Ariell, there was no guarantee Zaniel would feel the same.

"What's Lucifer's game in sending you to me?" I asked.

"I do not understand what you mean," he said.

"Are you normally his errand boy, or is this a new thing?"

"This is the first occasion in which Lord Lucifer has entrusted me with—"

I cut him off. "So he sent you here for a reason. I just need to figure out what that reason is."

"It is not for us to know Lord Lucifer's ways," he said.

"It is for me. I'm the one who's always getting screwed over by his plans."

While Zaniel and I had our little exchange, Nathaniel took the letter from my hand, opened it and read it.

"I do not see that you are 'getting screwed,' as you say. Lord Lucifer showers you with honors far beyond your status. You are only a distant heir in the bloodline, not even an immediate child." There was a strong note of jealousy in his voice.

"You want my 'honors'? You can have them. Every time Lucifer has some shit job he wants done that involves bloodletting some freaky monster, I get the privilege of handling it."

"That is the right of the Hound of the Hunt," he said. "By making you, one of his own bloodline, the Hound, Lord Lucifer sent a clear message to all his children that you are preferred."

"Yeah, well—" I started, but was cut off by Nathaniel.

"Madeline," he said.

I looked at him. He handed me the paper without a word, and I finally read the missive that was so important that Zaniel had to interrupt my day.

I'd been wrong. It wasn't an assignment from my darling great-grandfather.

It was an invitation.

And boy, I did not want to attend this party.

5

IT READ, IN FANCY ITALICS:

You are cordially invited to share in our joy
At the marriage of

Lucifer Morningstar, First of the Fallen

And
His One True Love,

Evangeline of the Bone-eaters Tribe

At our home
Saturday, May 15th at 5pm
Dinner to follow
RSVP Immediately

I couldn't decide whether to laugh or cry. Lucifer was formally marrying Evangeline, my psychotic, eyeless, one-armed, many-greats-grandmother. That meant that her child, the one they'd conceived while Lucifer visited Evangeline in the land of the dead, would become his heir, no question about it.

And that meant me and my offspring were out of it, which was absolutely a relief. Hopefully Evangeline would act less crazy once her position was secured.

However, I did not think it was a good idea for me to walk into the parlor of the spider. A confrontation with Evangeline in her own home would probably go badly for me.

The wedding would be a farce in any case. Would Lucifer wear a tuxedo? Would Evangeline wear a giant confection of a wedding dress? Would all the fallen do the Electric Slide and the Chicken Dance? I did not want to be a party to any of those things, although Beezle would want to videotape the whole thing and upload it to YouTube, I was sure.

I folded the paper and handed it back to the messenger, who did not take it.

"You can tell Grandpa that I respectfully decline," I said.

He shook his head, a malicious glint in his eye. "Lord Lucifer expected this response and instructed me to tell you that attendance is not optional."

"This wedding is only three days away. I've got pressing business here to attend to," I said.

"Your presence is required. And so is yours," he said to Nathaniel.

Nathaniel nodded, like he had expected this. *Oh, no, no.* I did not like that at all. Nathaniel's presence in my life had only been tolerated by Lucifer since the Morningstar had discovered Nathaniel was Puck's son. Prior to that, Nathaniel had been serving a debt to Lucifer for his part in Azazel's rebellion. His life was forfeit to my great-grandfather, and if Lucifer chose, he could kill Nathaniel without a second of justification. I did not want Nathaniel under Lucifer's eye for an extended period of time. The Morningstar might kill him in a fit of pique.

I opened my mouth to protest, but Nathaniel's look stopped me. I could almost read his mind. *Not now, get rid of the messenger.*

I folded the paper and put it in the pocket of my suit, smiling brightly. Zaniel appeared taken aback by my expression.

"Tell Lucifer we happily accept," I said.

Zaniel schooled his expression back to neutral. I got the sense that he was disappointed, that he had hoped for more protest from me. That made me wonder why.

Was he looking for an opportunity to pick a fight with me? And if so, was that fight sanctioned or encouraged by Lucifer for some reason? Or was the messenger willing to go off the reservation in order to exact revenge for his mother's death? This was why I hated dealing with the fallen. I usually ended up with a migraine.

"I will express your acceptance to Lord Lucifer," Zaniel said, and turned away, his back stiff and straight.

Nathaniel and I watched him go. He went to the corner near Pearson and Michigan. A black limousine seemed to appear out of nowhere. Zaniel climbed in and the limo pulled into traffic on Michigan, heading south.

"Why didn't he take a portal?" I asked.

"Perhaps he wished to do so in a more unobtrusive place," Nathaniel said. "There are many potentially curious people in this area."

"No," I said, staring in the direction the car had gone. "That's not it. Why not slip into an alley? He's taking the car because he's meeting with someone else."

Nathaniel looked troubled. "Sokolov?"

I nodded. "He's the only big player left here besides Alerian. And I can't imagine Lucifer sending that boy to deal with Alerian."

Nathaniel gave me a small smile. "That 'boy' is several thousand years older than you. Ariell's affair with Lucifer long predates Lucifer's original relationship with Evangeline."

"It doesn't matter how old he is," I said. "For someone who's been around for a while, he's not very good at hiding his emotions. Alerian would eat him alive."

"Perhaps that is what Lucifer wants. Perhaps he is going to meet Alerian."

"Clearing the board of his less-favorite offspring to make room for the new one? It doesn't seem likely. Lucifer is fanatical about anyone with the same blood as his. It seems more likely that Zaniel is going to meet Sokolov. If he's going to meet Sokolov, I want to know why."

"It would also be helpful to know whether he is meeting at Lucifer's behest or another's," Nathaniel said.

"I can't imagine what Lucifer would have to say to Sokolov," I said. "But it seems like Zaniel is too much of a bit player to have the power or authority to go to the Agency on his own. There could only be one topic of conversation, anyway."

"You," Nathaniel said.

"Not that I think I'm the center of the universe or anything," I said hastily.

"No, it is logical that any discussions with the Agency would involve you," Nathaniel said. "Who could direct Lucifer's son against you if not Lucifer himself?"

"Zaniel doesn't seem to like me very much," I said. "A smart person could play on that emotion easily."

"Which smart person?"

"Take your pick," I said. "I have too many enemies to try to narrow it down without more information. Too bad J.B. is away trying to be a good king. He might be able to get some extra information for me if he was actually in the office. It's really bizarre that he's not there. He spends more time sleeping at his desk chair than he does in his own bed."

"At the very least he would be able to confirm our speculation that the messenger is going to the Agency."

"Yeah," I said. "We might as well head home and see if Jude and Samiel turned up any information on that shapeshifter."

As I spoke I realized something was buzzing in my pocket. I pulled my cell phone out, surprised I'd even remembered to bring it. Then I reasoned I likely had not remembered, but that Daharan had known I would forget and put it in the pocket of the suit. The screen told me it was J.B.

"Hey," I said. "I was just talking about you. I thought you didn't think it was a good idea for us to talk while you were playing King of the Fae."

"I'm not playing," J.B. said. "Don't you even say hello anymore? Your conversational skills are actually getting worse as you get older."

"I can't help it. I graduated from the Beezle school of interpersonal relationships. If I let you talk first, then I might have to suffer slings and arrows against my character."

"I didn't call to listen to you mangle Shakespeare," he said.

"Is that from Shakespeare?" I asked. "I had no idea."

"Not really," he said. "Hence the mangling. I called because a messenger just showed up in my court. A messenger from Lucifer."

"Let me guess. He gave you an invitation and 'no' was not an acceptable RSVP response," I said.

"He gave me an invitation, but I wasn't foolish enough to say no," J.B. said. "I'm sure you were."

I decided to ignore that comment because it annoyed me that I was so predictable.

"I wonder who else was invited," I said.

"Everyone who's ever come to Lucifer's attention, I imagine."

"Which would include those who've crossed him," I said. "Why tempt fate by gathering your enemies in one place?"

"I'm sure he's got something up his sleeve besides marrying Evangeline," he said. "If I hear anything before Saturday, I'll let you know."

"Speaking of hearing things—have you got anyone you trust at the Agency that you can get in touch with?"

"Lizzie," he said. Lizzie was his secretary. "And a couple of others. Why? Did you do something?"

"No," I said. "Why does everyone always assume I've done something?"

"Your track record speaks for itself," J.B. said. "Don't make me start listing all the property you've destroyed."

"Slings and arrows," I muttered. "Anyway, I want to find out if the messenger who delivered the invite from Lucifer to me went to see Sokolov. And if he did, I'd love to know if he went there on his own or under somebody's orders."

"I'll see if I can find out anything. See you in a few days." He clicked off.

I looked at Nathaniel. "You heard all that, so there's no need for a recap, right?"

Ever since Nathaniel had come into his legacy from Puck, he had super-werewolf-like hearing. He nodded in acknowledgment. "J.B. is certainly correct. Lucifer will doubtless invite all his allies and enemies to this event."

"I notice you didn't say 'friends,'" I said.

"In all his long history, the closest thing Lucifer ever had to a friend was Michael," Nathaniel said.

"The archangel," I said. "I wonder if he will be invited."

By silent and mutual consent we walked to a semi-secluded spot where we could veil ourselves from human eyes and fly home.

"I do not think you should concern yourself excessively with Lucifer's wedding," Nathaniel said. "As you told the messenger, there are other, more pressing issues at hand, including Alerian's anger with your defiance. I am concerned about the stress you are under in your condition."

"I'm pregnant, Nathaniel. I'm not dying," I said.

"You are a human on the verge of giving birth to a child of mixed and extremely powerful origins. I believe you are underestimating what changes this baby has wrought in your body. All I suggest is taking each problem as it presents itself and not worrying about what may happen on Saturday at this time."

"But what if Lucifer is collecting all his known associates in one place so he can squash them in the most efficient manner possible?"

"You need not worry. If Lucifer were to do such a thing, your life would no doubt be spared," he said.

I frowned at him, knowing he could see my face despite the veil. "You think it would make it okay if I lived even if everyone else died?"

"All I am attempting to say is that Lucifer would not permit harm to come to you."

"Yeah, as long as I'm carrying the little prince," I said. "After that I'll be just as expendable as anyone else."

"I know you do not wish to hear this, but if you had accepted Lucifer's protection in the first place . . ."

"I'm not going to have this argument with you. Again."

"Very well," Nathaniel said, but I could tell he didn't want to let it go.

Beezle had made the same argument once I'd discovered I was pregnant. Both of them seemed to think I would be safer with Lucifer. But I didn't think it was a good idea to stay in such close quarters with the Prince of Darkness.

We landed on the lawn of the house. Everything seemed quiet and normal on the street. Our usual mail carrier was about half a block from my house, whistling as he jogged up porch steps to drop off catalogs and bills. I could hear the happy cries of kids released for recess at the school down the street.

For some reason, though, tension wound tight in my belly. Beside me Nathaniel appeared stiff and alert.

"Something's coming," I said.

He pushed me toward the house. "Get inside."

"You've got to be freaking kidding me," I said. "No way."

"Do not be stubborn for a change. For the love of the gods, let me protect you."

I shook my head. "I'm not being stubborn. You hear those kids playing down the street? There's no way I'm going to go inside and hide and let whatever's coming take out its frustration on them. Enough innocents have died in this city."

He did not argue anymore after that. We moved so that we were back-to-back, and waited.

There was still no sign of whatever was making us so tense. The mailman approached the house, working his way cheerfully down the block. I gave him a good hard stare, wondering whether he was the shapeshifter in disguise, but it didn't do me any good. I didn't have Beezle's powers.

Beezle. Right. What was I thinking?

I pulled out my phone. Nathaniel gave me a startled look.

"You are making a phone call now?"

I dialed the house phone. After five rings the answering machine picked up. "Damn. Beezle must still be out with Samiel. But where's Daharan? He's usually at home all day."

The mailman reached my front walk. He stopped whistling abruptly as he noticed us, tense-faced and ready for a fight.

"Um, good morning," he said, sidling past us like whatever was wrong with us might be communicable.

"Morning," I said through my teeth. The knot in my belly tightened. It was about to happen.

The mailman offered the rubber-banded bundle of envelopes to me. "Do you want to take it, or should I just leave it in the—"

I grabbed it from him and tossed the packet to the ground.

"—box," he finished.

"Thanks," I said. I wanted him to leave. I wanted him to leave *immediately*, before he was caught in the cross fire.

The mailman started to walk away, then stopped. "Are you by any chance the same Madeline Black who—"

"Alerian," Nathaniel and I both said simultaneously.

The mailman appeared confused. "Alerian? I was going to ask about the vampires."

"Get down!" I yelled just before the world seemed to explode.

There was no warning rumble, no indication that anything was going to happen. The grate flew off the sewer opening that was right in front of my house. The street seemed to cave in on itself before bursting outward, chunks of cement flying everywhere. I watched in horror as the pieces of the street crashed through the windows of people's homes. And then the first tentacle emerged.

"What the hell is that?" the mailman screamed. "Just what in the hell is *that*?"

My sword was in my hand before I even considered what I was doing.

"Go in the house!" I shouted, hoping the mailman would have the sense to take cover in the foyer, but the man seemed paralyzed by fear.

I couldn't blame him. I was feeling fairly paralyzed myself. A small, still-thinking part of my brain realized the gigantic tentacled sea creature rising from the rubble wasn't Alerian himself but an avatar, a sending to do his dirty work.

Nathaniel and I moved toward the thing, defying my very natural instinct to move away from the monster that wanted to eat us.

And I was pretty sure that it *did* want to eat us, as it seemed primarily composed of teeth and tentacles. Its mouth was a giant maw of rotating layers of teeth that seemed to circle in its jaw like razor-sharp gears. I could not see any eyes, but its front two tentacles shot toward us with unerring accuracy.

I did the only natural thing in those circumstances. I slashed at the tentacle that reached for me. The tip of the arm sliced off under the blade of the sword. Black blood, like cephalopod ink, poured out of the wound, splashing over us, smelling of salt and the sea.

Nathaniel took a different tack. When the second tentacle curled toward him, he grabbed it. And set it on fire.

"Hey, that's my M.O.," I said.

"I have learned by observation," Nathaniel said. "This is your way of effectively ending a conflict."

Flames sped up the appendage, making the monster roar and slap the burning tentacle on the ground. Chunks of oversized sea-monster flesh flew everywhere. I heard a woman scream, but I couldn't see her. All I could see was teeth and flailing squid arms.

The fire had panicked the creature temporarily, but I noticed the flames were going out. That limb was charred and useless, but the monster still had six more. And now it was angrier than ever.

"Apparently you haven't been watching me closely enough," I said. "When you set something on fire, you have to really set it *on fire*."

"At your pleasure, then," Nathaniel said, indicating that it was my move.

I looked at the thrashing, howling monster and realized pretty quickly that there wasn't a lot of point messing around with the tentacles. I reached inside me, where the heart of the sun burned, where Lucifer's magic called. Then I held my hands before me and let the fire fly.

It arrowed straight into the kraken's open mouth. Such was my connection to my magic now that I felt the flame descend deep into the cavity of its body, burning flesh, causing the creature unimaginable agony. For just a moment I felt its confusion, too. Alerian had created this thing to cause pain, not to receive it. It didn't understand the burning inside.

I deliberately drew back from the spell, broke the connection. The magic was doing its work. The monster was dying. There was no need to feed the shadow inside me by relishing its death throes.

The fire spread from the inside out, smoke pouring from the creature's mouth in thick black plumes. The stench was horrific. I covered my nose and took a few steps back, halting only when I bumped into the mailman. I'd half forgotten he was there.

He seemed unable to tear his gaze away from the spectacle of a giant octopus-squid-monster burning to death in the middle of a Chicago street.

I put my hand on his shoulder. He was so still I was afraid his mind was broken. "Hey, are you okay?"

My touch seemed to awaken him from his trance. He turned to look at me, blinking. "I guess you *are* that Madeline Black. The one with the vampires."

"Yes, I am." I felt I owed him the truth after what he'd just witnessed.

"This kind of thing happen around you a lot?" he asked. He seemed unnaturally calm.

"Unfortunately, yes," I said.

"Uh-huh," he said.

He walked away from me and toward his mail cart, which had fallen to one side when Alerian's monster emerged from the street. The side of the cart was smeared with blackened squid flesh. He righted the cart, collected the spilled mail, and then looked at me.

"I'll be asking for a different route," he said.

I nodded. That was to be expected. It was what any sane person would do after spending five minutes in my company.

He nodded back and pushed the cart down the sidewalk toward the house next to mine, carefully maneuvering around the buckled cement and the large chunks of the street scattered everywhere.

The street was quiet. Every sensible individual had gone inside, where they were probably frantically trying to explain to the 911 dispatcher what had just happened.

Beezle landed on my shoulder, his claw covering his beak. "What have you done? I may never be able to eat fried calamari again after this."

"Where have you been?" I asked.

"With Samiel, like you told me to," Beezle said. "We were nearby and saw smoke so we figured it could only be you."

Samiel appeared beside Nathaniel. He looked at the mess in the street and then at me. He appeared resigned.

"It wasn't my fault," I said, feeling defensive. "It just came out of the street there."

"Uh-huh," Beezle said, echoing the response of the mailman. "Well, the fire alarms have sounded so I would say that's your cue to go inside and pretend this had nothing to do with you. If you're standing on the lawn covered in squid guts, plausible deniability becomes a lot more difficult."

"He is right," Nathaniel said. "The proximity of your home to this event will already be a red flag for the authorities."

"And others," I said. "Jack Dabrowski will have a field day with this."

"You should be less worried about Dabrowski and more worried about what this means for the mayor's imprison-the-supernaturals plan," Beezle said as we trudged into the house. "The giant burned carcass is going to end up on the afternoon news. And I'm sure lots of our panicked neighbors will say they saw the two of you fighting that thing. Heck, a lot of them probably filmed it with their smartphones."

"We were *defending* our panicked neighbors from that thing," I said. "I should think that would tip the scales in our favor. If we're locked up, who will keep people safe from stuff like that?"

Beezle flew ahead of me as we entered the apartment and landed on the dining room table. He shook his head at me. "You're not looking at this the right way. There's already some anti-supernatural sentiment, and the mayor's announcement will only stir up more. People will argue that the monster wouldn't even be here if not for you."

That gave me pause. I sat down heavily in one of the dining table chairs. "Well, they would be right. Alerian sent that thing for me and Nathaniel."

"I take it you behaved with your usual tact at the meeting, then?" Beezle asked.

"Yes," Nathaniel answered. "Madeline, you should use the shower before I do. I believe Samiel is cooking, and you will need to eat."

Sure enough, I heard the familiar clatter of pots and pans in the kitchen. Samiel always liked to cook after a crisis. It was one of many reasons why Beezle adored him. Beezle's affection was easily bought by anyone with halfway decent kitchen skills.

"Why is Samiel cooking?" Beezle asked. "Where's Daharan? I thought he was going to increase the protection on this house. If he had done his job, maybe that gross tentacled nightmare wouldn't have found you."

"The protection was for the house. I was practically in the street," I said. "And it was supposed to make it harder for humans to find me. He never said anything about monsters."

"But where is he?" Beezle persisted.

"I don't know," I said, annoyed that Beezle, like Nathaniel, wanted to read sinister implications into Daharan's behavior. "I'm not his keeper. I'm going to shower."

"Good, because you smell like you've been on a fishing boat for the last two months," Beezle said, exchanging a look with Nathaniel.

"I'm going to leave now so the two of you can discuss Daharan without me," I said loudly.

I started down the hall, then stopped. Something had been nagging at me since we'd arrived home, and I'd only just realized what it was.

"Where are the dogs?" I asked, returning to the dining room.

Beezle and Nathaniel both looked at me blankly.

"They were here when I left with Samiel," Beezle said.

"Did Jude take them?" It seemed like a possibility. The dogs and Jude seemed to have formed an immediate bond.

Beezle shook his head. "He left with us."

"Where is Jude now?" Nathaniel asked.

Beezle shrugged. "He stayed with us for a while; then we split up. We figured it was more efficient that way."

"And he's not back yet," I said. "So that's another thing to worry about. Lock! Stock! Barrel!"

There was no answering bark or scrabble of claws on the floor. The truth was they usually enthusiastically assaulted me as soon as I walked in the door, so I should have noticed immediately that something was wrong.

I went through the kitchen, where Samiel appeared to be making soup. He didn't even glance up from the pile of vegetables he was chopping when I entered.

I crossed to the back door and opened it, half expecting

to see the three dogs on the landing leading to the back stairs. But they weren't there.

Fresh air drifted up the stairwell. I hurried down the stairs as fast as my increased bulk would allow, gripping the handrail. I'd nearly reached the bottom when I heard footsteps on the stairs above me.

"Madeline?" Nathaniel called.

"The back door is open," I said.

"Do not go outside," he shouted down the stairs. "Do not go outside without me."

I paused on the threshold, my backyard framed by the door.

Through the door was a sliver of the yard, the weather-proofed planks of the small back porch, the top corner of the garden shed, a few of the overhanging leaves from the tree in the corner. I shifted so I could peer more to the left, then to the right.

A dark shape hung from the tree. It was attracting flies.

6

"NO," I SAID.

I took one step toward the open door, felt Nathaniel's hand close around my wrist.

"Where are you going? I told you to wait," he said. "You do not know what is out there."

"She's never done what she's told," Beezle said, landing on my shoulder.

In response I pointed out the door to the hanging thing.

Nathaniel put his hands on both my shoulders and gently moved me to one side. "All the more reason for you to wait."

He paused at the threshold, listening. A little trace of magic filled the air, the pulse that Nathaniel sent outside searching for danger.

"Whatever was here is gone now," he said.

Nathaniel stepped onto the porch. I held my breath, expecting something to attack. But there was nothing, only the soft spring breeze carrying the scent of the trees and the lingering stench of roasted kraken. I followed Nathaniel outside and down the porch steps.

Lock and Barrel sat under the tree, staring up. .

That was when I realized what the shape was. It was Stock, his belly slit open, hanging from his own entrails.

I gagged, bile rising in my throat, covering my mouth with my hand as I turned away. The sound made Lock and Barrel give up their silent vigil. They turned toward me with mournful faces, automatically moving in my direction.

Then they stopped. And growled.

"Hey, guys, it's only Nathaniel. You know him," I said, approaching them with my hand out.

They growled again, showing their teeth.

"I do not think it is me they are upset with," he said.

I glanced behind me, just to make sure there was nothing scary standing at my back, and then looked back at the dogs.

"Me?" I said, pointing to my chest.

Lock and Barrel growled again.

"The shapeshifter," Beezle said. "While we were hunting all over the city, he came back here."

"And pretended to be me, and killed one of my dogs," I said.

I felt sick, and sick at heart, and tired of losing those whom I loved. I couldn't even take comfort in the other two because they thought I had slaughtered their companion.

"Reach out to them," Beezle urged. "You have a connection with them. It's how you brought them to heel in the first place."

He was right. The shapeshifter had already taken one of the dogs from me. Why should I let him take the other two?

I stepped closer, even though this caused both dogs to

increase their growling. I lowered to the ground, holding my hands out. Lock barked at me, his hackles raised. The dogs were only a few feet from me, their eyes glowing red. It reminded me that these were not ordinary dogs, that the memory of their life as Retrievers was still inside them, and so was their power.

"It's me," I said, and I sent out a breath of magic to touch them, so that they would know it was me, really me.

At the first brush of power they stopped growling. I felt their confusion, their sense that I was the person they loved and trusted, but there was Another, and that Other smelled the same and looked the same but then did a bad thing, such a bad thing, and when they saw it they were confused, and then the other changed to something else and went away, and they should have stopped the other but it looked like her, it smelled like her, and now here she was again, so was it her, or was it the other? It feels like her, it smells like her, but we don't know . . .

"It's me," I repeated, and sent my magic around them, wanting them to know, to understand I could never hurt them that way. I could never be that way.

Memories flashed through them, the shapeshifter calling to them, luring them outside. The doors were opened to them, the shapeshifter standing in the middle of the backyard, smiling, looking like me, seeming like me.

That was not me. This is me. I pushed harder with my magic, to make them feel that connection that had bound us in the first place. Lock whined in his throat. Barrel lowered his body to the ground and rested his head on his paws. *It is you.*

I scooted closer to them. Barrel put his head on what was left of my lap. Lock licked my face.

"Let's go inside, boys," I said, attempting to stand.

Beezle snorted with laughter as I fell back on my bottom. Nathaniel helped me to my feet, brushing grass from my suit. It seemed like a pointless gesture since I was still covered in goop from the fight with Alerian's monster.

"I will tend to this," he said, jerking his head at the tree.

Beezle, the dogs and I went back up the stairs. Samiel stood in the kitchen doorway holding a spatula and looking confused.

What happened? Everyone disappeared all of a sudden and nobody said anything to me.

"Sorry," I said. "It just sort of happened."

I'd never really thought about what a disadvantage it was for Samiel to be deaf. He seemed so strong and capable, but all three of us could rush past him, and if his back was turned, he would never know. And even though his battle instincts were pretty accurate, it would be easy for someone to sneak up on him and slit his throat, especially if he was somewhere he felt comfortable. Like, say, the kitchen.

I paused on the threshold, cursing as I realized what kind of danger we were all in now.

What now? Samiel signed.

"The doors. Somehow the shapeshifter was able to unlock and open the doors from the outside," I said.

Beezle whistled. "That's some magic. To be able to overcome the safety of the domicile—I've never heard of anything like it before."

"The shifter wasn't able to come inside, though. I saw in the dogs' memories that it had to lure them outside. As you know very well, though, there are plenty of creatures that can cross the threshold of a home without a spoken invitation."

"Great," Beezle said. "We need to check for infestations."

"Yeah," I said. "And bugs, video cameras, things like that."

"Thinking of Jack Dabrowski?" Beezle asked.

"Oh, yeah," I said. "If he came back here and the door was open, he would not be able to help himself. He'd have planted some kind of recording device."

The front windows were open, and the sound of emergency personnel in the street drifted up. Several male voices cursed, and I could hear the familiar click, beep and static of two-way radios. As if on cue the front doorbell rang.

"That would be the police." I sighed. "I might as well go downstairs and deal with them now. They're only going to come back later if I don't."

"You can't go down there now," Beezle said. "You never made it to the shower, remember?"

As soon as he said that, I was aware of how terrible I smelled. I looked down at my clothes, saw the blood and the smoke stains, imagined my hair and face looked a horror. Beezle was right. There was no way I could go downstairs and pretend not to know what happened outside.

"What about Nathaniel?" I asked. "He's out back, and he's just as much of a mess as I am. Plus, he's cleaning up the remains of a dog massacre. That won't look suspicious or anything."

The police have no reason to go into the yard, Samiel said.

"Sure they do," I said. "If any witness says they saw me fighting Alerian's monster and we don't answer the door, then the cops will feel free to poke around. And there's no gate in the walkway that leads back there—which means they could probably justify wandering around the property."

The doorbell rang again, and it might have been my imagination but it sounded insistent.

I'll answer the door, Samiel offered.

"You?"

I know how to play dumb, he signed, smiling a little. *When you're deaf a lot of people think you're dumb anyway.*

"I'll go warn Nathaniel," Beezle said as Samiel went out the front door and jogged downstairs.

My gargoyle flew toward the back, leaving me alone with Lock and Barrel, who gave me panting-doggy looks.

"I'm going to shower, I guess," I said; then something else occurred to me. "Why don't you two go help Samiel at the front door?"

I knew Samiel could handle himself, but I figured the presence of two large black mastiffs might help discourage any officers inclined to be pushy. I had the utmost respect for our police department, but now was really not the time for me to be interrogated. There was too much going on, and I couldn't afford to be tied up at the police station.

In the bathroom I peeled off my disgusting clothes and shoved them in the wastebasket. There was no salvaging that suit, and anyway Daharan had made it magically appear out of thin air. It wasn't as if I was losing money on an investment.

I scrubbed my hair until I felt like most of the smoke/squid smell had been rinsed away. I washed up quickly after that, taking the time only to note that my belly seemed like it had gotten bigger since I'd woken up that morning. I was never going to make it to nine months. Nobody had any idea how long the gestation period might be of a child with bloodlines like mine, but this kid was definitely popping out sooner rather than later.

But how much sooner? I wasn't ready to be a mom. So many things in my life were uncertain. Hell, I didn't even have a crib for this kid. Or diapers. Or any of those little sleeper things with the feet.

And I didn't have any friends to throw me a baby shower and "ooh" and "ahh" over cute little patterned blankets and baby socks.

I wrapped a towel around my hair and a robe around my body and went to the bedroom to put on the biggest T-shirt I owned and a pair of fleece pants.

I passed Nathaniel in the hallway. "Everything okay outside?"

He nodded. "The dog's body has been disposed of and the authorities have been diverted. Now I must get rid of this clothing and wash before I smell like the rotting sea for all eternity."

Samiel and Beezle were at the table eating soup and grilled cheese sandwiches. Samiel had thoughtfully put the stack of sandwiches on a platter in the center of the table and covered them so they would keep warm. I sat down and Samiel spooned soup into my empty crock.

"So what happened with the cops?" I asked.

Samiel grinned. *I signed at them and pretended I couldn't read their lips. They seemed fairly frustrated.*

"So they won't be back, then?" I said. "That's nice."

Maybe, Samiel signed. *There were a bunch of regular emergency response people in the street, but the guys who came to the door were wearing fancy new jackets with "STF" stitched on the lapel.*

"STF?" I said blankly. "Is that a nickname for a firehouse?"

"Supernatural Task Force," Beezle said. "They must have had this in the works for a while if they've already got gear."

"Did they seem unusually interested in talking to me?"

I asked. I was starting to wonder how alarmed I should be by this resettlement plan.

Of course, Samiel signed. *Then the dogs came downstairs and they decided you didn't live here and it wasn't worth it.*

"Maybe Daharan's spell actually helped there," Beezle said. "It did seem like it was pretty easy for Samiel to bamboozle them even with his look-at-my-innocent-green-eyes act."

"Where *is* Daharan?" I asked. "And Jude?"

As if in response to my query, the lock turned in the back door and Jude called, "It's me."

I frowned. I was glad Jude was home safe, but Daharan's continued absence was troubling. Since I'd met him, there was only one other occasion when he'd been out of touch for so long—when he'd gotten the Agency off my back and then met with Alerian. I heard Jude pulling on the clothes he'd stashed by the back door.

He entered the dining room, his face more exhausted and gaunt than it had been in the morning. Samiel got up to get another plate as Jude collapsed in a chair, rubbing his face with both hands.

"Nothing," he said. "I've been all over this city and couldn't find a trace of him."

"That's because he was here, killing Stock, while we were all out," I said.

Samiel returned with a plate and bowl and Jude dove into the platter of sandwiches as he asked, "Who?"

"Stock," I said. "One of my dogs."

Jude glance over at the other two, curled up on the sofa together. Lock picked up his head for a moment, as though he knew what we were talking about, and then put it down again.

"How the hell did that happen?" he asked.

I explained about the shifter duplicating my appearance, and how it had lured the dogs outside.

He finished one sandwich and immediately started on the next. "I've never heard of a creature able to work its magic over a threshold like that."

"I know; that's what I said," Beezle said.

"And if the creature is charismatic, as your uncle said, it could lure any one of us outside easily," Jude said. "Especially when we are asleep and vulnerable."

Nathaniel entered the room, wearing a white t-shirt and jeans, his wet hair pushed back from his face. Like Jude, he looked tired and hungry. The only one at the table who didn't appear wiped out from the day's events was Beezle, but he had probably spent a good portion of his time out napping on Samiel's shoulder instead of scanning for the shapeshifter like a good gargoyle.

"You are going to have to put added protection on the house to guard against hostile magic," Jude said.

"Yeah, and we still have to search the house for any potential infestations," I said, and explained about the back door being left open.

"Let us hope there are no more rat-demons in the house," Jude said.

I remembered cooking one of the horrid little things in a pan, torturing it so I could find out who had sent it to spy on me. That had been a real low point in my recent history.

"I hope so, too."

"One point is certain," Nathaniel said. "There is no need to exhaust ourselves chasing down the shapeshifter. His master is clearly interested in you, and thus the creature will find some way to approach you, either in the house or on the street. Perhaps the gargoyle should escort you whenever you leave the house."

Beezle paused in the act of shoveling half a sandwich in his mouth, his expression horrified.

"You do realize that you're proposing he sacrifice both his daytime television habit and the illicit snacking that he thinks I don't know about, right?" I asked.

"I should think," Nathaniel said with a pointed look at Beezle, "that your safety would take precedence over talk shows and soap operas."

"It does," Beezle said. "But I'm not sure it takes precedence over chips and dip."

Samiel smacked him in the back of the head and Beezle spewed out the half-chewed sandwich. "What was that for?"

You know.

"Oh, come on, Maddy is more important to me than snacks," Beezle grumbled. "Anyway, I didn't think you were paying attention."

I can read lips.

"But I thought you were looking at your food."

"Most people don't focus on their meal to the exclusion of everything else," I said.

"So it is settled, then?" Nathaniel said, cutting us off before our bickering spiraled down further. "The gargoyle will stay with you whenever you leave the house. He is the only being that can see the true essence of the shapeshifter. It would be too easy otherwise for the creature to approach you in the guise of J.B. or someone else you know."

"He's going to have to stay on my shoulder at the wedding like a mutant parrot. It would be too easy to approach me there."

"Wedding? What wedding?" Beezle asked. "I don't know anything about a wedding."

"Uh, yeah," I said, patting my pockets. "I left the invitation in the suit that was covered with squid blood."

"So whose wedding are we going to?" Beezle demanded.

"Lucifer and Evangeline's," I said.

Beezle looked from Nathaniel to me. "When did this happen?"

"When we were at the Ghirardelli shop," I said.

"Wait—you had time to go to the Ghirardelli shop between confronting Alerian and completely destroying our block? And you went *without me*?"

"Isn't this business of a wedding more pressing than chocolate?" Jude asked.

"*Nothing* is more important than chocolate," Beezle said.

"I don't like the idea of you at Lucifer's wedding," Jude said. "Too many opportunities for an attack on you."

Or for someone to attack Lucifer and for you to get caught in the cross fire, Samiel said.

"I will be with her," Nathaniel said.

"And J.B. will be there, too," I said. "Unfortunately, attendance is not optional."

Samiel stood up abruptly. *I just remembered. I noticed something when I picked up the mail outside.*

"Oh, the mail," I said. "I forgot about it after I tossed it on the lawn."

Samiel retrieved the packet from the side table near the front door and brought it to me, bottom side up. Lucifer's seal was on the back of the envelope.

I pulled the letter out of the rubber band and turned it over.

"This is for you," I said to Jude.

The werewolf took the envelope from me with a fierce frown. He did not like anything that had to do with Lucifer.

"There's another one," Beezle said.

I turned it over. This letter was addressed to Samiel. There was another for Daharan, and even one for Beezle, who seemed thrilled that he had gotten a personal invitation.

"I'm totally bringing a video camera," Beezle said. "I know people who would pay good money for video footage of Lucifer in a cummerbund."

"So we're all invited," I said slowly. "Even Beezle."

"Like I would have stayed at home anyway," he said.

"But the point is that Lucifer made absolutely sure you would show up. All of you," I said, looking around the table.

We are your team, Samiel said.

"But does he want you there to back me up in case things go pear-shaped? Or does he want to take you all out in one shot so I'm left alone and vulnerable? Or does he want to hold you hostage in order to get me to do what he wants?"

"Regardless, you are not going alone," Nathaniel said.

"And who's to say we could all be, as you put it, 'taken down in one shot'?" Jude asked. "None of us are weaklings. Even the great and mighty Lucifer won't be able to destroy us without a fight."

"I just wish I knew what his game was with this wedding in the first place." I said. "He's a law unto himself. He doesn't need an American wedding to give Evangeline legal rights. And for all his talk of an heir, I can't see that he needs one. Lucifer and all his brothers are immortal, older than the galaxy. Their parents are creatures that were born with the formation of the universe, and according to Daharan they are still alive, although sleeping. Which is apparently a good thing for humanity, because they are powerful and short-tempered."

"Not like anyone we know," Beezle muttered.

"The point is, why now? Why marry Evangeline? Why

all the fuss about an heir? Why threaten the relative stability of his kingdom by bringing everyone together in one place? He's practically guaranteeing a war will start," I said.

"Alerian is attempting to start a war also," Nathaniel said.

"Are they looking for an excuse to go at one another?" I asked.

"I think it's pointless to try to anticipate Lucifer's plans," Jude said. "Unless we get more information between today and the wedding day, we should focus on the problems before us. The shapeshifter. Alerian. The mayor's plan to fence off anybody magical and different."

"The giant dead squid in the front of our house that's not going to get moved anytime soon and already stinks to high heaven," Beezle said. "And it's not even rotting yet."

I pushed away from the table. "And we still have to check the house for infestations. Samiel and I can start up on this level. Nathaniel, you and Jude can check the apartment downstairs."

I gave Nathaniel the spare key. He looked at me. "What if Daharan is in the apartment?"

"I don't think he is," I said. "I can't believe he would have ignored that ruckus up front. Or that he wouldn't have come upstairs to check and see that I survived the encounter with Alerian. Anyway, it's my house and he's not paying rent."

"Very well," Nathaniel said, his face doubtful. He and Jude went out the front door so they could start searching from the foyer.

I was getting really sick of defending Daharan. None of the others would trust my instincts on this but I knew he would not harm me. Or double-cross me. I knew it.

Samiel seemed to sense my irritation and resultant need

for space. *I'll just clean this up and then start looking around the kitchen.*

I nodded and went into the living room. Instead of starting the search, I went to the edge of the picture window, peering out at the activity in the street while trying to stay out of sight of anyone looking up.

"Why don't you just veil yourself?" Beezle said.

"I shouldn't have to veil myself in my own house," I said.

"But it's okay to hide in the shadows like a criminal in your own house?"

"I'm trying not to flaunt the fact that I'm here. Why waste Samiel's cute-dumb-guy routine?"

Beezle muttered something to himself that I could not hear.

"What was that?" I asked.

"Nothing," Beezle said, but he had a look on his face like he was continuing to mutter in his head, and whatever he was muttering wasn't very complimentary.

I moved away from the window. There wasn't much going on right now anyway. Several police cars and fire trucks were parked around the monster's carcass. The street was blocked off at both ends by police barriers.

We lived close to the end of the block, and a crowd of people and a couple of news vans were on the other side of the police tape. I wasn't sure what human infrastructure would be able to do about the dead nightmare in the street. Drag it away with a crane?

Maybe later, when Daharan came home, we could figure out a way to clear it out. Since I'd made the mess, I should probably clean it up. Although half the responsibility was Alerian's. Unfortunately, he probably wouldn't see it that way. He'd just be pissed that I managed to escape his monster.

For now I needed to focus on the very real possibility that something small and nasty had taken advantage of the open back door. Pretty much every magical creature was unable to enter a home without a verbal invitation. Some little things, though, had such a weak magical aura that the rules were a bit more flexible. An open door could be an invitation to a creature like that. They followed the letter of the magical law, but you never actually asked them in.

Certain creatures behaved a lot like their real-world counterparts. If you got a pair of rat-demons in your wall, good luck getting them out. They were proficient breeders, and once the female started dropping litters, the only way to get rid of them was to hire a magical exterminator. In the meantime the demons would eavesdrop on every conversation you had and sell your information to the highest bidder.

No, this was definitely not a problem that I needed right now. I cast out my power like a net, my eyes closed. I could "see" all the magical energy within the reach of my net. The shapes of Beezle and Samiel were clear in my mind's eyes, as were the dogs, the aura of their power showing up inside my net.

I scanned the walls and the furniture thoroughly, looking for anything out of the ordinary. There were no living creatures on this floor that didn't belong, but there was *something* on the floor, something that looked almost like a rapidly dissolving paint trail.

"The shapeshifter," I said.

7

I DROPPED TO MY HANDS AND KNEES TO PEER AT IT more closely. The trail was dissolving even as I looked at it.

"No," I said, crawling along the floor, my nose pressed to the ground.

The dogs thought I must be playing some kind of game and hopped off the couch to join me, their tails wagging playfully.

"Not now," I said impatiently as I scurried along after the trail.

"What on earth are you doing?" Beezle asked. "I can't decide if you look like a basset hound or a really fat cockroach."

"I'm not fat. I'm pregnant," I said automatically. "And I think I found the magical signature of the shapeshifter, the spell he used to lure Lock, Stock and Barrel outside. If I could just get a good look at it, I might be able to lock on to it and track it."

As I said this I continued following the trail down the hall between the kitchen and the dining room. Lock and Barrel padded after me curiously.

"So what's the problem?" Beezle said, landing on my shoulder and pressing his cheek against mine so he could peer down at what I was looking at.

"It keeps dissolving," I said. "Almost as soon as I look at it. Do you see that?"

I pointed to the disintegrating trail.

"Yes," Beezle said, sounding intrigued. "It's almost like the act of focusing on it is making it disappear."

"What am I supposed to do, then, glance at it out of the corner of my eye? Pretend I'm not looking at it? How am I supposed to track this thing down if there's no magical signature to trace, no scent trail to follow? It doesn't even have the same appearance from one moment to the next."

"It is pretty much the perfect enemy," Beezle agreed. "It seems when Alerian designed these creatures, he thought through every permutation and possibility and made absolutely sure those doors were closed."

I came to my knees and fisted my hands on my thighs. "And if Alerian did that when he was creating a monster, then what chance do I have at stopping any of his other plans?" I said. "He's sure to have considered every angle already, and I don't even know where to start."

Beezle patted my head as I watched the magical trail disappear. "Don't worry. I'm sure you'll figure it out. And if you don't, you can always fall back on your de facto solution—flames, explosions, total destruction."

"You know, I try *not* to use those methods," I said.

"There's a giant octopus outside that would beg to differ if only you hadn't set him on fire," Beezle said.

"You're the one who told me that fire destroys all things," I said.

"I didn't realize I'd created a pyromaniac," Beezle said.

There was a sudden thunder of footsteps on the back stairs, like someone was running up in a hurry.

"That doesn't sound good," I said, trying to stand. "Help me get up."

"You want *me* to help *you*? Do I look like the Hulk?"

"Then get Samiel," I said, breathless and annoyed.

I couldn't seem to figure out this whole weight-on-the-front thing when I was on the ground. Every time I tried to get up, I'd roll back on my butt like a Weeble.

A second later the back door flew open and Jude came in, his face pale. He paused in the kitchen, his gaze moving toward the center of the room. It was out of sight from where I was in the middle of the hall, but I could hear the clatter of porcelain and running water as Samiel washed the dishes, which meant his back faced Jude.

Jude looked indecisive for a moment, then came to me and helped me to my feet.

"What is it?" I asked, searching his face. "Was there something in Daharan's apartment?"

He shook his head. "You need to come to the basement. And make sure Samiel stays here for now."

A cold ball of dread formed in my stomach. "Beezle, will you stay here and distract Samiel?"

"Aww, but I want to see whatever they found," he said.

"Gargoyle, can you not do as you are told for once in your life?" Jude snapped.

"Jeez, okay," Beezle said, flying off my shoulder and down the hall. "Fly off the handle, why don't you?"

"You know he doesn't mean any harm," I said.

Jude indicated I should follow him. "Sometimes levity is not appropriate."

I followed him though the kitchen. Beezle had Samiel crouching in front of the open refrigerator so that the door blocked any view of us passing. I felt like we were unfairly taking advantage of Samiel's deafness.

I didn't speak until we were on the stairs. "It's Chloe, isn't it?"

"Yes," Jude said. "Nathaniel does not want you to see what was done to her."

"He's worried about the effects of stress on the baby."

"And normally I would agree with him," Jude said. "But this is your home, and I feel you have the right to see what has happened inside it."

"And you're correct," I said. "He can't protect me no matter how much he wants to."

Nathaniel stood at the bottom of the stairs, his arms crossed and his eyes snapping. I knew he had heard every word.

"Is it not enough for you to know she has died? Must you personally witness every spatter of blood?"

"You act like I'm a rubbernecking ghoul," I said. "Jude's right. It's my home. If it's been violated, then I should know how."

Nathaniel did not respond. He dropped his arms and led us through the laundry area to the door of one of the two storage rooms. This one was for the tenant of the first-floor apartment, but as far as I knew, Daharan had never put anything inside it. The coppery-tang scent of blood was strong here even before Nathaniel pulled the door open.

It took a long time before my eyes could figure out what they were seeing. The small space looked like a slaughterhouse. It's easy to forget how much blood the human body can hold. That is, until you see it painting the walls and floors.

All of Chloe's organs had been removed and then diced and tossed around. The only reason I knew it was Chloe was because her head was intact, her eyes wide and accusing.

"She must have suffered horribly," I said. I was too sad to be angry. "There was no reason to make her suffer. She wasn't a threat to anyone. I don't want Samiel to see this."

"I did not want you to see this," Nathaniel said.

"So noted," I said, sighing. Chloe and I had not always seen eye-to-eye, but I would never have wanted this for her. And Samiel loved her, and I didn't know how I would tell him about this. Every death was another weight on my heart, and some deaths hurt more than others. This was one of them. "What I want to know is who did it, and how. Anything magical and powerful enough to do this wouldn't have been able to get in, right? So it would have to be a human. But what human would break into my house just to kill Chloe?"

"A human who came at the behest of some master," Jude said, his eyes sad. Jude had always liked Chloe, who had figured out how to restore the memories of the pack's cubs after they were kidnapped. "A human who came for one of us, but instead stumbled on Chloe, who was likely poking around looking for Samiel. And that human didn't even have to break in. The back door was wide-open."

"I think the two of you are deliberately ignoring an obvious perpetrator," Nathaniel said. "Chloe is in Daharan's space. And Daharan is missing."

I stared at Nathaniel. "Daharan wouldn't do this."

"You think he is not capable of murder?"

"Well, no. Everyone is capable of murder if pushed," I

said. "But there's no reason for Daharan to do something like this to a woman he's never met. Whoever did this . . . they enjoyed it."

"You forget that Daharan is Lucifer's brother," Nathaniel said. "I have seen Lucifer do all this and more simply to relieve his boredom."

"Daharan is not Lucifer," I said.

Nathaniel opened his mouth to argue some more but stopped when a very loud thump came from the other storage space.

"There's someone in there," I said, my heart quickening.

Nathaniel and Jude immediately stepped in front of me.

"It may be the killer," Nathaniel said.

"You couldn't smell an intruder?" I asked Jude as the two of them cautiously approached the other storage area.

Jude shook his head. "Too much blood. It overwhelms everything else."

I nodded my head, remembering the time we had stumbled upon Azazel's lab and something similar had happened.

Nathaniel and Jude moved in fluid synchronicity, silently exchanging glances as they moved into place. Nathaniel yanked the door open and Jude rushed in with a roar, Nathaniel directly behind him. Their footsteps stopped abruptly, and I moved around the door so I could see what was going on. The two of them had stopped just inside the entrance, staring at a figure on the floor. All I could see was a pair of legs clad in blue jeans and pale bare feet.

Not another body, I thought.

But it wasn't. The two men moved aside as I joined them, staring down in surprise. It was Jack Dabrowski.

His hands were bound behind him, his mouth covered with tape, and his eyes were terrified. As soon as he saw me his gaze widened and he kicked out his feet, trying to move away. He shouted through the tape, shaking his head back and forth.

I had a strange sense of déjà vu as I looked behind me, saw no one standing there, and pointed a finger at my chest. "Me?"

"The shapeshifter again," Nathaniel said. He knelt down to try to help Dabrowski, who'd been able to flee only a foot or two before he came up against the boxes of who-knew-what that filled most of the room.

Most of the boxes had been there when my mother was alive. Interestingly, when Daharan had rebuilt the house after the Retrievers burned it down, he'd duplicated the original structure and contents down to the last detail. It was almost as if the house had never been destroyed at all.

Jack wriggled around on the floor, making it impossible for Nathaniel to take the tape off his mouth and cut his bonds.

"For the love of all the gods that are and ever were, hold still," Nathaniel said through clenched teeth.

Jude joined him, holding Dabrowski's legs to limit his movement. Nathaniel managed to rip the tape from Dabrowski's mouth and the blogger immediately began yelling his head off.

"Get her away from me! Get me out of here! I saw what you did. I saw you. And everyone in the world is going to know you're a monster." His face was pale and sweaty and his eyes rolled in his head like a wild horse.

"Jack," I said. "Whatever you think you saw, it wasn't me."

"Of course you would say that. You don't want your reputation as the savior of Chicago to be tarnished," he said.

I was trying to be patient and sympathetic because he'd

obviously been through an ordeal, but I'd been through an ordeal or two myself since waking up that morning and my patience was stretched pretty thin.

"My reputation as 'the savior of Chicago,' as you put it, was nothing I wanted in the first place. It was your fault, anyway. You're the one who went online advertising what I'd done. All I ever wanted was to live anonymously."

"So you could carry out your atrocities without the glare of the public eye on you!" Jack shouted.

"Seriously? Where do you get your dialogue from?" I said. "You're like a scene from a bad movie. Look, why don't you tell us what happened?"

"You know what happened! You did it!"

"Let's say I have a case of temporary amnesia, then," I snapped. "Just give me the recap in your own words."

Jude had by this time cut the rope that bound Jack's hands. He scrambled to his feet, rubbing his wrists, which had been chafed raw by the bindings.

"I don't have to tell you anything," Jack said. "I'm leaving. I have a murder to report."

I was still close to the door, so I moved to stand in the frame. Jude and Nathaniel both reached for Jack, to hold him back, but I shook my head at them. I wanted to see what Jack would do when confronted by me, and only me. I wanted to see whether he really believed I was such a monster.

He stopped about a foot away from me. He was several inches taller than me (as most people seem to be) and I was hugely pregnant. Jack could probably muscle his way past me if he wanted. To all outward appearance I didn't seem to be much of a threat. Yet sweat beaded on his upper lip and ran down the side of his bloodless face.

The shadow inside me, the dark magic that slept under

the surface, awoke with a snarl of pleasure. The darkness was a predator, and here was prey. I refused to let the shadow run free, but I could use it to my advantage for the moment. Jack took a half step back, and I knew he had seen my eyes change.

"Madeline," Nathaniel said, the word filled with warning.

I ignored him, speaking only to Jack. "If I'm a murderer, as you say, what makes you think I would let you go?"

He took another half step back, shuffling away from me.

"These guys will stop you," Jack said in desperation. "The only reason you did what you did before was because no one was around to witness it."

"Neither of them has enough power to stop me," I said, and in saying it I knew it to be true.

Nathaniel's magic almost made him my equal. Almost. But I was the stronger one. The two strains of Lucifer's power that were alive inside me, plus the magic that came to me from Azazel, had combined in such a way that there wasn't much out there that could stop me if I didn't want to be stopped.

Jack looked at Jude and Nathaniel, who watched him impassively. "What do you want from me?"

"All I want is for you to tell me what happened," I said. "How is it that you were on the spot? I just told you to get lost and stay lost this morning."

"As if I would let a threat keep me from reporting the truth to the public," Jack said, a trace of his usual zeal back in his voice. "Anyway, I put micro cameras and bugs all around outside so I would know what you were up to. I knew all of you had left the house because I saw you leave, even that guy who usually hangs around the house all day."

"Daharan?" I asked. "I don't suppose you know when he left."

Jack shrugged. "It was right after the wolf and the gargoyle and the angel. He walked out the back and into the alley."

"Did you see where he went?" I asked.

"Nah, the cameras don't go that far," he said.

He seemed to be relaxing, getting more comfortable as he told his story. Which meant on some subconscious level, he knew I had not done anything wrong. Anyone who truly believed they could be brutally slaughtered at any moment would not be bragging about the bugs he'd set around my house.

The shadow did not like this. It wanted Jack to be afraid. I pushed that feeling down, away from conscious thought. Of course I didn't want Jack to fear me. I just wanted to get to the bottom of this mess.

"So what happened after Daharan left?" I asked.

"Well, I jumped on my bike and rode over here, thinking you might have left a window open or something and I could get in here and look around."

"That's called breaking and entering," Jude said.

Jack waved his hand, as if to say breaking and entering was just a technicality in pursuit of truth and justice. "Anyway, I got here and I left my bike in the alley. I was gonna open the fence when I heard you talking to that girl. The one you killed."

His voice had gone flat as he remembered. "Then I saw that one of the dogs was dead, and the girl looked angry. The back door to the house was open. And then the weirdest thing happened. It seemed like everything froze somehow—the girl, the dogs, me—and the only thing that could move was you. You turned your head, like you'd known I was there all along, and you smiled."

Jack shuddered. The shapeshifter's smile had clearly *not* been a pleasure to behold.

"Then—I don't know how it happened or how I got there—but somehow I was standing in the doorway of the room next to this one. And the girl, she was being torn to pieces." He was crying now, a steady stream of tears running down his face as he remembered. "Why did you make me watch that? Why did you make me see?"

He covered his eyes with his hands, his whole body shaking. I hated to press him, but I needed to know more. I needed to know how such a thing could have been done.

"But how did the shifter get in the house?" I said. "He shouldn't have been able to cross the threshold to bring you and Chloe inside."

Jack looked up, his face confused. "Shifter? What are you talking about?"

"How did I get inside?" I asked impatiently. "How did I kill Chloe in front of you?"

"How in the hell should I know?" Jack said, his face taut and angry. "I don't know anything about magic. Like I said, somehow I was here and she was there and she was getting ripped up, and she was screaming . . ."

"Was I in the room?" I asked. "This is important, Jack."

"No!" he shouted. "I don't know why you're asking me all these questions. I don't know how you did it, but you were still outside and we were here and somehow she was being torn to pieces."

Jude, Nathaniel and I shared a horrified glance.

"It doesn't *need* to come in the house," I said. I was cold all over, and I covered my belly with my hands. "It doesn't need to see us or touch us to do its magic. We're not safe here. We're not safe anywhere."

I glanced around at the walls of my house, feeling betrayed. This was my childhood home. It had always been a refuge against the madness outside. I should have been safe there. It had always sheltered me and mine.

All magical creatures were bound by the same basic laws. The sacredness of the domicile was paramount. You could not enter without an invitation. You were bound by the host's terms of hospitality. These were basic things that all magical beings knew to be true.

Even the most powerful creatures in the universe were forced to submit, which was the reason why I had never invited Lucifer into my home. But this shifter had overcome the protection of the house, something I had never seen or heard of before.

It had obviously been forced to follow the letter of the law. Its physical body had remained outside. But its magic had somehow found a way through our defenses, lured my dogs outside and killed one of them, then dropped Jack and Chloe inside and killed Chloe by remote. If it could do all those things, then it didn't matter if its body stayed outside. It could slaughter all of us in our sleep.

"We can't fight it," I said. "We can't fight something that can look like any of us, smell like any of us. It can kill from a distance, and the rules of magic don't appear to apply. How can I protect my baby against something like that?"

Nathaniel came to me then, put his arms around me, held me close. "We will find a way. We will increase the protection on the house. Daharan is more than powerful enough to plug the holes, so to speak. And if he is not, then we will go to Alerian again. It was he who created this creature. He should know how to stop it."

I laughed bitterly. "The last encounter didn't go so well.

Did you already forget the giant sea creature that trashed the street? I don't think Alerian is going to be volunteering to help us anytime in the near future."

"I will not allow you to be terrorized in your own home. There must be something we can do, and I will discover it," Nathaniel said.

We all heard the sound of footsteps descending the stairs. Jude immediately rushed out of the room to intercept.

I gave Nathaniel a panicked look. "I don't want Samiel to see Chloe that way."

"We will take him upstairs," Nathaniel said, pulling away from me. "Should I tell him?"

"As gently as you can," I said. "But don't let him come downstairs, even if you have to knock him out."

Nathaniel hurried out after Jude.

"Shit," I said, leaning against the wall and rubbing my eyes. "It really should be me. I should be the one to tell him. I owe him that much."

Jack Dabrowski had been observing all this rather avidly for someone who had just witnessed a traumatic event. Now he cocked his head to one side like a curious dog and spoke.

"So, am I to gather from all of this that you actually didn't kill that girl and tie me up down here?"

"Of course I didn't, you moron," I said tiredly. "I told you I didn't."

"Excuse me," Jack said stiffly. "I just witnessed something horrible and it may have confused me for a few moments."

"You shouldn't have been here in the first place," I said. "I told you that—jeez, was it only this morning? This is turning into one of the longest days ever."

"And there's some kind of shapeshifter running around

that duplicates anyone's appearance?" he asked. "And that's what actually murdered the girl and tied me up down here?"

"Yes," I said. "And if that ends up on your blog, I will personally come to your house and take a sledgehammer to your computer."

"Don't you think people have a right to know that there is a creature running around that can copy the appearance of their loved ones, and then kill them while under the guise of that person?" he asked.

"No. All that will do is make everyone doubt those close to them, to create more fear and paranoia in a city that's already seen plenty," I said. "And anyway, it's not a threat to the average individual. It's only interested in me."

"So it's only a threat to anyone who hangs around you—is that what you're saying?"

"Yes, and don't you think you should take that as a hint to run as fast as you can away from here?" I said. "You saw what happened to Chloe. That could have just as easily been you. Why can't you appreciate that?"

"I do," he said, and he did appear sincere. "I know it could have been me. But it's because it wasn't me, because I saw it happen, that I need to warn everyone else. I don't want anyone else to witness that."

"I can't believe this," I said, and walked to the door of the storage area.

Jack started to follow me. I held up one hand, using my power to keep him in place.

"No, you stay here for now," I said. "Until I figure out what to do with you."

"You can't do that," he said angrily. "You have no right to keep me here."

"I have every right," I said. "I have people to protect,

too. And I don't need curiosity seekers hanging around the house getting eaten up by the bad things that come looking for me."

I shut the door and put a spell around it to keep it sealed. Then I released the hold on Jack. A second later he was pounding on the door, yelling for me to let him out.

8

"HE'D BETTER NOT KEEP THAT UP ALL NIGHT, OR Daharan will come down here and gag him," I said to myself.

I felt a little twinge of sick worry in my stomach as I slowly climbed the steps. Where *was* Daharan? If he had been at home, as he always was, the shifter wouldn't have been able to kill Chloe or Stock. He might have even been able to capture the creature. We could be on our way to confront its master right this minute.

Instead I had a slaughtered friend in my storage room, and a trio of dogs turned to a duo. I didn't feel safe in my own house, and I didn't know what to do about it. I pushed open the kitchen door slowly. Nathaniel stood by the refrigerator. Jude was directly opposite him, leaning against the counter. Both of them looked helpless. Beezle perched next to the coffeemaker, his eyes sad. I couldn't see Samiel.

I moved around Jude and found Samiel collapsed on the ground, his arms around his knees, his face buried in his arms. I waved the rest of them out of the room. They went, looking relieved. I approached Samiel cautiously. I didn't know what he would think, or say. I didn't know if he would blame me.

He looked up as I crouched down beside him. His beautiful green eyes were red with grief, and his face was wet with tears.

"Samiel," I said.

I thought I knew. I thought I understood. But I didn't.

"Understood what?" I said, confused. I'd expected him to rail at me, to shout at me, to hold me responsible for Chloe's death.

I thought I understood what you felt when Gabriel died. I was sad and grieving, too. But it's not like this. I didn't know it was like having your heart and your lungs ripped out.

"Yes, that's what it's like," I said, and there I was again, in that memory that looped forever, the memory that never left me even when I wanted it to.

Hot blood and cold snow and dead eyes, eyes that loved me once and were gone now.

I took a deep shuddering breath, drawing myself back to the present. I could drown there in that memory still, under the water of my grief.

"That's what it's like," I repeated. "But you keep breathing. Your heart keeps beating. And you live."

I don't know if I want to live with this.

"You have to," I said. "Where she has gone you cannot follow."

But you can. You went into the land of the dead. You took Evangeline's soul out and returned it to Lucifer. You could do that for Chloe.

I shook my head at him. "You know that what I did was unnatural, and only because I was forced to. Once something is dead, it should stay dead. That's the natural order of things. Anyway, you didn't see Evangeline when I brought her back."

My many-greats-grandmother had been forced to pay a price to the universe for defying death. When she had returned to her body, both her eyes and her arm had been missing. And I honestly wasn't sure that her brains were all there, either. Of course, it was hard to tell with Evangeline. She had been somewhat unhinged to begin with.

I don't care what she looks like. I just want her back.

"I know," I said, touching my chest with my hand, the place where my heart was always bruised, never completely whole. "I know. But I saw Gabriel in the land of the dead before I returned here from that place Puck sent me. And I didn't bring him back. I didn't bring him back because it isn't right. He's dead; Chloe's dead. Our burden is to live, to go on without them."

His eyes filled up again, and I put my arms around his shoulders. He rested his head against mine, and cried, making no sound. I cried, too, cried for Samiel and Chloe, for Stock, for Gabriel. I cried for Patrick, the best friend I'd had before I'd discovered I was the daughter of a fallen angel. I cried for all the grief I'd caused and been given, cried for the lives I'd taken and the innocent lives that had been caught in the cross fire when monsters walked the Earth.

We cried until there were no more tears, and then we sat quietly together while the sun went down outside and darkness crept through the house.

Still Daharan did not come home.

After a long while Beezle came in the kitchen and turned on the small light above the gas range.

"I hate to interrupt," he said, and for once he looked like he actually meant it. "But we have a couple of pressing problems to deal with."

"The shifter could come back," I said. My voice sounded rusty.

Beezle nodded. "Since Daharan appears to be missing in action, you and Nathaniel are going to have to combine your magic and figure out a way to lay some better protection over the house."

"Otherwise the shifter could stand out in the street and kill us all without even coming inside," I said. "I know."

"Also, there's the matter of the . . ." He trailed off, looking at Samiel uncertainly.

Body, Samiel signed. *I'll take care of her. It should be me.*

"No," I said. "Absolutely not. I don't want you down there at all."

I have the right to see her.

I thought of the room, all of Chloe's inside parts on the outside. "You don't want to remember her that way."

Just what did the shifter do to her? Nathaniel wouldn't say. Samiel stood up, helping me to my feet.

"Can't you just trust me?" I said. "Do you have to see the horror for yourself?"

Something in my face must have convinced him, because he stared at me for a long time, then nodded.

"All right, then," I said, relieved. "Oh, and I might have left Jack Dabrowski locked in the second storage unit."

"Might have?" Beezle asked.

"I wasn't sure what to do about him," I said. "He's only going to run straight home and get on the computer, and I don't think it's in the public interest for the whistle to be blown on a freaky shapeshifter right now."

"I agree," Beezle said. "But you can't keep him in the storage unit forever. And you can't have him living in the house. He'll only pick up more intel that you won't want disseminated on the Internet."

"Have you been reading?" I asked. "You didn't learn such fancy words on TV."

"You'd be surprised what you can learn from TV," Beezle said loftily.

We went into the living room, where Nathaniel and Jude were watching the news with grim faces. I knew both of them had heard every word that was spoken in the kitchen. That was the advantage of supernatural hearing.

"It's already begun," Jude said, indicating the screen.

The film showed several people handcuffed with black bags over their faces being led away by police. The voice-over said that the individuals were a family of supernatural origin and that police had been led to the offending family by a tip from their neighbors.

"It's not just the shapeshifter we've got to worry about," I said. "My neighbors know unnatural things happen in and around this house all the time. J.B. and the Agency used to make sure all the nine-one-one calls were intercepted so I wouldn't be arrested. Whatever protection spell we use has got to deflect the human authorities as well. Otherwise we'll be on the news with black bags over our heads."

There was something else to consider, too. Lucifer was rather possessive of me, and his responses to different situations tended to be unpredictable. If by some strange chance the police managed to arrest me and lock me up, Lucifer might lose his mind and, say, smash the entire city of Chicago into oblivion. So it was definitely in my best interest as well as the people of the city that I not get taken.

Jude stood up. "Since night has fallen, we should dispose of Chloe's remains while the shadows can hide us."

You're just going to throw her away like garbage? Samiel signed, his face angry.

"I don't want to," I said. "But what else can we do? We

can't risk someone finding her in the basement, and we can't bury her in the backyard. Freshly turned soil is kind of a giveaway that you've been up to no good."

"It would be safest to burn her," Nathaniel said. "That way nothing will remain to direct the authorities to us."

"It will be like cremation," I said to Samiel. I could hear the pleading tone in my voice even if he could not. "You'll be able to keep her ashes."

"Of course, a giant conflagration in the yard might attract attention," Beezle said.

"There are two fireplaces in this building," Nathaniel said. "There is no reason to bring her outside."

I sat down abruptly on the couch, my stomach churning. "This is sick. This is sick and horrible. Why are we standing here talking about burning Chloe like she's just a logistical problem we need to work around? What is the matter with us?"

I expected Samiel to have another angry outburst, but he surprised me again by sitting beside me and taking my hand. *It's okay. I understand. I do. Something horrible has happened, and we're not in a position to behave normally about it. You can't call the police; you can't have a funeral. Nathaniel's right. Burning is the best way. It's only her body, anyway, right? Her soul has gone through the Door.*

My fists clenched involuntarily as I was seized by a flash of panic. What if her soul hadn't gone through the Door? What if her death was so strange and unnatural that her ghost would stay and haunt me forever? For the second time that day, I wished J.B. were still at the Agency. He would be able to check the paperwork and verify that she had been taken by an Agent. I didn't even want to consider what my former colleagues might think of one of their own being brutally murdered in my basement. And that led to another panicked thought. What if word spread around the Agency about what happened to Chloe, and I got blamed? What if a bunch of Agents were on their way here in the form of an angry lynch mob?

Stay calm, stay focused. Don't borrow trouble, I thought. If a mob of angry Agents was on their way, there wasn't much I could do about it, at least until they got here.

"I don't want her burned up here," I said. "I know it's selfish. But let's do it in the downstairs apartment."

"Daharan's a dragon. He won't care," Beezle said.

"Honestly, I don't care if he cares," I said. "I just don't want to look at my fireplace every night from now until forever and remember that someone I liked and respected met her final end there. Daharan isn't going to be here for the rest of his life. I am."

"Let us take care of this now," Nathaniel said. "Then we can focus on the protection spell."

Nathaniel started toward the back stairs and I followed, indicating Jude, Samiel and Beezle should stay behind. When we reached the back door Nathaniel turned to me.

"I do not think this is a task for you," he said.

"Believe me, I'm not volunteering to scoop up body parts," I said. "Something Samiel said made me wonder if Chloe's soul might be hanging around, and I want to check."

He nodded. "I did not consider that. You are correct. It would not do if her ghost were lurking about your home. At any rate, it will not be necessary to physically clean the room. I believe I will be able to do it without touching anything. I will use nightfire to destroy the body so the burning will be quick. I will be able to collect the ashes for Samiel."

"Then why don't you want me there?" I said as we went down to the basement.

"Do you really need to see her again?" Nathaniel said.

"Does not the argument you made to Samiel apply to you as well? Do you need to wallow in the pain in order to feel it fully?"

"No," I said, suddenly angry and not knowing why. "But you don't need to treat me like I'm some helpless little girl. I've faced plenty on my own without you to protect me."

He turned to me suddenly. Because I stood a couple of steps higher than him, our faces were at the same level for a change instead of his looming above me as normal. He was angry, too, and I could tell he'd been holding it in for a while.

"But you will not let me protect you," he said, his voice low and furious. "You must always push me to one side, determined to face the monster on your own, to prove that you do not need a shield. You will not let me do as I should do, as a man is supposed to do. You will not let me show that I love you."

"It's got nothing to do with love," I said. "I'm not going to let someone else take punishment that should be mine. Why should you suffer when it's my responsibility?"

"It is about love," Nathaniel said, the anger draining away from him suddenly. "It is about your love for Gabriel, and his for you. He stood in front of you when Azazel was there with his sword, and you have never forgiven yourself for that. You have never accepted that he died in your place."

All the emotions that had been stirred up by the events of the day were tangled inside me—love, grief, anger, fear, guilt. I didn't know what to do with all of this emotion. I didn't have anywhere to put it, and I was afraid. I was afraid that if I loved Nathaniel, or if I let him protect me as he wanted, the worst would happen again.

"Do you want me to be left like that again?" I said. "Will you feel that you've done your duty if I'm left standing over your body as I was with him?"

"Will you feel that you have done your duty if I'm left that way instead?" he said. "Do you think I could live with the loss if I thought I could save you?"

"No," I said, my voice small.

He put his arms around me. I resisted for a moment, then relaxed. There was comfort here, and I needed to learn to accept it.

"You are not being weak if you allow me to share the burden with you," he said.

"I know," I said. And I did know, in my head. But my heart was another matter entirely.

It was stupid of me to fight over every little thing. Didn't I have enough conflict in my life without picking a fight with my friends and allies? But I was afraid of weakness, afraid of exactly what Nathaniel had said. Death had been the first companion of my life, and Death never seemed to leave me.

"I'm sorry," I said.

He didn't respond, and I pulled away from his shoulder to look at his expression.

His face was frozen, a mask of pain, and blood was seeping from his mouth and nose.

"Nathaniel!" I screamed as his body started to crumple. I grabbed him as he went limp in my arms, but his weight was too much for me when I was already off balance from pregnancy. He tumbled away to the first-floor landing.

"Jude!" I shouted. "Jude, help me!"

I heard Jude and Samiel running. A moment later Jude shouldered past me, picking up Nathaniel's limp form and carrying him back up the stairs past me.

Samiel and Beezle stood at the top of the stairs watching as Jude carried Nathaniel into our bedroom. I huffed up the steps after him.

"The shapeshifter has to be nearby," Beezle said. "You've got to protect the house before he comes after you."

"Nathaniel," I said, trying to follow Jude, but Samiel grabbed my arm.

Beezle's right. You're the only one who's strong enough to protect us.

"I don't know what to do," I said. "I've never done a spell like this on my own. Nathaniel's the architect. I just put power into whatever he designs. The only thing I know how to do on my own is destroy. And you need to let me go because I have to help him. He's bleeding from the inside. He's going to die if I don't do something."

Nathaniel had almost died once protecting me, when I'd killed Azazel and the result had triggered a violent explosion of magic. But back then I hadn't cared about him. He'd been an unwanted bodyguard, a replacement for Gabriel who could never replace my husband.

Now he was something else to me. I wasn't sure what that something was, or what I wanted him to be, but I wasn't going to lose him five seconds after we'd argued about this very thing. I wasn't going to stand over another bleeding body knowing that my enemy had taken someone else from me.

I know how to do a healing spell. Gabriel taught me that much, Samiel signed. *But you've got to protect us. You've got to protect your baby.*

It was hard to think when part of me was panicking, picturing Nathaniel in his death throes on the bed where we slept together. It was hard to accept that Samiel could fix this when I needed to do it myself. I needed to see with my own eyes that Nathaniel would be all right.

And as I thought this, I felt a questing thread of power swirling around me, seeking, hunting. It wanted me. It wanted to destroy me and my child.

I didn't think. I pushed my own power out, against the thing that shouldn't be here, that shouldn't be able to violate the sanctity of my home but somehow had.

The other's magic resisted. It pressed back against my will, and the resistance *hurt*. This magic was a strange and alien thing. It was not the product of its own will but another's, and as such it wasn't affected by emotion as I was. The shifter had been told to do something and it would exert whatever force necessary to achieve that task.

I pushed harder, drawing deeper into the reserves of my power but not dipping into the well of darkness. I didn't know what might happen if I tapped into my black heart when I was in my present confused emotional state. There was a good chance that I wouldn't have control over my magic, and then I might end up destroying us and everyone on the block in an effort to keep the shifter out.

On the upside, the shifter problem would be solved.

I exerted more will, more magic, pushing against the shifter's power. I needed to get that thread out so I could seal up the house. The shifter's spell receded against me, and I could actually feel it draw its attention away from Nathaniel to me. The spell crept toward me again.

But Nathaniel is safe, I thought. The knowledge that the shifter was no longer killing him by degrees while I fought its magic helped me relax, helped my own magic flow more freely. I gave a great push with my power, envisioned it shoving the shifter's spell out of the house.

The creature did not expect the sudden surge, and its magic seemed to rear back for a moment. That allowed me to send my own spell around the house like a protective bubble. I slumped against the wall, panting with effort. It shouldn't have been that difficult to get rid of the shifter. I had enough magic to kill some of the most powerful creatures that had ever walked the Earth.

Too much of myself was bound up in the darkness now, I realized. By not accessing that part of my power, I was cutting myself off from my strength.

I noticed Samiel had left the kitchen, and Beezle was sitting on the counter watching me.

"I saw some of that," he said. "Didn't expect something so low could give you so much trouble."

"I didn't expect it, either," I said. "Did Samiel go to help Nathaniel?"

"Yeah," Beezle said.

I straightened, intending to go to the bedroom to check on Nathaniel, when I suddenly buckled in half with pain.

"What is it?" Beezle asked, alarmed. "Is it the baby?"

"No," I said. "It's the shifter. He's shoving against the protective spell, trying to make it break."

Because I put so much of myself in the spell, I could feel the probing magic of the shifter, looking for cracks, and realized I would not be able to relax and let the spell do its work. As long as the creature was outside, it would try to get in.

"This thing is like the effing Terminator," I said, pouring magic out to reinforce the bubble. "It's not going to go away."

"I'm not sure this is good for you," Beezle said. "You look kind of sick."

"It's not going to be good for any of us if it gets inside," I said.

Rivulets of sweat poured down my face as I chased the shifter's attempts to crack my spell, patching weaknesses as I went.

Samiel and Jude came out of the bedroom and saw me

slouched against the wall. Jude's shirt was covered in Nathaniel's blood.

"What's happening?" Jude demanded.

"The creature is trying to break Maddy's protective spell," Beezle said. "It would be really helpful if Daharan came home right now."

Is this good for the baby? Samiel signed.

"Not a lot of better options," I said through gritted teeth. "I need you all to go away. I can't concentrate when you're talking to me."

"If the creature is performing a spell, it's probably nearby. This is our chance to catch him," Jude said.

"You can't go outside," I said. "If you go after the shifter, you'll break the circle and then we'll be right back where we started."

I lowered my head to the cool tile of the kitchen floor, lying on my side, and closed my eyes. I don't remember a lot about what happened that night. The shifter's magic tried to break, and my magic blocked. And this seemed to happen over and over again. I never sensed any anger or frustration on the part of the creature, only a relentless determination.

There was darkness and pressure, and I resisted it with everything I had. Then suddenly it was morning, and the sun was streaming in through the windows. The pressure abruptly eased, and I opened my eyes.

Nathaniel sat beside me, cross-legged, on the floor. He was pale and somehow appeared thinner. But he was alive. His eyes had dark circles under them.

"You're okay," I said, reaching my hand toward him.

His fingers wrapped around mine. "As are you."

There was a lot unspoken between us, as usual. And as usual, it didn't really seem like the time to go into it.

"The shifter's gone," I said, slowly easing into an

upright position. Every part of me was stiff from spending the night on the kitchen floor.

"Did your magic force it to leave?" Nathaniel asked.

I shook my head. "It was all I could do to keep it out. I think maybe its master called it back."

"Why was it so difficult for you to hold the creature away?" Nathaniel asked. "I have felt, and seen, the breadth and depth of your power. This should have been child's play for you."

I explained my theory about my power being bound up in the darkness inside me.

Nathaniel nodded. "And you did not wish to lose control, yes?"

"I thought that would be a bad thing," I said.

"We must find a way for you to draw upon that magic again," Nathaniel said. "Without it, you are too vulnerable to threats."

"I don't know how I'm going to do that without becoming a tool of Lucifer," I said. "No matter how hard I've tried, it seems that he's winning."

"That is not my Madeline talking," Nathaniel said. "My Madeline does not give up. She spits in the eye of immortals."

I gave a little laugh. "Your Madeline is really tired right now."

"Then you must rest," Nathaniel said.

And he reached for me. I thought he was going to put his arms around me, help me up or even carry me.

Instead he put his hands around my throat and started to squeeze.

9

HIS EYES CHANGED, BLED FROM JEWEL-BRIGHT BLUE
to red as I clawed at his hands, kicking my feet in attempt
to get away from his killing touch.

Madeline!

Someone was calling me, but I couldn't tell who it was.
My hearing seemed to be fading in and out. Nathaniel's
eyes were disappearing beneath the splotches of black on
my vision.

Madeline!

Hands on my shoulders, someone shaking me roughly.
A stinging slap across my face, and I opened my eyes, and
saw Nathaniel.

I moved without thinking, jerking away from him.

He moved toward me, and I scooted farther away. His
eyes were hurt and confused.

"Madeline?"

I put my hand to my throat, which felt sore and bruised. "You were choking me."

He shook his head. "It was not me. But you were being choked. I could see the shape of hands around your neck as you slept. That is why I woke you."

It was hard to shake off the sense that Nathaniel was lying to me. It had seemed so real, like the kind of conversation we would have together. Was that the intention? Not to kill me, but to plant a seed of suspicion against someone I trusted?

"It must have been the shifter again," I said, struggling to rise to my feet. "It wasn't able to break through the protection I put around the house, but when I fell asleep I was vulnerable and it found a way in. It was a dream, but it seems that if it tries to kill me there, then it will kill me here."

Nathaniel held out his hand to me, and I took it with some reluctance. It was a mark of the fragility of our relationship that I could believe so easily that he would try to strangle me. I was a little angry with myself about it.

"How are you feeling?" I asked, trying to push away the lingering unease.

"Much better, thanks to Samiel. But do not concern yourself with my health. I have been up and about for several hours. I am much more worried about the notion that the shifter can reach you when you are asleep and hurt you through your dreams," Nathaniel said as he led me to the dining room. Jude, Samiel and Beezle sat around the table eating waffles and bacon.

"Yeah, Freddy Krueger has nothing on this guy," I muttered.

"Who?" Nathaniel asked.

"Nobody," I said. "Just a horror movie character."

Beezle snorted. "A horror movie character who scared the bejesus out of you until you were about fifteen years old."

"Apparently I was right to be terrified, because the shifter just tried to kill me in my sleep," I said as I took my seat at the table. "And how is it that there are waffles and bacon? Wasn't I lying on the floor in the kitchen?"

"We just stepped around you," Beezle said. "Some of us were hungry, and we didn't know if you were going to lie there all day."

"I was trying to protect the people in the house," I said. "I wasn't taking a nap."

"From what I can hear, you *were* taking a nap," Beezle said. "Since Freddy was trying to get you and all of that."

"Have I survived so many murder attempts that you just don't care anymore?" I asked.

"It is kind of getting old. But I much prefer live Maddy to dead Maddy," he added hastily as Nathaniel glared at him. "So what's up with the shifter? Is he still trying to get in?"

I shook my head. "No, I can't feel him anymore. I think the attempt to get into the dream was a last-ditch effort."

"The shifter has endless power at its disposal, and it obviously is out to get you," Jude said. "So why would it leave?"

I shrugged. "Perhaps its master called it away."

"We will have to design a better form of protection for your home," Nathaniel said. "One that does not require so much effort and difficulty on your part."

"Yes, and allows us to get in and out of the house when the creature is nearby," Jude said. "It doesn't sit well with me, cowering inside while it runs unfettered outside."

"Where is Daharan?" I said. "It's not like him to stay away so long."

"There was no sign of him downstairs in the apartment," Nathaniel said. "And I should emphasize *no sign*."

"Meaning?"

"Meaning there is not one stick of furniture, article of clothing, or morsel of food downstairs. I do not know if Daharan simply conjures that which he needs when he needs it or if he leaves this dimension when he leaves your apartment, but there is nothing there."

"And you think that's suspicious," I said.

"It is certainly odd."

"What were you doing down there anyway?" I asked, feeling defensive about Daharan, as usual.

"I took care of the arrangements we discussed earlier while you slept."

I gave him a blank look for a moment before I realized what he was talking about. Chloe. He'd burned Chloe's body in the fireplace downstairs as I'd asked. Which reminded me . . .

"Shit, Jack Dabrowski is still downstairs in the storage area," I said. "I totally forgot about him."

"What should we do with him?" Nathaniel asked. "If you release him now, you will have the same problem as yesterday. He will run straight home to his computer and publish everything that occurred in this house."

"All in the name of 'warning' the public," I said. "I know. I wish there was somewhere we could stash him until the wedding was over."

"Why until the wedding's over?" Beezle said.

"I'm hoping by then to have solved the shifter problem and it won't matter what he publishes."

Since Samiel was at the table, I did not add that the burning of Chloe's body would protect us from any murder charges that might come up if the authorities happened to read and believe Jack's blog.

"Awfully confident, aren't you?" Beezle said. "We haven't found a way to track the shifter yet, and you think you'll have the problem solved before tomorrow?"

"The wedding is on Saturday," I said. "Today is Thursday. That gives me two days. I think. Unless I slept longer than I thought."

"No, it's still Thursday," Beezle said. "But Lucifer lives in California, and you'll be expected as an overnight guest. You don't arrive for a wedding on the same morning as the festivities."

"Why the hell not?" I said. "I don't want to spend one second more than necessary in Lucifer's house. And I certainly don't want to sleep there."

"This is one of those things you really don't have a choice about," Beezle said. "Lucifer expects you on Friday night, whether you want to be there or not."

"What, you can read Lucifer's mind now?" I asked.

"No, he sent me a message on Facebook," Beezle said.

"I don't even want to know what Lucifer is doing on Facebook," I said.

"Reposting pictures, like everyone else," he said. "Lucifer's home has very strict private portal access, and he's allowing you to transport directly there, along with the rest of the crew."

"Gee, what a privilege," I said. "So what am I supposed to do about Lock and Barrel? What am I supposed to do with Jack Dabrowski?"

Beezle shrugged. "The dogs can probably take care of themselves for a day or two, believe it or not. They are supernatural creatures that only act doglike because of you.

As for Jack, let him go and deal with the consequences. Or keep him here and deal with the consequences."

"Either way I don't like the consequences," I said.

"Which would you like least?" Beezle asked. "Jack telling a wild story about a monster that can kill people from afar, or Jack possibly finding out about Lucifer's wedding and following you there?"

I shuddered at the thought of Dabrowski at Lucifer's wedding. "Let him go, then."

"Shall I simply throw him in the street?" Nathaniel asked, rising from the table.

"No, escort him nicely out the back door and encourage him to forget anything that happened here yesterday. Not that it will do any good. Anyway, he said he rode his bike here so he can probably get himself home without too much trouble."

Nathaniel left the room to take care of the Jack problem. This was going to continue to be a problem until Jack figured out it was in his best interest to keep his mouth shut about me or until he was killed, whichever came first. In the meantime, he would probably be pretty irritated about being locked in my storage area all night long, and I wasn't in the mood to deal with him.

"So, just to update the status of our various situations," Beezle said. "Alerian is unhappy with you and will probably send another monster to kill you soon since the first one didn't do the job. The city's plan for locking us all up is going forward and you haven't come up with a solution to stop it. The shifter has way more power than we first thought and we have no idea who its master is. The most famous supernatural blogger in the city witnessed a horrific killing in your house and then you pissed him off by locking him in your basement for twelve hours. And the first of the fallen is getting married in two days and all of your friends and enemies are invited to the party."

"Seems pretty standard for us, doesn't it?" I said. "Lots of insurmountable situations to surmount. Let's start with the protection for the house. We've got to have a way to keep the shifter out; otherwise none of us will be able to sleep again."

"While you were passed out in the kitchen I went online and looked up some information about domicile protection," Beezle said.

"I wasn't passed out; I was focusing," I said.

"Whatever. Anyway, I talked to some witches and they gave me some tips," Beezle said.

"Shouldn't you know all about domicile protection since you're a home guardian?" I asked.

"My job is to watch for intruders. I can't do a damn thing to actually keep them out. The threshold is supposed to do that," Beezle said. "Luckily the witches did know a thing or two about spells that can get past the protection of the home. It seems that some of them have cast those kinds of spells in the past."

"Isn't that handy," I said dryly.

"Totally," Beezle said. "The point is that you and Nathaniel should be able to seal the house up pretty tight."

"What's going to happen when we go to Grandpa's house tomorrow?" I asked.

"I would hope that this creature's master would have the sense to not attack you while you're in the presence of the Morningstar," Jude said.

"I'm not sure we can count on that," I said. "Beezle will be with me all the time so we'll be able to see any direct attack coming, but what if the shifter tries to pull the same trick? Stand outside the house and attack from a distance?"

Beezle shook his head. "Lucifer is going to have that mansion protected from anything and everything. Remember, he's a lot more powerful than you are. And he's had a lot more time to collect enemies. He would never risk being caught off guard in his own home. There will be layers upon layers of protection. I don't think you'll have to worry about murder by remote control."

"So just the direct kind of murder, then," I said.

"Anyone who attends the wedding would conform to the laws of hospitality. Most of the creatures attending are old, and many of them have conflicts with each other. But they know that if they air their grievances in Lucifer's home, they'll be violating some ancient understandings. You may actually be safer in Lucifer's presence than you would be anywhere else."

"There's something really wrong about that," I said.

Nathaniel returned to the dining room, looking disgruntled. "That boy doesn't have the sense to be terrified, even after what he witnessed."

"Let's not worry about Jack right now," I said. "Beezle apparently got some info from witches that will help us protect the house."

The five of us discussed the spells, worked out a plan, and Nathaniel and I spent the rest of the morning sealing off the house. While we did that, Jude and Samiel went to see Alerian as my "ambassadors." The hope was that he would either 1) call off any additional giant monster attacks that might traumatize the locals, or 2) help us figure out a way to track down and defeat the shifter and its master. Or both.

But when Samiel and Jude returned, they told me that Alerian had checked out of his room that morning. Jude had attempted to track him, but the trail had gone cold next to the river just outside the hotel. Now we had two super-powerful creatures missing in action on my watch.

They might be holed up somewhere together, plotting, as Nathaniel and Beezle suspected.

Or they might have been taken out of the picture by some other player, something strong enough to remove two ancient and extremely magical beings.

Neither option was particularly comforting.

There was a third option. Alerian and Daharan were off somewhere pursuing their own agendas, and those agendas didn't necessarily mean destruction for me or anyone else.

But I had trouble believing that Daharan would go off for more than a day without telling me where he was going and what he was doing. A low-level knot of anxiety had permanently lodged in the back of my brain.

So there was no Alerian to negotiate with. The shifter seemed to have disappeared and there was no point wasting energy trying to hunt it down. There seemed to be no way to tackle the other problems at the moment, so we waited.

All of us were exceptionally bad at waiting except for Beezle, of course. Beezle thought he'd died and gone to heaven. He had four people in the house to annoy and all the snacks and TV he wanted. There was no blood and no crises for twenty-four hours, although there were an awful lot of reporters and whatnot lurking outside, making pointed remarks about the wisdom of the mayor's plan while standing in front of the squid carcass.

The rest of us were snarling at one another like restless lions. Somehow there just wasn't enough space in the apartment for an angel, a werewolf and a couple of mixed-bloods with too much power and nowhere to put it.

Beezle spent plenty of time on the computer. By Thursday night he reported that Jack had posted an extremely detailed account of what he encountered at my home and far too many details about the shifter itself. He thankfully spared me the stress of identifying my house as the site of the murder, but I was still pretty sure that he wasn't going to survive much longer if he kept doing stuff like that. Once the shifter's master got word of Jack's report, the blogger would be counting the remainder of his life in minutes rather than days.

By Friday afternoon it was almost a relief to be packing for Lucifer's wedding. It freed me from the tension of waiting for something to happen—waiting for Daharan to return, waiting for Alerian to appear, waiting for the shifter to attack, waiting for the police to show up to take me away to their camp for magical creatures. Now I had something to focus my energy on.

Beezle flew into the bedroom and landed on the dresser as I threw things into a suitcase.

"What are you packing?" he asked, disgust evident in his tone.

I pointed at the various articles of clothing I'd put in the case. "Little black dress. Heels. Second-nicest dress for whatever you do the night before a wedding."

"Dress rehearsal," Beezle said. "The dresses are cheap and they look it. And I see you've also packed your crummy jeans and black T-shirts. Why can't you ever shop for anything new?"

"Kind of busy saving the world," I said, nettled.

"Buffy saved the world all the time and she always had leather pants and kick-ass boots," Beezle said.

"Buffy had a stylist," I said. "And apparently she had money that I don't have. I don't have the magic to make new clothes the way Daharan and Puck can, but I think I figured out how to make the belly part stretchy enough to fit."

"You know, you probably do have money," Beezle said.

"Azazel died. You were his heir. Sooner or later a lawyer is going to show up at the door with a big check and some papers for you to sign."

"I'm not holding my breath," I said. "Besides, I don't need a million dollars. I just need to be able to take care of my baby."

"But first you need to *not* show up at Lucifer's wedding dressed like the country mouse," Beezle said.

I threw some underthings and a brush on top of my clothes. "I don't have anything else to bring, and I'm not going shopping now. So Lucifer will just have to deal with the indignity of having a poorly dressed relation."

Beezle muttered something that sounded like "But what about my dignity when I'm sitting on your shoulder and you're wearing that off-the-rack dress?"

"What was that?" I asked.

"Nothing, nothing," Beezle said. "Nathaniel said to tell you that he's getting the portal ready now. He's waiting for a signal from Lucifer. Once the portal opens, you'll only have a short time to use it, so get a move on."

"I'm sure Nathaniel didn't say to get a move on," I said.

"No, I did. Get a move on." He flew out of the room after throwing one more black look toward my suitcase.

I fingered the cheap material of my dress. So what if it wasn't a designer label? Did that make me less valuable as a human being? Why were immortals so damned shallow? Didn't they have more important things to worry about than who was wearing what and when? They were all trying to outmaneuver one another every second of the day. You'd think they wouldn't have room in their brains to think about clothes.

"Madeline!" Nathaniel called, and his voice was impatient.

I zipped up the case and hurried into the living room. That is, I hurried as fast as a pregnant woman carrying a suitcase can waddle, which isn't very fast.

Everyone else was gathered in the living room. Jude and Samiel both had backpacks slung over their shoulders. Nathaniel carried a garment bag. The dogs lingered around the edges, their ears curled in question. I patted their heads gently.

"You guys will be okay without us for a day or so, right? Beezle says you don't have to be dogs if you don't want to."

They rubbed their faces against my legs, telling me without words that they would be fine. I still didn't want to leave them. I was worried about what might happen if the shifter returned while we were away.

Beezle landed on my shoulder, settling himself in for the trip.

"And where are your fancy clothes?" I asked.

"I'm perfect the way I am," Beezle said. "I don't need clothes."

"Are you telling me that Lucifer won't be offended that you don't have a bow tie or something?"

"Children, please," Nathaniel said. He had one finger pressed to his ear like he was listening to an in-ear microphone.

"Is Lucifer talking in his head or something?" I whispered to Beezle.

The gargoyle nodded. "Interesting that he chose to have Nathaniel open the portal and not you."

"Am I supposed to read some dread portent in that?" I asked. "Maybe he just didn't want to trouble me."

"He didn't want to trouble his Hound of the Hunt?" Beezle said skeptically. "I think it much more likely that he wants you to conserve your energy for whatever is waiting on the other side."

Nathaniel beckoned us all closer. He pointed his finger toward the floor and drew a circle in the air. A line of energy left his hand and the portal opened in front of our feet, a swirling vortex that bore a strong resemblance to Alice's rabbit hole.

I moved toward the portal, and Nathaniel put his hand on my arm. "Let me go first."

The argument we'd had the day before rang in my ears, and I started to shake my head no.

But before I could raise a protest he'd stepped forward and disappeared into the hole.

"Dammit," I swore as Samiel dropped in right after Nathaniel, almost as if the two of them had coordinated it ahead of time.

Jude looked at me and gestured toward the portal.

"You're not going to try to go in front of me to make sure the helpless woman is safe?" I said.

"No, because it's my job to stay here until you're through in case anything comes out of the woodwork at this end," Jude said, smiling a little.

"So they did arrange it ahead of time," I said.

"You didn't have to take twenty years to pack," Beezle said. "They had too much time to discuss things among themselves."

"Just hold tight," I said, and stepped into the portal.

I expected the usual feeling of having my brain squeezed between my ears, but this portal felt sort of light and floaty. If that was Lucifer's doing, then I was grateful, although I would never tell him so. It would be nice to arrive at the other end without feeling nauseous for a change.

The trip was over almost before I knew it. One second I

was in the portal, and the next moment I had landed softly on a plush carpet, blinking in surprise at my many-greats-grandfather, who stood waiting for me with the beaming smile of a game-show host.

"Air Morningstar," Lucifer said, winking. "The only way to travel. Much more comfortable than your usual portal, yes?"

This was not the first time that I'd had the disquieting feeling that Lucifer could read minds, although he strenuously protested otherwise.

"Nothing but the best for my future grandson," he said, a greedy light in his eyes as he looked at my burgeoning belly. "You may want to step to one side, Madeline. I believe my friend Judas is arriving."

Lucifer lightly pressed my shoulder and guided me to his side so that we could see Jude arrive. The wolf narrowed his eyes at his old enemy.

"Morningstar," Jude growled.

"Judas," Lucifer said merrily, ignoring the malice in Jude's tone. "Welcome to my humble home."

I glanced around the room and thought that Lucifer's idea of humble and my idea of humble were two very different things.

The room had quite obviously been decorated by someone with piles of money and the taste to go with it. He'd eschewed the baroque-madness look favored by so many other ancient creatures and gone with clean, modern lines and simple colors. It didn't look like a comfortable room for cozying up with a book, but neither did it look like the kind of place where you'd be afraid to sit down because you might break the furniture.

Samiel and Nathaniel stood off to one side, holding their bags. I opened my mouth to yell at Nathaniel for going into the portal before me and realized that Lucifer watched me closely. Was he looking for a wedge to drive between Nathaniel and me? Everything I did for the next few days was going to be observed. I'd better start acting accordingly.

"Thanks for having us here," I said, trying to sound sincere.

Lucifer's eyes crinkled in laughter. "You look as though you just swallowed a toad, Granddaughter."

I guess fake sincerity is not my best thing.

"Come, I will have Zaniel show you to your rooms and then you will join us in the main hall. Evangeline is greeting the other guests there," he said.

He led us to a door that opened onto a hallway. Zaniel, the messenger who'd delivered the wedding invitation to me, stood there like a soldier at rest.

"Show my granddaughter and her entourage to their rooms," Lucifer said. "Then you will escort them to the hall for cocktails."

"Entourage?" Beezle muttered. "We're her family."

Lucifer gave Beezle an amused look, and Beezle glared back at him.

Zaniel nodded his head once. "Of course, Lord Lucifer."

Lucifer bent to kiss my cheek, so he didn't see the flare of emotion in Zaniel's eyes. This kid really did not like me.

I steeled myself not to shrink away from Lucifer. At the touch of his lips on my cheek, the darkness inside me opened its eyes.

Lucifer pulled away from me after that brief touch, his eyes dark with anticipation. He'd felt the magic inside me, felt like call to like. And he was happy that I was here, where he could try to bend that magic to his will.

I gave him a steady look, so he would know that I wasn't scared, and that I wouldn't surrender.

The Morningstar only turned away from me, smiling.

10

ZANIEL LED US THROUGH THE MAZE OF HALLWAYS
and stairways that seemed to comprise Lucifer's house. It
reminded me quite a bit of Azazel's home, which had been
a warren of little rooms, most of them filled with horrors.
Lucifer might not be a scientist experimenting the way
Azazel had been, but I had no doubt there were plenty of
things I did not want to see behind these doors. He was
nicknamed the Prince of Darkness for a reason.

We were brought to the topmost floor of the mansion,
and Zaniel bowed.

"You and your people have the entire floor at your disposal, Ms. Black," he said.

"Okay," I said, passing my suitcase to Nathaniel. "Why
don't you three go find rooms? I just want to have a quick
word with Zaniel here."

Samiel and Jude looked uncertain, glancing at Nathaniel.

"Don't look at him like he's in charge of me," I said. "I'll be fine."

"What about him?" Jude asked, jerking his head at Zaniel.

"I won't break anything," I said.

Samiel and Jude seemed fine with that, and they turned away to choose rooms. Nathaniel, however, stubbornly stood his ground. I gave him my best death glare, but he ignored it. He wouldn't argue with me in front of Zaniel, but he wasn't going to leave me alone, either.

"In case you're wondering, this kid is not the shifter," Beezle said loudly, breaking the tension.

"Thanks, but I wasn't worried about that," I said.

"Then what did you wish to speak to me about?" Zaniel asked. He looked polite and attentive, and there was no hint of the hatred I'd seen earlier.

"Why did you go see Sokolov when you were in Chicago?"

He wasn't expecting that, and because he was caught off guard I saw the surprise in his face before he schooled his expression again.

Zaniel frowned slightly. "I am sorry, Ms. Black. I do not know this individual of whom you speak."

But it didn't matter what he said. I'd seen the truth in his face. He had gone to the Agency and spoken with Sokolov. Now I just had to find out why—and at whose behest.

"I must have been mistaken, then," I said lightly. "I'll be right back as soon as I drop off my case in the room."

"You do not wish to change for cocktails?" Zaniel said, looking at my scuffed combat boots, threadbare jeans and the T-shirt that didn't quite cover my belly.

"No," I said firmly.

Nathaniel followed me down the hall, carrying the

luggage like a bellhop. I picked the first room on the left and he followed me in. Beezle flew to the dresser so he could stretch his claws without hurting me.

I closed the door firmly behind me and gestured for Nathaniel to come closer. I was sure the room was bugged, and if by some strange chance it wasn't, then I didn't want Zaniel to overhear what I was going to say.

"We're going to have a lot of problems if you keep undermining my authority in front of everyone here," I said to Nathaniel. "There was no reason why you couldn't leave me alone with Zaniel for a minute."

"Madeline, you have no authority over me," Nathaniel said. "And the sooner we resolve that misunderstanding, the better. I will not leave you alone in this place, not even with a seemingly harmless errand boy. He is Lucifer's son and we know he bears you ill will."

"He wasn't going to try to attack me in the hallway with everyone watching," I hissed.

"How do you know?" Nathaniel said. "If he killed you under Lucifer's roof, then his father might be angry with him but the damage would still be done. And do not believe that he would play fair. You have too long faced enemies that want to stand and fight you. Zaniel knows he is not as powerful as you. He would not engage you in a battle. He would surprise you and you would be dead before you could blink. And so would your child."

I stared at Nathaniel. "I thought I would be safer with Lucifer than with anyone else."

"Safer does not mean perfectly safe," Nathaniel said. "There is still much danger here."

I sighed. "Fine, be my bodyguard if it makes you feel better."

"It does," Nathaniel said.

"Let's go down and get this farce over with," I said. "I can't imagine I'm going to enjoy mingling with a bunch of people who might slit my throat when Lucifer isn't looking."

"Are you truly not going to change?" Nathaniel said. He wore his usual black suit and white dress shirt, open at the collar. He looked perfectly respectable even if I did not.

"I have nothing to change into anyway, according to Beezle," I said.

"You weren't there when she was packing," Beezle said.

Nathaniel nodded toward the bed. "I believe Lucifer left that for you."

The bed was covered with a red silk comforter, and on the silk there was a perfectly lovely wine-colored dress with a fitted bodice and an A-line skirt. There was also a shawl that looked like it might be cashmere. A string of white pearls lay across the shawl, and on the floor was a pair of dangerous-looking heels.

I pointed at the shoes. "First of all, I'd kill myself in those things. Second, my belly is too big for the cut of that dress. It's made for someone with a small waist. I can't even find my waist. Third, if Lucifer wants me to wear that getup, then I am definitely not putting it on."

"Madeline, why be contrary for no reason? Pick your battles. It would please Lucifer to see you wear this. I think you would find it would accommodate your new figure," Nathaniel said.

"I am not interested in Lucifer's pleasure," I said. "If I wear the clothes, then I'm giving in. He doesn't get an inch from me. Not an inch. I won't be his caged bird. And maybe if he sees that, he'll give up this stupid quest to make me his heir."

"He will never give that up," Nathaniel said. "I saw his face when he kissed you. He knows the darkness is rising inside you. You become more powerful every day, and your child may be even more so. Lucifer will not risk you falling under another's influence."

"Too bad Lucifer still doesn't realize Maddy hasn't been influenced by anyone since she could talk. Her first word was 'no,'" Beezle said.

"I'm not changing," I said, and went into the hall.

Samiel and Jude waited there. Samiel had put on a gray suit that made him look very handsome. Jude was dressed like a Hell's Angel as usual, so I felt better. Jude wasn't going to give Lucifer an inch, either.

Zaniel led us down to the main hall. The room had double doors, like Amarantha's castle and Azazel's mansion. It was as if all the old creatures had used the same architect. I had a strange moment of déjà vu when the doors swung open as we reached them. I half expected to see Nathaniel standing there, golden and arrogant, as he was when I'd first met him. But Nathaniel stood at my side, his hand clasping mine, and we stepped into the room.

There were a lot of people. A lot. I did not recognize the majority of them, although Beezle started whispering in my ear as soon as we entered, pointing out dignitaries from the faerie world and various wolf packs and other assorted creatures. I heard none of it. Anyone who had caught sight of us was whispering and pointing, and the whispers followed us as we crossed the endless room. It was like Azazel's ballroom all over again, and I lifted my chin. None of these gossiping immortals mattered to me.

Someone grabbed my elbow. "Maddy, thank goodness."

I smiled up at J.B., who looked very handsome but as uncomfortable as could be in his suit. "Where's your entourage?" I asked, looking behind him.

"I ditched them as soon as I saw you," J.B. said. "I

haven't had a decent conversation for weeks. Faeries are so damned boring."

"The one thing Maddy isn't is boring," Beezle said from his perch on my shoulder. "Wait until you hear about the giant squid that destroyed our street."

"There was a squid?" J.B. asked, looking at me with a raised eyebrow.

"There was a squid," I said.

"And you probably dispatched it with the maximum amount of mayhem," J.B. said. "How many fire trucks showed up?"

Beezle chortled. "Does he know you, or does he know you?"

"It's not my fault that burning is the most effective way to get rid of giant monsters," I said. "If the giant monsters would just leave me alone, we wouldn't have a problem."

"Speaking of monsters, look who else is here," J.B. said. He jerked his head toward the left, where a familiar set of horns rose above the crowd.

"Focalor?" I asked, surprised. "Why is he being treated like a guest? He was a key player in the uprising against Lucifer."

J.B. shrugged. "I'd like to speculate on Lucifer's motivations, but that way lies madness and migraines. And look there."

He pointed at a tall man with golden hair and white wings. I could only see the back of the man's head, but there was something familiar about him. Of course, all angels sort of looked the same, with the wings and the blond hair and the unearthly beauty.

"Another angel of the host?" I asked.

J.B. shook his head. "How about an archangel?"

"Michael?" I asked.

As I said his name he turned toward me, almost as if he had heard me speak. I was unable to suppress a little gasp. It was his eyes that took my breath away. Instead of the usual angelic jewel-brightness, his eyes were made of flame. For a moment it seemed like that flame rose up around him, that he was wreathed in it. Then he nodded at me, and turned back to whoever he was speaking to, and the moment passed.

"Anybody else in need of extra oxygen?" Beezle asked.

"So I wasn't the only one who felt that?" I said.

Beezle shook his head. "In a room full of powerful people, he stands out. Kind of like you."

We were about halfway through the room, standing in a little cluster—me, Nathaniel, Samiel, Jude, Beezle and J.B. It was comforting that all of us were together in this place, that the friends I'd trusted over and over to help me through the apocalypse were with me one more time. Especially since the apocalypse could rear up again at any moment. That tended to happen around me.

Lucifer and Evangeline were in one corner of the room, surrounded by fawning guests. We had not yet officially greeted the happy couple, and I was reluctant to head that way. Once I joined that group, there would be more pointing and whispering, more speculation about me and my abilities. I just wasn't in the damned mood to deal with it right now.

The double doors at the end of the hall were thrown open, and a smartly dressed faerie marched in. "Presenting His Highness Puck, the High King of all Faerie."

All of the fae in the room immediately dropped to one knee as Puck entered, a satisfied smirk on his face. The only fae who did not kneel was J.B. I could tell by the look on his face that he really wanted Puck to say something about it. I think we all wanted to have a go at Puck for one reason or another. The rage that surged up as soon as I saw him made me long for an outlet—like, say, beating the manipulative little so-and-so bloody.

Puck strolled through the throngs, heading toward the corner where Lucifer and Evangeline held court. He wore a suit that would not be out of place at a Hollywood club. I noticed he had a shiny silver birdcage in one hand.

His path, naturally, took him right past our group. Beezle's claws dug into my shoulder, a warning against losing my temper. The darkness inside me had already awoken with my anger, and I was struggling to keep it under control.

Puck saw me looking at the birdcage and stopped in front of me with an impish smile. That smile made me want to knock his teeth out. My fists clenched at my side.

"Like my new accessory, niece?" he asked, holding up the birdcage. "I have you to thank for it, after all."

I realized with horror that Oberon was inside the cage. Oberon, the former High King of Faerie. Oberon, whom I had diminished during a battle in which he had cheated and attempted to kill me. Oberon, whose wife I had killed when she had refused to believe I was innocent in her son's death.

The fae could have fit in the palm of my hand. He gripped the silver bars of his cage and glared at me.

Puck looked from Oberon's face to mine. "If looks could kill, you would certainly be dead now, my niece."

"You're sick. Parading him around like that," I said. "And quit calling me 'niece.' I would much prefer that no one realize we are related."

"Oh, it's too late for that," Puck chortled. "On the joyous occasion of his nuptials, Lucifer has decided to reveal our long-secret filial relationship. So everyone will know you are related to me."

He then turned to Nathaniel, whose coloring precisely mirrored Puck's dark hair and jewel-blue eyes.

"And you, my son? Would you, too, prefer to disavow our bond of blood?" Puck asked.

"I cannot disavow what is apparent to everyone," Nathaniel said.

Puck's smile widened. "A very careful answer. Although I think you would like to sneak up behind me and slit my throat."

"There would be no sneaking," Nathaniel said, his voice hard.

Puck laughed. "Families are so much fun, aren't they?"

He gestured toward the group of flunkies that had followed him into the ballroom and continued on to greet Lucifer. We all turned to glare daggers into his back.

"You restrained yourself pretty well," Beezle said.

"There's no damned point in threatening Puck," I said. "He only laughs and makes you feel like a fool."

"Ah. So you would have threatened him if you thought it would make a difference—is that it?"

I spun around, deliberately putting my back to Lucifer and Puck and the fake display of affection that was occurring over there. The two of them were probably whispering death threats in each other's ears.

"I'm already sick of this," I said. "I want to go home."

"You can't," Beezle said.

"Why not?" I said. "Why must we all be in thrall to Lucifer and his desires?"

"Because he can squash us with one evil thought," Beezle said.

"Oh, yeah, that's why," I said. I felt abruptly fatigued, exhausted from the constant low-level buzz of stress and adrenaline that I'd felt for the last few days. "Can somebody get me a glass of water or something? I don't feel so good all of a sudden."

Nathaniel went to look for something to drink. There were roving waiters with trays of alcoholic drinks, but those were not for me in my current state. It was unfortunate, because an adult beverage would make a big difference in my disposition.

J.B. scooted closer to whisper in my ear. "Your buddy did go and see that individual we discussed."

"Yeah," I said, thinking of the expression on Zaniel's face. "Any chance you know what they talked about?"

J.B. shook his head. "The room was sealed with magic so no one could eavesdrop."

"So I know he was there but I still don't know why or who sent him," I said. "Maybe I can beat it out of him later."

"You're kidding, right?"

"Sort of," I said. "It gets very tiresome sometimes, trying to stay on the side of the right and the good when the bad guys get to do whatever they want."

"That's why they're *bad* guys," J.B. said.

"Speaking of bad guys . . . did you by any chance hear about what happened to Chloe?" I said, sneaking a half glance at Samiel to make sure he wasn't looking at me.

"I did," he said, his green eyes very grave. "The paperwork for her soul retrieval came across my desk, and Lizzie called me. I'm assuming there's something you want to tell me about that."

"Yes," I said, and turned a little so Samiel couldn't see me talking as I described what happened. I felt guilty talking about it in his presence, anyway, although he wasn't paying attention to me in the slightest.

Jude and Samiel had seemed like they were on alert

ever since we entered the room, both of them constantly shifting and scanning the area. Now that alert appeared to be heightened. "What's up with you two?"

"It's not safe here," Jude growled.

Samiel nodded. *Can't you feel it?*

Now that they mentioned it, it did seem there was an air of barely suppressed tension, a sense that something might snap at any moment. And it had started as soon as Puck entered the room.

I looked over to the corner where Lucifer and Puck were playing hail-fellow-well-met with each other.

"They're going to kill each other before the night is out," I predicted.

"Look on the bright side. If they kill each other, you'll only have to deal with Alerian," Beezle said.

"Yeah, I don't really see that as a bright side," I said. "I kind of half expected that he would be here, since Lucifer is all into gathering his family around his bosom."

As if my words were a summoning, the double doors at the far end of the room opened again and Alerian entered. He had no collection of hangers-on following him. He was not announced. But the power emanating from him was so palpable that a hush fell over the room.

Even Lucifer and Puck ceased their antics as Alerian strode toward them. His green hair was tied back at the nape of his neck. His face looked like it was carved from marble. Like Puck and Lucifer, he wore an expensive tailored suit. He walked so lightly that his heels did not make a sound on the floor.

The crowd cleared the way for him. No one whispered and gossiped. No one wondered who he was. But they understood power, and how to get out of its way.

I glanced over at Lucifer and Puck. Lucifer was frowning. Puck was trying to act like Alerian's display didn't bother him by talking to his underlings.

Because my group was apparently the first stop on the tour, my great-uncle paused before me, his face impassive.

"Disappointed to find me still alive?" I asked.

There was a long pause. "Very."

"Don't think about trying anything here," I said. "For some reason Lucifer likes me."

"I would not dream of violating my brother's hospitality," Alerian said.

"But once I leave it's a different story, right?"

There was a flicker in his sea-colored eyes; then he moved away without saying a word.

"I think you should take that as a yes," J.B. said.

"I didn't need to hear him say it," I said, watching him approach Puck and Lucifer. "He's a lot like Amarantha, or Titania. He's decided I've given him insult and there is nothing short of complete and total humiliating subservience that will make him happy."

"You never even respected my authority when I was your boss," J.B. said.

"Exactly," I said.

"Exactly," Beezle said.

Alerian greeted Lucifer and Puck, and then Evangeline. My many-greats-grandmother was resplendent in a red floor-length gown with long sleeves. One sleeve was pinned up to the shoulder because there was no arm there to fill it. A silk scarf was tied around her head to cover the empty holes where her eye sockets used to be. She was hugely pregnant, like she was about to give birth any second.

"I thought maybe Lucifer would have found some way to fix up Evangeline," I said quietly to Beezle.

My gargoyle shook his head. "She lost her eyes and limb as a result of the price paid for defying the magic of death. There is no fixing that."

Now that the three brothers were gathered together, all the air seemed to have gone out of the room. The crowd had resumed speaking, but conversations were low and furtive. No one seemed to want to attract the attention of the big three, which was unusual at a wedding. Normally people tried to monopolize the engaged couple. I put one hand on J.B.'s shoulder. My face was hot and my lungs were tight.

"What's the matter?" he asked. "Are you going to be sick?"

"No," I said, fanning my face with my hand. "I feel like I can't breathe. Where the hell is Nathaniel?"

J.B. scanned the crowd, looking for my escort. "I can't see him. I wonder where he got off to?"

I felt a moment of illogical panic. What if Lucifer had instructed his underlings to grab Nathaniel as soon as he was separated from me? But a moment later he was at my shoulder, holding a large glass of ice water. I grabbed it from him and guzzled it down quickly.

"More," I said.

Nathaniel stared at me. "If I had realized you were so thirsty, I would have brought a pitcher. I had to go to the kitchens to get this. There are only cocktails on the trays."

I put my hands over my throat, which felt parched. "I just feel so thirsty. And hot."

Nathaniel put his hand on my forehead. "You're burning up with fever. What happened while I was away?"

J.B. looked startled. "Alerian stopped here for a second. That was it."

Beezle flew off his perch to peer at me more closely from the front. "Someone is trying to hurt her," he announced.

"Someone in this room has got a spell going to make you sick. I can see the traces of magic on you."

"Can you trace it back to its owner?" I asked, my breath coming in short bursts.

He flew around me, looking for a trail to follow, and returned to my shoulder with a shake of his head. "No," he said. "It's like the shifter. The trail sort of peters out when you look at it."

"That means the shifter is in this room," Nathaniel said.

I slumped against his shoulder, barely able to stand on my feet. Jude, J.B. and Samiel huddled closer, the four men forming a protective knot around me. "But he's not trying to kill me right this second. He's trying to weaken me, make me sick."

It was working, too. All I wanted to do was lie down and close my eyes.

"I thought the gargoyle was here to identify the creature when it is in disguise," Jude growled. "Do your duty."

"There are a million people in this room," Beezle said. "If I fly around looking for the shifter, it could walk right up to Maddy while I was somewhere else and you would never know."

"Beezle's right. He needs to stay here," I said. "And I don't want to make a big fuss and attract everyone's attention."

"You've already attracted attention," Beezle pointed out. "People are looking at us, wondering what's wrong with you. In a second Lucifer will hear something's going on and come over here."

"That's exactly what I don't want," I said. "I'd like to try to keep Lucifer out of this."

"It is Lucifer's home. I doubt you will be able to do so," Nathaniel said.

Nathaniel's arm was around my shoulder to help keep

me upright as I swayed back and forth. I needed to focus, to push off the shifter as I had done before. But he was smart. A direct attack would have brought a full show of force on my part.

Instead the creature had chosen a subtle magic. That magic wormed its way inside, weakening me before I even realized it was there. If not for Beezle, I might not have known it was a spell at all. It felt exactly like a sudden illness.

"I do not like standing here while this monster does as he likes," Jude said. "It is infuriating that we can do nothing when we know it is so close."

"We could chase around and make a scene," I said through the haze of fever. "But it would just drop the spell and we wouldn't be any closer to finding it."

"In the meantime you're getting sicker by the minute," J.B. said. "Let's make a scene if that's what makes it stop."

It was getting hard to think straight. "No, I want to try to trace it back."

"How?" Nathaniel said.

"Beezle, you can see the effects of the shifter's magic."

"But the spell fades away when I look at it," he said.

"Right," I said. "But if I push back against the spell, push against the source, you'll be able to follow my magic back to him."

Beezle gave me an admiring look. "That's pretty good thinking, Maddy. I didn't think you had it in you."

Nathaniel shook his head. "I do not like it. The shifter will be able to continue to harm you. We should do what is necessary to break the spell now."

"Just trust me," I said, and my voice sounded little and breathless. "Jude, you get ready to follow Beezle wherever he says you should go."

I knew the wolf had personal reasons for wanting to

capture the shifter himself. I also knew that if I didn't give Jude something to do soon, he might start rampaging around just to burn off his excess energy.

Should I stay with you? Samiel signed.

"No, Beezle should go with you and Jude," I said. "J.B. and Nathaniel can stay here with me."

Beezle fluttered over to Samiel. His little face was concerned as he watched me struggle against the fever.

"Maybe Nathaniel's right. You don't look so good," Beezle said.

"This is our chance," I said. "He's here in Lucifer's mansion. I don't want to look over my shoulder for him anymore. Now be quiet."

I turned my focus inward, searching for the thread of the spell that was sickening me. My baby turned over and over in my belly. He could feel the magic, too. He could feel what it was doing to me. But it wasn't hurting him, and that was some consolation at least. The magic was so small and subtle that it didn't have the power to go after my child as well.

In fact, the subtlety was so great that it was hard to catch hold of the magic. It moved not like a river, as most magic did, but more like a fine mist. Now I could see the reason why I didn't notice the intrusive spell immediately. The difficulty was in pushing it away. I couldn't shove the magic back out by force when it was spreading in every direction. I collected the disparate pieces of the spell into a kind of arrowhead, and then blocked them with my own power.

I hoped that once the invading magic was drawn to that point, I would be able to bulldoze the spell out of me. Otherwise I would be using up a lot of energy when I was already in a weakened state. Then the shifter would be able to finish me off, and no one would be able to find the culprit.

As before, the shifter seemed to sense my resistance and redoubled its efforts. This actually worked to my advantage, for strengthening the spell gave it a more solid and consistent form.

Which meant it was a lot easier for me to push back, once I could clearly see what I was pushing.

A few moments later I felt significantly better as the shifter's power cleared my body.

"I see it," Beezle said. He directed Samiel and Jude in the direction of the spell I had sent in pursuit of the shifter's power.

The shifter seemed to realize that the magic was no longer affecting me. It strained back toward me, tried to take advantage of my physical weakness. The few minutes of illness had left me feeling drained, and it was extremely difficult to fight back without drawing on the darkness inside me. If I called upon that power in Lucifer's presence, he would surely be able to sense it.

The tug of magic back and forth between the shifter and me was almost like a rope, a long rope that joined the two of us. I was slightly shocked that in a roomful of magical creatures no one else seemed to be aware of what was going on. Then I realized that any little pulses of magic that came from me or the creature would be easily drowned out by the show of power coming from Lucifer and Evangeline's corner. The shifter had timed his attack perfectly.

Even though Alerian, Puck and Lucifer were pretending to get along, each was clearly trying to outmuscle the other in presence. The guests were fascinated by the display while trying not to notice it, because gawking openly might draw the attention of one of these big, bad immortals.

In the meantime the shifter was able to attack me under everyone's nose.

Beezle, Jude and Samiel disappeared into the crowd as I continued my battle with the shifter. I wanted to make sure to keep its attention long enough for Beezle to track my magical signature back to the creature.

There was a sudden surge of power, like the creature was pouring everything it had into one shot. I staggered back, my grip on my magic tenuous for a moment. That was when the darkness inside me, waiting so patiently, seized its chance.

11

I MIGHT NOT WANT TO USE THAT POWER, BUT DARK magic has a life of its own. If I had not been weakened by the shifter's spell, there was a chance I could have suppressed the darkness. But it sensed a threat, and I wasn't strong enough to hold it.

The darkness surged forward in a great explosion of power, which was immediately noticed by everyone in the room. Unfortunately, the shifter sensed the change in me and abandoned its efforts almost immediately. Its desire to remain anonymous was obviously greater than its need to defeat me, at least for the moment. I hoped that Beezle had been able to find the creature before it dropped the spell.

Nathaniel had pulled me into his embrace when I staggered, and I knew the darkness inside him answered the call of my own. His eyes changed color for a moment, burning midnight-dark.

"None of that, now," J.B. said briskly, and he scooped his arm around my waist and pulled me away from Nathaniel, breaking the connection.

The surge of dark power was also broken, like water had been thrown over me. I gave J.B. a grateful glance as he settled me back on my feet.

"Thanks," I said.

"No problem," he replied softly. "I just didn't want a repeat of what happened in the basement of my building. I didn't think you'd appreciate it if everyone in the room was watching you and Nathaniel."

The whole room was quiet, and I could feel the curious glances of the guests. I also felt the pleasure that Lucifer had experienced when he witnessed my little display. Pleasure, and curiosity. He was surely wondering what had caused me to lose control.

I kept my eyes steady on J.B. "Everyone is watching me, aren't they?"

"Oh, yeah," he said. "But if we're lucky, something more interesting will happen in a minute and they'll go back to their business."

"I'm not usually that lucky," I said.

As it turned out, I was. A servant entered the room from side doors and announced that dinner was to be served. The guests immediately queued up at the door to the dining room. I guess that free dinner trumps all things, even if you're a supernatural.

Nathaniel, J.B. and I waited while everyone else flowed around us. A moment later we were rejoined by Beezle, Jude and Samiel. I could tell by the irritated look on Beezle's face that they had been unable to finish the tracking.

"You couldn't have held on to your control for one more minute?" Beezle said. "I almost had him. I think."

"Did you see anyone familiar in the area where the spell was going?" I asked.

Beezle shrugged. "It was going in the direction of Focalor's party. But let's not make any assumptions."

"Yeah, let's not make any assumptions just because Focalor has tried to kill me a few times before," I said.

"Sure, but he could also be fooled by the shifter pretending to be a member of his group. Jude said that the wolves didn't even suspect the shifter was among them," Beezle said.

"The gargoyle is correct," Jude said. "While Focalor may be involved, it's best not to assume he is. We don't want to miss the real culprit because of past prejudice."

"How about you give Focalor's table a good hard stare anyway?" I said to Beezle as we joined the rear of the throng making its way toward the dining room.

"Oh, don't worry. I will," Beezle said. "Even if he isn't the shifter's master, he's probably up to no good. He can't seem to help himself."

We were among the last to enter the dining room, which was already arranged for the reception the next day. There was a long table at the front of the room for Lucifer and Evangeline and Puck and Alerian. Other groups were seated at small round tables scattered throughout the room. I looked for Michael, since his status as Lucifer's only friend would seem to indicate that he be seated at the upper table. But he was elsewhere, with a small knot of angels who all appeared to have come from the same place as Michael. No fallen there, so they must have been Michael's entourage.

"So, do we just sit anywhere, then?" I asked. I was still feeling a little woozy and wanted to get in a seat as soon as possible.

A servant materialized at my left elbow. "Ms. Black, you and your guests are to come with me. King Jonquil is to join his party at table thirty-one."

It took me a moment to realize who King Jonquil was. J.B. frowned.

"I will take care of her," Nathaniel said quietly.

"I know you will," J.B. said. "I just don't want to go back to my own people."

I patted J.B. on the shoulder. "Don't worry. I'm sure you'll be able to ditch them at the reception tomorrow."

"Don't be so certain," J.B said. "I'm probably going to have to dance with every female in the group just so no one is offended."

He walked away toward the faerie table as we followed the beckoning servant.

There was an empty round table just underneath the raised front table where Lucifer, his brothers and his bride-to-be were on display in front of the whole room. The servant indicated that Samiel and Jude should sit. I started to pull out a chair, but the servant shook his head.

"Ms. Black, you are to join your grandfather at the main table, as is your escort," he said, indicating Nathaniel.

I gave the servant a dirty look. "No way."

He seemed taken aback at my vehemence. "But Lord Lucifer wishes . . ."

"I'm not sitting up there like a monkey on display," I said.

The servant hesitated, uncertain how to handle an intractable grandchild of his master. Suddenly Lucifer himself was there, speaking quietly to the servant, then guiding me toward the upper table. Nathaniel followed behind.

"There is no need to, as you would put it, shoot the messenger," Lucifer said. I thought he would remark on my inappropriate attire, but he said nothing about it. "The servant was simply doing as I asked."

"I don't want to sit where everyone can gawp at me," I said.

"But I do want you to sit where everyone can see you, especially after that little display," Lucifer said, and his voice was filled with deep satisfaction. "Everyone in this room has now felt what my granddaughter is capable of."

He steered me to the chair to his immediate left and seated Nathaniel beside me. There was a small plate in between our chairs for Beezle, who hopped down and rubbed his hands together.

"When's the first course? I didn't get any of those appetizers that were circling the room with the cocktails," Beezle said.

Servants were moving around the room spooning soup into bowls, so Beezle didn't have long to wait. I averted my eyes once he started eating. Soup and Beezle are not a good combination, especially since Beezle won't wear a bib.

Evangeline was on Lucifer's right with Alerian and Puck beside her. There was an empty chair next to Nathaniel's. Lucifer saw me looking at it.

"That is for Daharan. I am frankly surprised he did not arrive with you," Lucifer said.

"I haven't seen him for three days," I said. "He walked out of the house and never came back. I thought you might have something to do with his disappearing act, actually. You or Alerian."

"Not Puck?" Lucifer asked with a raised eyebrow as he sat down.

"My impression was that he liked to keep his distance from Daharan," I said.

Lucifer laughed, and Evangeline glared in my direction. That is, she glared as much as an eyeless person can. My many-greats-grandmother has no particular love for me. She does not like anyone who distracts Lucifer's attention from her. I really wanted to tell her she could have him and all the baggage that came with him.

I studiously looked down at my plate as dinner was served. I was more than a little irritated that Lucifer had managed to turn the attempt on my life into an advantage for himself. Especially since he'd expressed no interest in the reason why I was using magic in the first place.

Unless he knows why, I thought. *Unless he knows who the shifter's master is. Unless he IS the shifter's master.*

I paused, my soup spoon halfway to my lips. It was possible. It was just possible that Lucifer, like Puck before him, was manipulating me. Lucifer wanted me to come to the dark side. What better way to get me over there than to threaten my life again and again, make me lose my control of my power?

It would even fit in with Daharan's warning to Jude to look to his past for the reason why his pack was being targeted by an unknown enemy. Lucifer and Judas had a long and storied relationship, and Lucifer seemed to enjoy messing with Jude's head for petty reasons of his own.

I glanced at Lucifer from the corner of my eye, wondering. My grandfather was feeding Evangeline morsels from his own plate. Their overly affectionate display made me shudder. Beezle looked up from his intense concentration on his meal.

"What's the matter?" he asked.

"Nothing," I said, and went back to eating. It was some kind of squash soup, and it tasted pretty good.

After a bit, the soup plates were cleared away and out

came a salad. Beezle moved the greens around his plate in distaste.

"Rabbit food," he pronounced.

"Not everything can be deep-fried," I said.

"Even lettuce could be improved by the liberal application of beer batter and frying oil," he said. "And maybe cheese sauce."

The resulting image was so unappetizing that I pushed my salad fork away. "I don't want to talk to you anymore during dinner. Somehow I always end up losing my appetite."

Nathaniel opened his mouth, doubtless to inform me that I needed to eat to keep the baby healthy, but Lucifer beat him to it.

"You must eat, Madeline," Lucifer said. "My grandson needs plenty of nourishment. He is growing quickly."

"As is our own child," Evangeline cut in, possessively rubbing the bulge of her belly.

"Of course," Lucifer said. "But I do not have to fret over you eating enough. You are staying here under my watchful eye, which Madeline refuses to do."

"I am certain Madeline is old enough to take care of herself," Evangeline said dismissively. "I don't see that it is necessary for her to house with us."

Lucifer clearly did not care for Evangeline's attitude. "Madeline has been involved in many dangerous incidents since becoming pregnant. And every child of my line is important to me."

He said this with a finality that made it clear he would not tolerate any disparaging remarks about me or my offspring.

"Of course, darling," Evangeline cooed, but her face was wrinkled in distaste.

It was no secret that Evangeline wanted Lucifer to

prioritize her child over all his others—his many, many others. Lucifer certainly had not been faithful to Evangeline's memory in the years since she had been taken from him. But Evangeline had a special hatred for me, because I would not allow myself to be used as her tool of revenge against Ariell and Ramuell.

The funny thing was that the reason Lucifer held me in such high esteem was because I was the last direct link to the children he'd had with Evangeline so many centuries before. Evangeline didn't share his nostalgic feelings. She saw me as an obstacle to her goal—the complete and total monopolization of Lucifer's affection. She didn't just want to be queen of his kingdom. She wanted to be queen of his heart, and she would do anything to get that.

I had noticed that Zaniel was not seated at the main table, even though he was Lucifer's son. He was at a table with several other angelic-looking creatures, who were quite possibly his half siblings. I wondered why Lucifer had put his other children at another table when he was so interested in a show of family strength. Was it because those children had not shown themselves to be exceptional? Or was it Evangeline's influence? If she had her way, she would probably eliminate every child of Lucifer's bloodline, excepting her own and starting with me.

There were already plenty of people present who would be happy to see me dead. Focalor. Alerian. Oberon. Nameless members of the faerie court who hated me for killing Amarantha and Titania. In fact, when I glanced around at the tables full of guests talking and laughing, I did not see a convivial party. I saw a nest of vipers waiting to strike. I pushed the plate of salad away from me to indicate that it could be cleared.

"See, you don't want the rabbit food, either," Beezle said.

"I just don't have much appetite right now," I said quietly, hoping Lucifer would not overhear. He was engaged in conversation with Evangeline and Puck, any previous signs of strife forgotten. "For some reason I keep thinking about all the people in this room who want to kill me."

"Yes, I keep thinking of that as well," Nathaniel said.

He had been so quiet that I'd nearly forgotten his presence. Now I realized he was on high alert, like Samiel and Jude. Waves of tension radiated off him.

"Gargoyle, can you not see the shapeshifter in this room?" Nathaniel said. "His presence should be easy to discern with all of the guests before you."

Beezle shook his head. Despite his protestations of "rabbit food," I noticed he was gnawing on a piece of carrot. "He must have slipped out another door when everyone exited the main hall."

"So he's probably not disguised as one of the guests," I said. "The people who arrived with him would notice him missing, especially during dinner."

Beezle nodded. "It would be easier to impersonate a servant. You would have an excuse to come and go, then."

"Or to get close to your target," Nathaniel said as the main course was carried out on large trays. "I hope you are watching everyone who approaches Madeline closely, gargoyle."

"Don't tell me how to do my job, half-blood," Beezle said. "I've been a home guardian longer than you've had wings."

"Don't bicker," I said. "It's bad enough that we've got enemies all around us. I don't want us to fight among ourselves, too."

"You must be feeling bad if you don't want us to bicker," Beezle said. "You've perfected arguing to an art form."

"Says the gargoyle who taught me everything I know," I said.

The salad plates were taken away and replaced with a filet of beef stacked on top of root vegetables and artfully drizzled with some kind of sauce. Pink juice oozed from the steak and my gorge rose. There was no way I could stomach eating meat right now, especially since the effects of the shifter's spell were lingering. Beezle, naturally, dove into his plate like he had not eaten in a hundred years.

Nathaniel was making a show of eating, but I noticed he was picking at his food. When I looked over at Samiel and Jude, seated at the table just below ours, neither of them was eating, either. They weren't even pretending to communicate with each other. Both of them shifted restlessly in their chairs, glancing up at the head table and then around the room. I knew for sure that Jude would have preferred to shift into wolf form and walk the perimeter. Unfortunately, Lucifer seemed to want to give a more upscale impression.

I found J.B.'s table among the throng of guests. He appeared to fare no better than the rest of us. He was pushing food around his plate, twirling his wineglass and generally doing a bad impression of a person enjoying himself. I'm certain that any courtiers trying to get his attention were getting curt answers.

It was a fact that none of us could really relax in Lucifer's presence, and the additional bonus of Alerian and Puck wasn't helping. I know that Beezle and Nathaniel would disagree with me, but I would feel a lot better if Daharan were with us.

Daharan was the eldest, he seemed to be the most powerful, and the other three were respectful of his presence. Plus, out of all the brothers, Daharan liked me best, no matter what lip service Lucifer paid to valuing all of the children of his line. And it would be really, really nice to have someone big and superstrong who liked me the best backing me up.

But *where* was he?

Beezle polished off the filet on his plate with a smack of his lips. "Are you going to eat that?"

I shook my head. Lucifer glanced over at me, frowning, although he didn't make another remark about my need to feed the baby. Which meant that he was definitely listening to everything that went on at my side of the table no matter what impression he gave to Evangeline.

I had to get out of this place. Nothing good was going to come of my staying under Lucifer's roof.

Beezle shoved his empty plate away and pulled my plate in front of him. If nothing else, we had to get out of here before Beezle gained twenty pounds gorging himself on food from Lucifer's kitchen.

After the first course came a second course of gnocchi in pesto. I thought that the pasta course should have come before the meat course but, as Beezle pointed out, I knew nothing about etiquette and even less about formal dinners. Once upon a time I'd been a food writer, so I knew how to cook and could recognize good food when I saw it, but serving it was beyond me. I hadn't had many opportunities in my life to play entertainer.

I had a few bites of gnocchi so that Lucifer wouldn't pay any more attention to me than he already was. He nodded in satisfaction every time he looked over and saw me chewing.

Alerian sat at the opposite end of the table next to Puck, and he appeared to be steadily drinking his way through several bottles of wine. He did not speak to anyone and resisted Puck's attempts to draw him out by glaring every time his brother spoke to him. Nathaniel was equally silent and stoic at my end, so the two looked like a pair of frozen bookends.

Was Alerian anxious in the presence of his brothers? Or was he irritated at being away from water, the source of his magic? I wasn't an expert in geography and I had not seen the outside of Lucifer's home, but I was under the impression that his mansion was in or near Los Angeles. And I thought Los Angeles was at least kind of close to the ocean. Alerian could draw more power from the Pacific Ocean than from Lake Michigan, I would think.

Of course, it was entirely possible that Alerian was drowning himself in wine for none of those reasons, but simply because Puck was annoying him.

As if he had heard my thoughts, the new High King of Faerie looked over at me and winked. I resisted the very strong urge to leap across the table and punch him in the face. His eyes twinkled merrily, which meant that he could certainly read the emotion on my face if not what I was thinking.

After the pasta was cleared, there seemed to be a lull in the gorging. Beezle was flat on his back on the table between Nathaniel and I, rubbing his belly and moaning.

"Nobody made you eat your plate and mine for every course," I said without sympathy.

"I couldn't let good food like that go to waste," Beezle said. "But now I don't think I have any room for dessert."

"You probably don't have any room for breakfast tomorrow, either," I said.

Beezle lifted his head slightly to give me an incredulous look. "That's crazy talk. I'll be hungry again in a few hours. But that will be long after dessert, and there might not be leftovers."

He glanced hopefully at Lucifer. The Morningstar did not confirm or deny the possibility of leftovers. He gave no indication that he had heard Beezle at all. Instead, he rose to his feet, a wineglass in his hand.

"I'd like to propose a toast," he said, and all eyes in the room turned toward the table.

I tried to slouch down as low as possible in my chair but my protruding belly made it impossible to slide under the table, which was what I wanted to do.

"You look like a turtle," Beezle whispered.

"To my loving bride-to-be, Evangeline, for her loyalty and devotion throughout many eons," Lucifer said.

For a moment there appeared to be a legitimate light of affection in his always-calculating eyes. I remembered something I had thought once, a long time ago. Nobody had ever loved Lucifer except this one crazy girl. She had worshiped the ground he walked upon from the moment she first saw him, a shadow with eyes of starlight calling to her.

She loved him, and in his own way he loved her, too. That was why she was given this gift, this public declaration, that none of his other lovers or children of those lovers had received. That was why he valued me more than his closer kin. I was a child of the line of Evangeline.

Lucifer had continued talking while my mind drifted away. I came back to earth when Beezle nudged me.

"Hey, you're supposed to be drinking to your grandmother's health," he said.

I noticed everyone else in the room doing just that, and figured they all had their faces in their own glasses and couldn't see what I was not doing with mine. Lucifer noticed, though. He didn't say anything, but he noticed. He noticed everything.

After Lucifer's toast, Puck, not to be outdone by his brother, stood up and proposed a toast to the happy couple. I confess that I tuned it out entirely. I find toasts to be uncomfortable for everyone involved, and I didn't like that all this public speaking kept all the guests' eyes glued to our table.

Puck sat down finally, and then the dessert course was brought out. Beezle had sat up while Puck was entertaining the guests with his speech, and now he drew his dessert spoon toward him eagerly.

"I thought you didn't have room for dessert," I said as dishes of flan were set before us.

"All this talking gave me time to digest," Beezle said.

I rubbed my eyes. All I wanted to do was to leave this room and go to sleep. Of course, the presence of the shifter in the mansion made sleeping a much more dangerous proposition than it ought to be.

Nathaniel and I would be able to protect the room with a spell similar to the one we used on my home before we left. We would have to do the same for Jude and Samiel. There was no way I was leaving them unprotected in this house.

Finally, dessert was over and everyone was dismissed for the evening, with the promise of much revelry the next day. Several guests gathered in clumps to talk and drink more of Lucifer's wine. Others disappeared into the maze of the mansion, either to travel to outside accommodations or to head to guest rooms.

A bunch of people approached the table to thank Lucifer or pay fealty or whatever it was they wanted to do. I took advantage of Lucifer's distraction to escape before I was introduced to anyone. Nathaniel put his arm around me and hurried me toward the side door. Samiel and Jude followed.

Beezle wanted to stay behind and finish off any flan on the tables that had been untouched, but Nathaniel nixed that idea with a sharp look. My gargoyle came along with a grumble.

We had nearly made it to the door when Michael stepped in front of us. His power was almost overwhelming up close, a tangible thing that filled the air around him. I had the same feeling I'd had before, that there was something familiar about him. Maybe it was because his power infused the line of Agents? That would make sense. He'd used his own grace to disguise Evangeline's children, the original Agents, so many centuries before.

"I do not believe we have met," he said. His voice, too, seemed to occupy all the empty space around it. "I am Michael."

"Madeline Black," I said, reaching my hand toward him.

He looked at my hand impassively, but did not offer his own. "I know who you are. I said we have not met."

"Okay," I said, feeling impatient suddenly. I was tired and cranky and not in the mood to play games with an immortal. "What do you want?"

"To look upon the favored granddaughter of Lucifer," Michael said. "I have long watched you from afar."

"Why?" I asked.

"Your actions have been of great interest to many," Michael said. "Particularly your actions of late. We always like to know when there is darkness loosed upon the world."

I narrowed my eyes at him. "Well, aren't we judgy. You

want to worry about darkness? Why don't you have a conversation with your old pal Lucifer? He's forgotten more about evil than I'll ever know."

"Lucifer is not my concern. You are. You are an Agent," Michael said.

"Not anymore," I said.

"Whether you choose to exercise your privilege is irrelevant," Michael said. "The line of Agents is my province, and I watch it closely."

"Fine, keep watching," I said. I did not like the implication that I was somehow the problem here, and I didn't care for Michael's attitude. "And do nothing about the real problems, like Lucifer and his brothers trying to take over everything in sight. Just leave that up to me. As usual."

I stepped around Michael and stormed out of the room—at least, as quickly as a waddling pregnant woman can storm. I turned back after a moment to make sure everyone was following me, and saw Michael staring after us. He wasn't looking at me, though. He was looking at Jude, who didn't seem to notice the attention.

"Did you call the first archangel 'judgy'?" Beezle asked.

"You were there. You have ears," I said shortly. I pulled Jude close to me as we walked away. "Why is Michael staring at you?"

Jude appeared startled. He glanced back over his shoulder. "I don't know."

"Watch your back," I said. "We have enough interest in our party as it is."

"Says the woman who called Michael 'judgy,'" Beezle said.

"There are a lot of people staying here," I observed as we climbed the stairs. "Just how big is this place?"

"As big as Lucifer wishes it to be, I imagine," Nathaniel said. "If there are insufficient guest rooms, he can always add more."

"Why would he want so many of his enemies under his roof?" I said as we passed a hallway while climbing to the next level. A quick look that way showed me Focalor's distinctive curved horns disappearing into one of the guest rooms.

"He is keeping them close so he can observe them," Nathaniel said. "They are much less likely to conspire with one another while under his nose. Additionally, some of them will feel it is a great compliment that Lucifer has favored them thus."

"I don't know why anyone would think it's a compliment," I muttered. "It feels more like a prison sentence to me."

Nathaniel and I carefully put the safe-from-the-shifter's-magic spell over Samiel's and Jude's rooms. The two would be able to come and go as they pleased, but while they were asleep no hostile magic would be able to attack them.

Beezle chose to sleep in Samiel's room. "There's isn't enough privacy with you two in there," he said. "Besides, with the spell you won't need me to check everyone who comes to the door. Just don't go wandering around the mansion without me."

After we sealed up our own room, Nathaniel and I changed and climbed into bed. I wanted to talk about what had happened that day, about my suspicions that Lucifer might be behind the shapeshifter attacks, but I was so exhausted I closed my eyes almost immediately.

I only opened them again when I heard a woman screaming right outside my door.

12

IT WAS PITCH-BLACK IN THE ROOM. BOTH NATHANIEL and I sat up abruptly. He threw on a bathrobe over his pajama pants, which was all he wore.

"Stay here," he said. I could see the angelic aura around him in the darkness, moving toward the door.

"You shouldn't go out there, either," I said, swinging my legs to the side of the bed and using the bedpost to help me stand. "It could be a trick from the shifter to draw us out."

He paused. "You are correct. We should scan the area first."

There was a sound outside in the hallway like a body being dragged along, and then fingernails scraped across the surface of our door. For a moment I was a child again, frozen in place, terrified about what might be outside scratching to get in. Then I came to my senses.

"Or maybe someone is bleeding to death out there while

we stand here and debate about it," I said, following Nathaniel's glow until I joined him.

"If it is the shifter, then he would know you would think that," Nathaniel pointed out. "Your heroic tendencies are well documented."

A voice came from under the door, small and faint. "Help. Help me."

"Dammit," I swore, lunging for the door before Nathaniel could do anything about it. I couldn't leave someone out there, hurt and asking for help. I couldn't bring myself to value my own safety first over someone in need.

When I opened the door, though, I sort of wished I'd waited. Because Evangeline lay on her back, bleeding from several stab wounds to the chest. The blood made a patchwork of wine-colored stains on the same red dress she had worn during the festivities earlier in the evening. Whoever had stabbed her had removed the scarf that covered her eyeless sockets. Those empty holes looked horrible, endless pockets of night in her face.

The bulge of her belly looked like it was writhing under the skin. Her baby was dying, too. My own child fluttered inside my body, safe for the moment.

She could not have picked a worse place to be attacked. I would get blamed for this, without a doubt. And while the loss of Evangeline would be bad enough, Lucifer would fly into a rage such as we had never seen when he realized the child was gone.

Nathaniel cursed behind me and nudged me out of the way to check her pulse. "She is still alive, though barely."

He gripped her hand. I felt the pulse of energy that came from the angelic healing power. But Evangeline's wounds continued to bleed. Her breath was shallow, a sound so close to death it chilled me to the bone.

Nathaniel pulled away, confused. "My power cannot heal her. Perhaps you can try."

I knelt on the floor beside Evangeline. The blood pooling underneath her stained the knees of my pajamas. They were flannel Eeyore pajamas, my favorites.

I took Evangeline's hand in mine, as Nathaniel had done. It was small and cold. Her life was almost gone. I pushed the power of the healing spell into her, and something happened that had never happened before.

The healing spell rebounded on me.

I tried again, only to have the same result duplicated.

"It's like the healing won't go into her," I said.

"It's because she's died once already," Beezle said.

I looked up, and saw Samiel, Beezle and Jude emerging from their rooms into the hallway. Beezle fluttered to my shoulder, looking down at Evangeline with a sad, troubled expression.

"I died, too, but the healing spell has always worked on me," I said.

"Your soul never actually went through the Door," Beezle said. "And your bloodline is tied to Lucifer's, tied to the power of Agents of Death. The rules aren't going to be the same for you as they are for Evangeline. She's just an ordinary human. She's got a touch of power right now because she's carrying Lucifer's child. But it's not enough to overcome the fact that she's not supposed to be here. She died once, and Death wants her back."

Evangeline suddenly sucked in a deep breath, startling us all. Her hand tightened around mine.

"The . . . baby . . ." she said, taking great deep gulps of air in between each word. "You . . . have . . . to . . ."

She paused, and there was a long exhalation of breath as her body seemed to relax. I think we all thought it was over then. Her fingers loosened on mine for a moment, then gripped them tight again.

She sat up with a sudden strength and urgency that I did not expect. Her eyeless face pressed close to mine. Her breath smelled of rotting death.

"You must take the baby from me," she said, her voice fierce. "You must save Lucifer's child."

"What? How?" I said. I didn't want to say that the baby could already be past the point of saving.

"Cut him from my belly," Evangeline said. "For your grandfather, you must do this."

"This is crazy," I said as she fell backward to the floor again.

"You should do it," Beezle said decisively. "Saving the baby might be the only thing that will save all of us from Lucifer's wrath when he finds out what happened."

The thought of cutting Evangeline's stomach open and pulling the baby out in some kind of half-assed caesarean section made my own stomach turn.

Jude pulled a huge gleaming hunting knife from his boot and presented it to me. Nathaniel knocked his hand aside.

"Do not be so crude," he said harshly. "Madeline can perform this task with her magic. It will be safer for the child, in any event."

"If you know how it's done, then you do it," I said. "I'm no baby doctor."

"Her life is slipping away as we speak," Nathaniel said. "She is holding on to the last of her strength to preserve the life of the child. You must do it now. Now."

He placed my hands over Evangeline's stomach. I could feel the writhing mass beneath, and knew that her child still lived.

"I don't know what to do," I said. "I don't understand what I should do."

"That which you have always done," Nathaniel said. "Defy death."

The living heart of Evangeline's child seemed to reach for me, reach for my magic, and the child within me responded to the call of the blood, Lucifer's blood. I understood what I had to do.

I spread my hands apart on her stomach, and as my palms separated a split appeared in her dress. Through the open seam I could see the swollen skin of her belly, so like my own. Except . . .

Now that her stomach was exposed I could see that this child was not like mine. The limbs that pressed against the surface of the skin were not those of a human child. I paused, unsure of what I should do.

"I don't think I can," I said. "It's not human."

"You must," Nathaniel said. "The gargoyle is correct. Lucifer's rage will know no bounds if he loses the child. You were not with him when first he discovered the loss of Ramuell or Baraqiel. I was. His anger was terrifying to behold. But at least he had some time with those children. To lose this one, a child of his beloved Evangeline, without even seeing it—I do not want to consider what may happen."

"Ramuell and Baraqiel were monsters who murdered dozens of people. What if this child is, too? How can I knowingly let it loose upon the world?"

"There is no time," Nathaniel said.

There was no time. And yet I hesitated.

"Lucifer will kill us all if you do not at least attempt to save the baby," Nathaniel said.

"What if what's inside there kills us all when it grows up?" I said.

"Better the devil you know," Beezle said.

I was not sure. I really was not sure. But it seemed that, like so many times before, I was out of options. I put my hands on Evangeline's belly, felt the thing that moved under the skin. Repulsion coursed through me. It was wrong to do this, but it was happening anyway. My magic knew what to do almost without my guiding it. It overrode my disgust and hesitation. The line of Lucifer would always seek out its own.

Evangeline's belly came apart under my fingers as if I had sliced it with Jude's knife. Blood spewed out and splattered us all. Beneath the layers of dermis and fat and muscle, there gleamed a pulsing sac of fluid. Something dark darted beneath the surface.

"She is nearly gone," Nathaniel said. He held Evangeline's hand in his own. "You must do it now."

My palms hovered over the final layer that divided Evangeline's child from the world. I could let it die and damn the consequences. There was still a chance for humanity, a chance to be free from whatever monster she was carrying inside her.

But the darkness that lurked inside me had other ideas. Magic surged from me without warning and through the thin membrane. Black fluid spilled forth as the amniotic sac broke open. A wet cry, alien and terrible, came from the open wound of Evangeline's stomach. At the same time, Evangeline gave a long exhalation of breath, and then lay still. She was dead.

"Take the child," Nathaniel urged.

I shook my head. "You do it. I don't want to touch it."

Nathaniel gave me an exasperated look, but he reached inside the cavity anyway. I was disturbed that the dark magic I'd been trying so hard to suppress was now working on its own. It wasn't simply that the power was difficult to control. It was developing a kind of sentience. Soon I would not be able to control it at all. It would control me, and then I would be the monster that Beezle feared I would become.

Nathaniel's hands disappeared inside the hole I had cut in Evangeline's body. He could not disguise his horror as he touched the baby inside and pulled it out into the open air.

It was terrible to behold, a nightmare made flesh. Lucifer and Evangeline's child had been conceived in death, while Evangeline's soul was on the other side of the Door. It was black as pitch and covered in the glop from Evangeline's belly. At first all I could see were the tiny horns at the top of its head, and then other features became visible.

Its limbs unfurled from its body as Nathaniel held it up. The legs were furry spider's appendages, although it had six instead of eight. Wings unfolded from its back, articulated like a bat's. The mouth was hidden in its blank, insectlike face, although it continued to make a kind of metallic keening noise. The eyes were not in the least bit human or angelic. They were large red orbs slightly off center, again reminiscent of a bug.

Lucifer's child was a hideous thing to look upon, and it was certainly carrying some power that would not be pleasant for any human that encountered this creature. I was seized by a wild impulse to grab the little monster and run to the nearest window and toss it out. Or maybe fly out over the ocean and drop it there. This wasn't a baby, a child to be cherished and loved. This was a blight on the Earth, and I had helped bring it forth.

Nathaniel still held the creature away from his body, his arms outstretched. "Someone must cut the cord."

"What? Oh, right," I said, shaking my head. We had all fallen briefly under the spell of this thing, frozen in contemplation of its horrible form. "Jude, you've got that big knife handy."

I considered my duty done. I had delivered the damn thing, whether I wanted to or not. Let the others deal with the rest.

Jude neatly sliced the umbilical cord so that the monster was separated from Evangeline. The creature made weak, struggling movements in Nathaniel's hands.

Now what do we do with it? Samiel said.

"Find Lucifer," I said. "It's his kid. It's his problem."

"Yeah, but what about this mess?" Beezle said, gesturing toward Evangeline's body.

I looked down at her, my many-greats-grandmother, the woman who had cast my fate centuries ago by falling in love with Lucifer in the first place. I felt a little sad for her. Could she have known that she was carrying this horrible thing inside her? Had she been dreaming of little fingers and toes, of soft downy hair and chubby cheeks?

And would I suffer the same fate as she? My child, too, was born of the line of Lucifer, and my baby's father had been the son of a nephilim. Those little wings I felt fluttering inside me—were they the wings of a monster?

"I will take my son now, Nathaniel," a voice said behind me, icy cold.

I shifted on my knees, and saw Lucifer standing in the hallway, just a few feet away. I had not felt him approach, and I was slightly shocked that I had not. His eyes burned like starlight, and his magic was a palpable thing. Normally I could feel Lucifer's power coming near.

Nathaniel rose to his feet as the Morningstar stepped forward. Nathaniel's shoulders were hunched in tension as he handed the kicking, mewling thing to Lucifer. My grandfather took the baby, looking down at it. The creature ceased making noise once it was in Lucifer's arms. It seemed unnaturally aware, as though it knew it was with its parent. Lucifer's face softened in a gross parody of fatherly affection.

Nathaniel backed away from Lucifer to rejoin us. I came to my feet, as did Jude and Samiel. Evangeline's body lay inside the circle we made, and all of us were studiously avoiding looking at it. The silence that hung over us was heavy and fraught with peril. None of us could predict what Lucifer would do, and we were all afraid of what might happen.

For several moments Lucifer appeared to be communing with his offspring. Then he looked up, and snapped his fingers.

Two flunkies appeared out of nowhere. They took the child from Lucifer without a word and disappeared back into the walls or wherever they had come from.

Now Lucifer looked at the five of us—me, Beezle, Nathaniel, Jude and Samiel—and the body that was partially hidden by our feet.

"I want to see her," Lucifer said.

We all moved aside. I glanced down at Evangeline—the stab wounds in her chest, the open cavity of her abdomen still leaking fluid, the gaping sockets where her eyes used to be. It was a horrifying sight.

Lucifer walked to her body and crouched on the floor. He still wore the expensive suit he'd had on earlier in the evening but didn't seem the least bit concerned about blood on his shoes or the cuffs of his pants.

His face was a mask of stillness though his eyes burned bright. I could not tell, or guess, what he was thinking. Nor could I feel his emotion as I had done in the past.

After a long while he stood, and gave each of us a measured look. "What has occurred here?"

I explained what Nathaniel and I had heard, how we had found Evangeline dying outside our door, how we had been unable to save her but had saved the child at her request. Throughout my narrative Lucifer showed no emotion.

When I was finished he said, "And none of you thought to investigate the area for her attacker? Did you not care that a murderer has managed to kill my fiancée in my own home?"

"We were kind of preoccupied with trying to save her and the kid," I said, my natural inclination to defy authority reasserting itself. It wasn't fair of Lucifer to act like we'd somehow been negligent. "Where were you, anyway? How come she was up here all alone in the first place?"

"I am not answerable to you, Granddaughter," Lucifer said, and for a moment I felt the surge of his anger. Then he leashed it again, and I realized how tightly he held himself in check. He was saving his wrath for the culprit, and when he found whoever had killed Evangeline, there would quite literally be hell to pay.

"However," Lucifer continued. "I will tell you that I do not know why Evangeline was here. Perhaps she wished to speak with you."

"In the middle of the night?" I asked.

"You and your party are among only a few guests who have retired. Many others remain awake. It is not unthinkable that Evangeline would think she could approach you at this hour," Lucifer said.

"I can't imagine that we would have much to talk about," I muttered, but Lucifer heard me.

"I realize you and Evangeline had quite a difficult history, but I requested that she attempt to make amends with you for my sake," Lucifer said. "After all, you are both precious to me. She may have decided not to wait until tomorrow."

"Or maybe it had nothing to do with me at all," I said. I started to say, "Maybe she was meeting someone else," but didn't think that would sound too good.

It implied that either she was cheating on Lucifer (unlikely) or she was up to some nefarious plot, and I don't think Lucifer would believe his darling Evangeline capable of such a thing.

He seemed oddly naïve about her. Evangeline would never in a million years have shown up in the middle of the night to apologize to me. She might have come looking for me to threaten me, or to make sure I understood the order of things now that she was to marry Lucifer. But to "make amends"? Never.

I'm not sure I would have accepted her apology in any case. I tend to get unreasonable when people try to possess me from beyond the grave and use me as a tool of their will.

"Whatever she was doing here, someone took advantage and murdered her," Lucifer said. "I intend to find that person and punish them."

"How are you going to do that?" I said. "There are dozens of guests here. You have servants and whoever else normally lives with you. Plus, most of the creatures you invited to your wedding are magical and know very well how to hide their tracks."

"But not from me," another voice said.

My eyebrows rose to my hairline as Puck appeared behind his brother. "What are you doing here?" I asked. "Your room isn't on this floor."

"Not happy to see me, niece?" Puck said, but the merriment that usually danced in his eyes was banked.

"Why would I be?" I said. Nathaniel put his hand on my shoulder and squeezed it in warning.

Puck ignored me and turned to Lucifer. "As you know, I can see into the past. There will be no need to interrogate the entire household. I can show you what happened and you will be able to identify the culprit."

"How can you do that?" Jude asked.

"With a wave of my hand and some pixie dust," Puck said offhandedly. "How it works is really none of your business. But the fact remains that I can do it."

"Yes, he can," I said, thinking of the way Puck had "animated" the lost tribe on that faraway planet, a race of faerie dead for centuries. "He can show the past, but he can also manipulate it."

"How do we know that you will not show Lucifer some trick?" Nathaniel asked. "You could use this as an opportunity to present an enemy of yours in a bad light."

"Worried I'll put my own offspring on the chopping block, dear boy?" Puck said.

"You've done it before," I replied. He'd killed Bendith, Nathaniel's half brother, just to set me up for the fall. He knew I would have to get rid of Titania, Bendith's mother, whose rage knew no bounds. And because I had killed her to defend myself, he was now free from the chains that had bound him to the Faerie queen for centuries.

I knew Puck was angry that I had "ruined" Nathaniel, whom he had designed as a kind of walking time bomb to assassinate Lucifer at some future point. This would be the perfect opportunity for Puck to clear the board of me or Nathaniel or both.

I turned to Lucifer. "He can show you the past, but I wouldn't necessarily trust it."

"I know quite well what my brother is capable of," Lucifer said, his voice cold as winter. "You and Nathaniel have nothing to fear as long as you have done no wrong."

That wasn't true. Titania hadn't believed a word I'd said despite my protestations that I'd had nothing to do with Bendith's death. The murder looked like I could have committed it, and I was on the spot when it happened. Therefore it was my fault.

Now Evangeline was dead outside my door, and I was covered in her blood. No matter what Puck showed us, I had a feeling things were not going to end well for me. Somehow I was always blamed when things started to go wrong.

Puck waved us away from Evangeline's body. We all moved to one side, even Lucifer. Puck held his hands over her for a moment, murmuring quietly.

At first nothing seemed to be happening. Jude shifted restlessly against the wall, his nose sniffing the air.

"What is it?" I asked.

He shook his head. "I can't tell. It may be the shifter."

"Silence," Lucifer said, and Jude and I ceased our whispering.

Then, suddenly, Evangeline seemed to rise a few inches from the floor. Everything that had occurred in the hallway happened in reverse, as real as if we were watching a live performance. We saw Nathaniel remove the baby (which looked even more horrible the second time around), saw me cut Evangeline's stomach open (also not particularly pleasant on review). Since the "film" was running backward, it looked like we all went into our bedrooms instead of coming out of them, and Evangeline crawled the wrong way down the hallway, away from our doors. At the end of the hallway, near the windows, Evangeline came to her feet.

A second figure materialized in the frame. Someone in a dark cloak stabbed her, a shiny silver knife sliding into her chest over and over. Evangeline struggled, throwing her arms out. The figure stepped away from her, back into the shadows. Just before the figure disappeared, the face under the hood turned toward our end of the hallway.

It was my face under the hood.

Of course it was.

13

I SIGHED. "SERIOUSLY. YOU COULD HAVE PREDICTED that would happen."

I expected Lucifer to dismiss what he had seen out of hand, or turn on Puck and accuse him of manipulating the memory of what had happened here. But he did neither of those things. Instead, he turned on me with a look so cold and frightening that I took a step back.

"I thought you did protest too much, Granddaughter," Lucifer said.

"You've got to be kidding me," I said. "You believe all that? You think I killed Evangeline? Why? I have enough aggravation without adding on a murder rap."

"We all witnessed it," Lucifer said. "My eyes have told me the truth."

"Your eyes have lied to you, or he has," I said, pointing at Puck.

Puck shook his head. He looked at me with speculation

and, I thought, surprise. "I have done nothing to change what happened here, niece."

"And you believe him?" I said to Lucifer. "You do know what he's been up to for the last few months, don't you?"

"Puck cannot lie to me," Lucifer said.

"Since when?" I said.

"Since always," Puck said. "We cannot speak or show falsehoods to one another. It is a price of our magic."

"Madeline could not have done this," Nathaniel said. "She was with me for the duration of the evening. She never left the bedroom."

"We are all aware that you would lie for Madeline," Lucifer said. "It is the natural instinct of the protector."

"Yeah, and how did I get in and out of the bedroom without anyone seeing?" I asked.

"There are paths in these walls, just as in Amarantha's home," Lucifer said. "And you discovered those easily enough."

"How do you know that?" I asked. "Just how closely do you watch me?"

"Closely enough," Lucifer said.

"Then you should know I didn't kill Evangeline," I said.

"I was not watching earlier this evening," Lucifer said smoothly. "I had guests to attend to."

"It was the shifter," Jude said. I could tell that he was strongly resisting the urge to pick a fight with Lucifer. He had a grudge against the Morningstar to begin with, and now Lucifer was casting aspersions on my character.

"Damn right," I said. "And it framed me for the third time."

"What shifter do you speak of?" Lucifer asked.

Nathaniel, Jude and I fell over one another trying to explain about the shifter and what it had been up to—how it had slaughtered one of the Retrievers, how it had murdered Chloe, how it had betrayed and hunted Jude's pack.

Lucifer listened, his expression unchanged. "And you say this creature is something created by Alerian? How is it I have not heard of it if this shapeshifter was formed to fight me and my armies?"

"Daharan said that he made Alerian destroy the creatures. I don't know why you never heard about them. You can take it up with Daharan and Alerian," I said. "And Alerian claims that the current iteration has nothing to do with him."

Lucifer appeared deep in thought, brooding. He snapped his fingers and another servant appeared at the end of the hall.

"How does that work?" I said. "Do they lurk just out of sight or do you have little portals for them to use to walk through the walls?"

My grandfather only gave me another icy glare. It was shocking that he was taking all this so seriously. Not Evangeline's death—of course he would take that seriously, especially if he truly loved her as much as he seemed to. But I couldn't believe he was actually considering the possibility that I had been the one to harm her.

He told the magically appearing servant to fetch Alerian. He also gave instructions for the removal of Evangeline's body and the cleanup of the hallway. A second servant appeared while he was speaking to the first.

"Search Madeline's room for a black cloak or a large knife," Lucifer said.

My indignation was growing by the minute. "There won't be anything in there. And even if there is something in there, do you know how freaking easy it is to plant a murder weapon? Don't you ever watch TV?"

"No," Lucifer said shortly.

"Well, Beezle watches a ton of it, and I've picked some stuff up by osmosis over the years," I said.

"Again, the protestations," Lucifer said, his voice silky. "As I said, you will have nothing to worry about if you have actually done nothing."

"I *have* done nothing, and yet I'm still getting worried," I said. "Because you're obstinately refusing to listen to reason."

Lucifer turned on me then, his eyes blazing like the sun. "I am still master in my own house, Granddaughter. Whatever leniency I had allowed you in the past will not be considered if you are Evangeline's killer. My justice will be swift and absolute."

I covered my stomach with my hands, an unconscious gesture that drew Lucifer's gaze there.

"My grandson will not be harmed, of course," he said. "But you will certainly suffer."

I narrowed my eyes at him. "It sounds like you've already decided."

He turned his back on me then, saying nothing.

I knew I shouldn't have come to this damned wedding. I should have stayed at home and taken whatever consequences came with ignoring Lucifer's invitation. Anything would be better than being trapped in his house, at his mercy.

The only way we would get out of here was if Nathaniel and I joined our powers and blasted the whole place into oblivion. And even then it was a certainty that Lucifer and Alerian and Puck would put aside their differences to stop us. The resulting boom would probably look a lot like a nuclear apocalypse, and a lot of innocent people would be killed in the process. Lucifer might not care about those innocents, but I did.

It came as no surprise when Lucifer's flunky emerged from my bedroom holding a bloody cloak and a knife covered in rust-colored stains.

"I'm being railroaded," I said to Nathaniel as Lucifer turned to me in triumph, the cloak and knife clutched in his fists. I felt strangely dazed about the whole thing. It seemed as if it had all been planned from the start.

"You certainly are," Nathaniel replied.

Through the haze of my bewilderment I became aware of something. Nathaniel was angry. He was very, very angry. The connection between us was choked with his rage. He kept such a leash on his emotions that I was almost never aware of him and our connection. But now I felt it acutely.

I took his hand, forced him to look at me before he did anything foolish.

"Don't," I said. "I'm already in trouble. Don't give him an excuse to hurt you, too."

His eyes were brilliant blue in his fury. "Do not ask me to stand by and watch harm come to you."

Puck watched us with avid interest. "And what will you do to prevent it, my son? The evidence points in one direction only—toward Madeline."

"Quite conveniently. We are all very well aware that Madeline would not and could not have murdered Evangeline," Nathaniel said through his teeth. "Lucifer is allowing this farce to continue for reasons of his own. I know what you wish to do with Madeline."

"At the moment I wish her in a cell," Lucifer said. "Which is where she will go, to be held until the court of the Grigori can be assembled for her trial."

Samiel looked at me in panic. He'd been captured by Lucifer's men and held once before. I'd intervened on his behalf and ended up as Lucifer's Hound of the Hunt. The outcome had been better than Samiel's execution, but had saddled me with another connection to Lucifer. No matter what was decided at this trial, Lucifer would get something he wanted out of it. Lucifer always got something he wanted out of every situation.

"You haven't asked Alerian about the shifter yet," I said. "Wait until your brother gets here before you decide to lock me up for no damned reason."

Alerian appeared at that very moment, silently entering the hallway.

"Waiting for your big entrance?" I said.

He did not dignify my remark with a response. Instead, he looked at Lucifer with no small amount of resentment. "You requested my presence?"

It was pretty clear that Alerian didn't think much of Lucifer's request.

"Yes," Lucifer said, passing the "evidence" back to his servant and waving him away, along with anyone else hanging around. "What do you know of this shapeshifter that Madeline claims has been lately in Chicago, and now here?"

"I know nothing of this creature," Alerian said calmly.

"I thought you couldn't lie to one another," I said.

"I am not lying," Alerian said, narrowing his eyes at me. The sound of the ocean crashed inside my head. Every time Alerian got angry with me, I felt like I was about to drown in some metaphorical sea.

"If you're not lying, then you're definitely parsing the question," I said. "You know something about this kind of shifter in a general, if not specific, sense. Especially since it's your personal Frankenstein's monster."

"I answered the question my brother asked," Alerian said.

"Ask him more directly," I told Lucifer.

"I do not take orders from you, my granddaughter. It is, in fact, the exact opposite. You are beholden to me and my will, as my Hound of the Hunt."

The implications were clear. Because I carried this curse as Lucifer's Hound, he could make me do whatever he damned well pleased. And that meant that if he ordered me into a cage and told me to stay there, I would have to do it. I'd been afraid for a long time that it would come to this, and now it finally had.

The second implication was that he would not challenge Alerian, or make him answer any further questions. Lucifer was steering this event so that he would get the outcome he wanted. All that remained for the rest of us was to wait.

The only people left in the hallway were my group—Nathaniel, Samiel, Jude, Beezle and myself—and the three brothers.

And Evangeline, whose body had been left in the middle of the floor like an accusation.

"Don't you want to cover her with a sheet or something?" I said to Lucifer.

"Cannot bear to see the evidence of your crime?" Lucifer asked.

"No, I just think it's unseemly to leave her out in the open like that, all carved up," I said. "You were going to marry her. You'd think you would have more respect for her remains."

Lucifer reached for me then. I don't know what he would have done—slapped me or grabbed me or just put his hand on my chin—but Nathaniel stepped in front of me before he could do it.

"Do not touch her," he said. His voice vibrated with an intensity I'd never heard before.

Nathaniel had always been the one who counseled calm, who recommended the wisest course. He always kept a lid on his feelings. He was always impatient when I lost my temper, or when I defied a being much older and more powerful than I.

Now he was facing down Lucifer, practically chin to chin. Lucifer had finally crossed some line that Nathaniel would not tolerate.

Or maybe it was just that he really, truly loved me. But my head was already on the chopping block, and I didn't want his there, too.

"Nathaniel," I said, taking his face and turning it toward mine. "Don't. Don't do something that can't be undone."

His anger was a palpable thing. I was shocked that Lucifer hadn't struck Nathaniel down for insubordinate behavior already.

Nathaniel's eyes searched mine. I wished desperately for the ability to read his mind, and for him to see into my own thoughts. Everyone in the hallway was watching us with varying levels of concern and curiosity.

Lucifer had taken a step away from us. He was probably calculating how to turn this to his advantage, but I didn't care. I needed Nathaniel to know that it was not acceptable to me if he died defending me from Lucifer's wrath. I would not go through that again. I would not watch someone else stand in the path of a sword meant for me.

There was only one way I could show him without speaking, and so I kissed him.

I am not usually a fan of public displays of affection, especially when I am being so closely observed. But if Nathaniel and I were physically joined, it tended to strengthen the emotional bond formed by our magic. So I kissed him, and I poured all of the things I could not say into that kiss. I told him that I cared, that I needed to protect him as much as he needed to protect me.

In that kiss I felt his love, his anger, his frustration and, finally, his resignation. He would not challenge Lucifer. For now.

I pulled away from him, put my mouth close to his ear. Everyone except Samiel and Beezle could probably hear us anyway, but I wanted at least the illusion of privacy.

"I'll need you to get me out," I said.

He nodded, though his anger had merely been banked, not eliminated.

Then I moved away from Nathaniel and toward Lucifer. "All right," I said. "Arrest me, since that's what you obviously want."

"No," Jude said, and Samiel shook his head rapidly. Beezle watched me carefully. I couldn't tell whether he approved or not. I know Nathaniel didn't.

His eyes narrowed in suspicion. "What game do you play now, Granddaughter? First you proclaim loudly to have nothing to do with Evangeline's death, and now you quietly permit me to lock you away?"

"I did have nothing to do with Evangeline's death," I said. "And I'll be proven right. In the meantime, you can stop wasting everyone's time with this farce."

Puck looked at me like he was trying to figure me out. "I cannot tell if you are being very wise or very foolish."

I shrugged in what I hoped was a mysterious fashion. Let Puck and Lucifer try to fathom my motivations for a change.

"I am certainly not going to allow the opportunity to imprison my fiancée's murderer to pass," Lucifer said. "Particularly not if you are going to be cooperative for a change."

He snapped his fingers, and for the third time two

servants appeared. I didn't know whether he could communicate with them telepathically or what, but these two appeared to be just what the doctor ordered—big, burly characters that looked like prison guards.

For a moment I thought Nathaniel would not go along with my half-assed plan. The sight of the two men flanking me seemed like it might be too much for him to take. But he stayed in control.

Outwardly, I did the same as the two guards led me away from the scene in the hallway. Inwardly, I was trembling. I hoped that I was making the right decision.

It had been pretty apparent that Lucifer wanted me to take the fall for Evangeline's murder. I didn't know if it was an act or if he sincerely thought I had done it. But I did know if I stood in that hallway any longer, he would have continued to marshal "evidence" against me. And my best chance of wriggling off this hook that Lucifer had me on was to go along until Nathaniel and the others found the shifter—the real culprit.

The creature was still somewhere in Lucifer's mansion. What I found shocking was that, if they were to be believed, neither Lucifer nor Puck nor Alerian could feel the shifter's power or identify him when he was in disguise.

For creatures so old and powerful, this struck me as suspicious, particularly in Alerian's case. If this shifter was like the ones Alerian had created so many centuries ago, then he should have been able to detect traces of its power signature. Alerian had expressed a decided lack of interest in the shifter. Lucifer, too, had been dismissive of the idea that such a creature could exist. All the evidence seemed to point toward the theory I'd developed earlier at dinner—that Lucifer was the shifter's master, that he was using the shifter to corner me.

If Lucifer *was* manipulating all this, then I might have made a huge mistake by quietly offering myself up for imprisonment. But if Lucifer was simply using the circumstances to move things in his favor, then there was hope for me.

It was a gamble, but I hadn't seen any other way to get out from under Lucifer's microscope. Any other way that didn't involve bloodshed, that is.

I was so involved in my thoughts that I'd barely noticed where we were going. Now I realized my two escorts were leading me down—and down, and down. We were on a curving stone staircase in a narrow passage, almost like one that would lead up to a high tower in a fairy tale. Except that in this case, the princess was going in the wrong direction.

We descended into the earth, far below Lucifer's mansion. I wasn't sure that any house built near Los Angeles could possibly have a foundation like this—more evidence that Lucifer magically manipulated his home to suit his needs. For all I knew this part of the house could be in a completely different dimension.

At the bottom of the stairs was a short row of cells on both sides of a hallway—metal bars that blocked rooms made of cold stone. There were no windows, and only a few flickering torches of flame provided light.

"Where did Lucifer learn about prison decorating? *The Count of Monte Cristo*?" I said.

Neither of the two men with me responded. One of them took out a bunch of keys on a metal ring. The feeling that I was suddenly trapped in a Dumas novel persisted. He opened the metal door and the other jail keeper ushered me in. There was a stone bench to sleep on, but nothing more.

As the door slammed shut behind me, I felt a moment of

profound panic. I was trapped, pinned like a butterfly on a board. Lucifer finally had me where he wanted me—under his thumb and unable to do anything about it. My baby, who had been so unusually silent and still during the events upstairs, fluttered his little wings in time with the rapid thrum of my heart. Would Nathaniel even be able to find me down here?

Lucifer's goons drifted back up the stairs. I was underground, in the dark, and alone. But I didn't have to stay here. I knew that as soon as I put my hands on the bars. There was no magic binding me, nothing to stop me from blasting the doors off and fighting my way out of the house.

Except that I would be leaving the others behind, who would no doubt pay a terrible price for my actions. I realized that I had essentially left my family and friends as hostages, and that Lucifer's plot to get us all under one roof would make his plans—whatever it was he had in mind— much, much easier.

I really wished Daharan were here. He would never have allowed it to come to this.

"I see that your sins have finally come home to roost," a voice slurred from the darkness.

I peered across the hallway, trying to make out the shadow hidden in the cell opposite mine.

"Who is it?" I said. "Come into the light."

The figure moved from the back corner of the cell, shuffling slowly. For a strange moment I thought that it was a zombie, or some other kind of monster imprisoned by Lucifer. Then the person's face emerged into the flickering light of the torch. The face had obviously been hit multiple times, but I still recognized it.

It was Jack Dabrowski, and I had only one thing to say to him.

"You are a moron," I said.

He shook his head, though it was obviously painful. "How could I pass up the wedding of Lucifer? Everyone online was talking about it."

"You could have passed it up by using your brain," I said harshly. "I warned you over and over again that it was dangerous to investigate things you don't understand. You're lucky Lucifer hasn't killed you already."

"He didn't kill me because I told him I was a friend of yours," he said.

"And as you can see I'm in the cell across from you," I said. "Not your best move. And we're not friends. Last time we met you were a little annoyed with me because I'd locked you in the storage area in my basement."

"Which was significantly more comfortable than Lucifer's accommodations, by the way. But I thought that saying I was with you was a safe bet. Everything I've read has indicated that Lucifer lets you do whatever you want because you're his favorite. What are *you* doing in the oubliette with me, anyway?" Jack asked.

"Just how much of my life is discussed on the Internet?" I asked, avoiding his question.

"More than you think," Jack said. "Even the average nonmagical person would probably be shocked to see what comes up if they Google their own name. And don't think I didn't notice that you didn't answer me. I can see the blood on your clothes, so I bet there's a body involved."

"What an investigator you are," I said. "You should have won a Pulitzer for your reporting by now."

"No need to be snide," Jack said. "The way I look at it, we're in the same boat. We should help each other."

"We are *not* in the same boat," I said. "I can leave this cell anytime I want to. You can't."

"You can get out?" he asked.

In demonstration I waved my hand in front of the door. The lock turned under my will and the door swung open.

Jack clutched the bars eagerly. "Let me out, will you? I snuck into the house. I could probably sneak out again."

I shook my head, pulling the door shut again, although I did not lock it. "You'll never make it out of the mansion. Lucifer's got servants everywhere, and he's going to be on alert now that . . ."

I trailed off, not wanting Jack to know about Evangeline.

"Now that what?" he said. "You might as well tell me. I'll find out anyway."

"Then you can ferret it out. I'm not your source," I said.

"Why are you always so hostile to me?" Jack said. "I could help you. I came to you from the start to help you."

"I think you're mixing up 'help' with unwanted publicity," I said. "I don't want my business published. I want my privacy."

"Did you ever think that if more people knew about you and what you did, then you would be protected?" Jack said.

"Protected from what?"

"From stuff like this," Jack said. "The more famous you are, the harder it becomes for someone like Lucifer to make you disappear. People would care. They would look for you."

"And they would find nothing," I said. "Even now, even when you've been beaten up and imprisoned, you still don't get it. Lucifer didn't have to do it this way. If you're alive and I'm alive, it's because he wants us to be, because it serves his purpose. He's not showing you mercy. In fact, if he had been in a bad mood when he found you, then you would be nothing but vapor right now."

"You mean he wasn't in a bad mood when he ordered his goons to beat the crap out of me?" Jack said. "I think my arm might be broken. It hurts like hell."

Now that he mentioned it, I could see that his left arm hung at a strange angle.

"Oh, yeah, that's broken," I said. "Now, that, I can fix. I think."

I pushed the door of the cell open again and crossed to the bars of Jack's enclosure. I hesitated for a moment. I knew the healing spell by heart, but I had never tried to use it on an ordinary human before.

"Having second thoughts about putting me out of my misery?" Jack asked.

"No," I said. "I was just thinking that the spell might harm you more than it helped. I'm not sure an ordinary human can handle it."

"I can handle anything," Jack said confidently. His face was eager, and I could tell he was more excited about the prospect of having magic performed on him than about fixing what was broken.

"Don't act like a child," I said. "If I don't do this correctly, or your body can't process it, who knows what might happen. You could explode from the inside out, or have a stroke right in front of me, and there would be nothing I could do about it. You would probably be wishing that you had just waited for a regular doctor to set your arm then."

"I know you won't hurt me," he said.

"Three days ago you thought I had mutilated a person right in front of you," I reminded him.

"Yes, but now I know better," he said. "C'mon, just fix my arm since you won't let me out of the cell."

He was putting on a brave face, but he was obviously in

pain. And I could make it better. And I probably wouldn't accidentally blow him up. Probably.

I reached through the bars, put my hand on his shoulder. He winced when I brushed my fingers across his arm.

A little pulse of magic flickered through me and into his arm. I was trying to find the precise point where the arm was broken, so that I wouldn't have to overload him with power. I used my ability to locate the fracture and then sent gentle waves of magic through to heal it.

Jack watched me with wonder in his eyes. "You could do so much with a power like this. You could heal cancer. AIDS. Kids with rare diseases. Why do you hide yourself from the world?"

"This power isn't an endless well, you know," I said. "Whenever I use too much magic, it takes something out of me. Can you imagine what would happen if everyone in the world knew that I could heal people? Thousands would descend upon my house, each of them with a story sadder and more horrible than the last one. And I wouldn't be able to say no. I'd help them, and I'd heal them, and eventually I would be too sick and exhausted myself to help anyone else."

"But what if you could just help the really needy?" Jack asked as I pulled my hand away.

"Who decides who's really needy?" I asked. "Does your arm hurt? Do you feel any aftereffects, like nausea?"

Jack bent and stretched his arm. "Nah, it feels great. I feel great, as a matter of fact. Like I just drank a lot of coffee. Wow. Magic is incredible."

He started doing jumping jacks in his cell, almost like he couldn't help himself. I noticed that even though I'd tried to pinpoint the fracture, my magic had still spread to other parts of his body. The bruises and cuts on his face were rapidly healing while I watched.

"Okay, I guess there are some side effects," I muttered as Jack began jogging in place. "Apparently magic makes you high."

I was about to tell him to quit it when I felt a sudden cramp in the side of my abdomen. The pain seemed to recede for a moment; then it twisted through me again. Something wet ran down the inside of my pajama pants.

"Oh, damn," I said. "The baby's coming."

14

JACK STOPPED WITH HIS EXERCISE-VIDEO ROUTINE AND stared at me. "The baby? You're having the baby now?"

"Yes," I said.

The pain was not intense, but it was definitely there. I could feel the baby moving inside me. I didn't know if normal human moms could feel that when they were about to give birth, but I certainly could.

"Damn," I said. "Damn, damn, damn, damn."

This was exactly what I had not wanted. I didn't want to give birth under Lucifer's roof. I especially didn't want to give birth while I was "imprisoned" on a murder charge. Lucifer would use my incarceration as an excuse to whisk my son away from me, which was what he had wanted all along.

I staggered toward the stone bench in the cell. I needed to sit down for a minute, to breathe, to think. It was all becoming clear.

It didn't matter, really, if Lucifer was the shapeshifter's master. He had seen the opportunity given by my look-alike's murder of Evangeline. Once I was locked up, I was under his power, and he could keep me locked up until I had the baby.

Once the baby was born, Lucifer would have everything he wanted. Two new heirs—my child and Evangeline's—and no rebellious granddaughter or jealous wife to get in his way. He could execute me without even having to justify his actions before the court of the Grigori. No one would question that he would want his fiancée's killer to receive justice.

And I had made all his plans easier by passively agreeing to be locked up in the basement. It had seemed like a good idea at the time, but as usual I'd been outmaneuvered by a master.

Now I needed to get out of Lucifer's house before this labor progressed any further. And to do that I needed Nathaniel.

I could easily fly to the top of the long flight of stairs. But once I got to the top, there was sure to be more security than there was down here. There was no way Lucifer would leave me in a cell with a door that I could easily unlock with magic.

My second problem was Jack Dabrowski. The moron had followed me here and gotten himself locked up by the Prince of Darkness even though I'd warned him about a thousand times about interfering in the lives of supernatural creatures. It would serve him right if I left him where he was, but my conscience unfortunately would not allow me to do that. So I'd have to take him with me. And he was going to be deadweight in a fight. Completely manic high-with-magic deadweight. He'd gone back to exercising, and was now doing squat jumps from the bench on the wall to the floor and back again.

I tried not to think about how completely terrified I was. It wasn't just the prospect of trying to fight my way out of the mansion while I was in labor. It was the possibility that my son was a horrific monster like Evangeline's child. He could rip his way out of me, kill me before I ever had a chance to see his face.

Even if he was a completely normal adorable little cherub, I was still scared. Because I didn't know how to be a mom, and I didn't know how I would keep him safe from my own family members, never mind the multitude of enemies I had. Many of those enemies were staying right here in Lucifer's house for the wedding that would now never happen, all of them conveniently placed for snatching my baby away or murdering me before he could ever be born.

I took a deep breath. The cramping feeling had intensified, although it was nothing like the way birth looks on television, with the mom all sweaty and screaming her head off with every contraction. It just felt like I had the worst menstrual cramps ever.

I stood up gingerly, using the wall as a brace. No matter what, I was not going to get far without Nathaniel, and I wouldn't leave him or Beezle or the others behind anyway. So I reached for the connection between us. We weren't able to send messages, per se, but I hoped that he would feel my need and my distress and find me.

The darkness inside me opened its eyes, lurking, waiting for me to drop my guard so that it could take over again. I ruthlessly put a lid on that part of my power. I didn't need to deal with an internal struggle for my personality and sanity right now. As usual, I had more than enough to deal with.

But I could feel the black energy seeping around the edges of my connection to Nathaniel, looking for an opening, looking for a way in.

"Nathaniel," I said aloud. I thought I felt him respond, but I wasn't sure.

Maybe we were, as I'd suspected, in another dimension here in the basement. When I'd been on that strange planet far away in time and space, I hadn't been able to feel Nathaniel. Which meant that I would have to at least get back up into the mansion before I could call him to me.

"I'm not Nathaniel. I'm Jack," Jack said.

He was soaked in sweat. He looked like one of those people from the P90X commercial, jumping around all over the place and seeming superhappy about it. I don't get those people. I'm not quite as lazy as Beezle, but how can anyone be that happy when they're expending that much energy?

"Come on, exercise boy," I said. "We're busting out of this joint."

I waddled over to his cell and waved my hand over the lock, opening the door.

"Yes!" Jack said. "What do we do now? Sneak out of the house?"

"I doubt there will be any sneaking," I said. "As soon as we get to the top of the stairs, there will be guards. And we will have to dispatch those guards before they raise an alarm if we want to have any chance of escaping at all. So I need you to calm the fuck down and stop acting like a toddler who just ate a bag of Halloween candy. Because if everything is blown because you're acting insane, then I will personally throw you to the bottom of these stairs."

"No, you won't," Jack said, swinging his arms back and

forth. "I know all about you now. You talk tough, and it's cute, but you're just a big softy."

I wanted to list off all the big, dangerous creatures I'd battled and defeated, but it sounded too much like bragging, and I didn't really like to brag about the murders I'd committed, however justified. Plus, there was not enough time to convince a half-crazed human that I was a hell of a lot tougher than I looked.

"Just stay close to me and don't make any noise. Got it?" I said as I started up the stairs.

It would have been significantly faster to fly, but I would have to carry Jack. Under normal circumstances I would have plenty of strength for such a task, even though Jack was about ten or twelve inches taller than me. But it took a lot of work to remain calm in the face of increasing contractions as well as maintain control over my lurking dark side. I didn't have much left over for carting around the wayward blogger. So it was climbing the stairs for us.

Jack immediately pushed ahead of me and started jogging up the stairs.

"Hurry up, won't you? Why are you so slow?" He started to sing the chorus from an old Duran Duran song.

"I *am* going to kill you when I catch up to you," I mumbled. "I have tried so hard to forget the eighties."

I fluttered up to the step behind him. There was no reason for me to trudge up the stairs and get out of breath chasing him if he wanted to run the whole way up.

We were about halfway to the top by my estimation when Jack suddenly ran out of gas. He slumped against the wall, sliding down until his butt hit the step. His face was white and pale, and he looked like he might boot.

"Don't you dare throw up on me," I said. "I'm the one

who's about to give birth here. I should be falling down and getting sick, not you."

My hands were wrapped around the shifting bulge in my belly. I was trying to slow my son down, trying to keep him from emerging into the world at that very moment. I didn't want to reach the top of the stairs and have the baby pop out right there, into Lucifer's waiting arms.

"I feel like crap," Jack moaned. "I don't think I can climb another step."

"Serves you right for behaving like a lunatic," I said, trying to pull him to his feet. "No one made you run up the stairs like you were in the Olympics."

"Go on without me," Jack said. "I'm going back to the cell to take a nap."

"Get up, you idiot," I said. "If you stay here, you're going to be executed by Lucifer in front of his whole court."

"Says you," Jack said. "Maybe he'll keep me as a performing monkey."

"I can't believe you would consider that a viable alternative," I said. "Now, get your ass up and moving before I have this baby right here on the stairs."

After much grumbling he rose to his feet and started moving again, albeit much slower than before. On the upside, he was much less likely to alert the guards of our presence when he was in his current (and much mellower) state.

I continued flying behind him. It took a lot less energy for me to fly than to try to climb. My whole stomach now felt like a sponge that was being wrung, and my breath came in pants. Sweat trickled around my face, and I imagined that I now closely resembled those movie moms in labor.

Jack glanced back at me. "You don't look so good. How are you holding up?"

"I just need to get to Nathaniel," I said.

"That tall black-haired guy who always stands near you and glowers?" he asked.

"Yes, him," I said.

"Is he the baby's dad?" Jack asked.

"No," I said.

I didn't want to explain that I had been married only a few short months before, and that my husband had been killed by my father. It seemed like the sort of thing that might end up on Jack's blog—if he ever lived to blog again, that was.

We rounded a curve of the staircase and suddenly there was a small landing and a door directly in front of us. It looked like a plain, ordinary metal safety door, like the kind that are in emergency exits in tall buildings. But there was something different about it. I couldn't put my finger on it. I put my hand on Jack's shoulder.

"Wait a second," I said.

I landed on the stair behind him and then nudged my way past. I reached out with my power, looking for a trace of a magical signature.

And boy, did I find one.

"That's no ordinary door," I said. "It's booby-trapped with magic."

The doors downstairs had been so easy to open because of this. I knew that Lucifer wouldn't have allowed anyone he considered a threat to be locked up with so little security.

I just hadn't thought there would be quite this much security elsewhere. Right away I could tell that the spell on the door would trigger at the slightest touch. There had to be a way to disable the trap from the other side so that the prison guards could come and go.

Unfortunately, I didn't have time to wait for Lucifer to decide to give us bread and water. We needed to get out of this stairway immediately. My contractions were getting closer together and more painful. However, I wasn't certain I could break down the spell without making everything go kablooey. It was a complex work of magic, and a highly dangerous one.

"I need Nathaniel," I said again. "Life would be a lot easier if I wasn't wearing pajama pants."

Jack stared at me, his eyes blank and tired. He was coming down hard from the effects of the magic. "What do pajama pants have to do with anything?"

"If I wasn't wearing pajama pants, I would have my cell phone," I said. "And if I had my cell phone, I could just call Nathaniel and have him come and get us out of here instead of trying to rely on a very tenuous emotional link through magic."

"I still don't understand what that has to do with your pajamas," Jack said.

"Never mind," I said. I concentrated hard on Nathaniel, on the connection between us. Now that I was out of the depths of the mansion, I was hoping it would be easier to sense him, and for him to find me.

Nathaniel, I thought. I didn't know if it would work or help, but I tried to send a mental picture of where I was and what I needed. It felt slightly silly. Even with all of the things I had seen and done that involved magic, telepathy seemed like it was still an "out-there" concept.

After a few minutes I had to stop. It was hard to concentrate on sending Nathaniel an S.O.S. when it felt like my stomach was being ripped in two.

And as soon as I stopped, I heard him.

I'm coming.

"Wow, I can't believe that actually worked," I said.

"Can't believe what actually worked?" Jack asked.

He had sat down on the stairs with his back against the wall while I did my human-telephone act with Nathaniel. His face was white and covered with sweat, and he was shivering. I probably did not look much better. It was a struggle to stay upright, and a couple of times I saw black dots in front of my eyes, like I was on the verge of fainting.

"Don't worry about it," I said. "The cavalry is on its way. Unless I'm hallucinating Nathaniel's voice in my head. Which is entirely possible."

"You know, I'm starting to wonder how you have such a powerful reputation," Jack said, his eyes closed. "You seem like kind of a flake."

"You'd seem like kind of a flake if you were trapped in a stairwell with an unhelpful blogger while you were in labor," I said.

I wondered whether I had really managed to reach Nathaniel, and whether he would understand where I was and how to get rid of the booby trap on the door. I wasn't really sure what our options were otherwise. There was not nearly enough time for me to try to take apart the spell from this side. If I tried blasting through the wall that surrounded the stairwell, I would most definitely alert Lucifer and his goons. I was still hoping that we could find some way to sneak out of the house.

How long should I wait, though? I thought. How long could I wait? I didn't really know anything about having a baby (somehow I'd never gotten around to reading the pregnancy book that Beezle and I had bought a billion years ago), but it seemed to me that the whole process was moving pretty fast. I should have expected this, since the baby had grown unusually large in a short amount of time. In fact, I wasn't anything close to a normal term for a human pregnancy, and yet here he was, on his way.

Suddenly I felt a surge of emotion inside, and I realized that two things were happening at the same time. One, Nathaniel was coming for me. I hadn't hallucinated his voice in my head. The bond between us, forged in magic when I'd released his legacy from Puck, had penetrated the barrier of the door and whatever dimension we were in.

Two, Lucifer had just discovered something that made him angry. I'd felt Lucifer's emotions occasionally in the past, though not often with clarity. Usually I could just feel him approaching, blood calling to blood. I wondered what had pissed him off this time, and fervently hoped it had nothing to do with me.

Another contraction hit me hard, and it was a struggle not to cry out. I didn't know how soundproof that door was, or if there were guards on the other side. If I started screaming, then they would come running—

I smacked myself in the forehead. "What a dope I am."

I opened my mouth and started screaming as loud as I could. A moment later there was an audible sound of fingers punching a keyboard, and the magical shield dropped away from the door. That was interesting. I'd never seen magic that could be programmed with a computer before.

The entrance swung open, and one of the big guys who'd escorted me into the oubliette stood there. I blasted him in the face with nightfire and he fell to the ground without making a noise, which was mighty convenient.

Jack had opened his eyes when I started screaming, but was still sitting on the steps with a dazed look.

"Come on, dummy," I said from the doorway. "We're busting out of here."

He came to his feet like a two-thousand-year-old man and climbed the steps at a pace so glacial that I almost screamed again in frustration. I cautiously moved into the passageway to scope things out while Jack shambled along behind me.

We definitely seemed to be in some kind of back hallway, away from the action of the mansion. That was good. It increased the probability that we would be able to sneak away out the servants' entrance or something like that. This particular passage was lit dimly with just one small bulb on the ceiling. There were two ways to enter it—from the basement and from the opposite end of the hall. There was an open doorway to the right, and yellow light streamed from it.

It is hard to walk quietly and cautiously when you're pregnant. It's even harder to walk quietly and cautiously when you're about to give birth at any moment. Every time a contraction hit, I had to bite back a cry of pain. I concentrated on keeping my breath quiet. Just to make matters more complicated, Jack was shuffling like a confused zombie behind me, heedless of any noise he might make.

I flattened myself against the wall beside the open doorway, and Jack copied me. I peeked around the frame into the room. It was empty, a storage room lined with pantry goods on shelves. There was another door opposite.

"Were you paying attention when they brought you into the cell downstairs?" I whispered to Jack. "Do you remember what's on the other side of that storage room?"

He shook his head. "Some big guy rang my bell pretty good. I mostly remember the floor tile."

"And I wasn't paying attention," I said, my breath

catching as another contraction hit. "Look, let's just try to proceed as quietly as possible. We could come upon someone at any moment who could raise an alarm."

We edged into the storage room. It wasn't very large, and while the walls were stacked high with food, the center of the space was completely empty. I felt exposed and on edge. Magic crackled across my fingers. If anyone came charging through that door, they were going to get blasted into oblivion.

Then I heard the sounds of a struggle in the next room, and smelled the ozone burn of nightfire. My heart surged.

"Nathaniel," I said.

He rounded the corner into the room, followed by Beezle, Samiel, Jude and J.B., and stopped short when he saw me. He looked slightly disappointed to find me there.

"Will you never allow me to rescue you?" he said. His expression was just a little grumpy, like I'd stolen his thunder by getting out of the basement on my own. That face made me want to kiss him until he smiled again, and that was when I realized I loved him.

I loved Nathaniel. It was a hell of a moment for a revelation, especially since another contraction hit at that very second. Freed from the restraint of silence, I cried out, my breath coming in panting bursts.

Beezle's eyes widened. "You're in labor *now*? Can't you ever make anything easy on yourself?"

"Not a lot of choice, Beezle. Rescue away," I said to Nathaniel. "This kid is going to pop out any second."

"And where did he come from?" Beezle asked, pointing at Jack. "And why does he look drunk?"

"Apparently he found out about the wedding on the Internet and couldn't resist the opportunity to have the crap beaten out of him by Lucifer and his flunkies," I said.

"You know, I've said a few times that you are too stupid to live," Beezle said to Jack. "It's nice to know that I was right."

"We must be away from here before Lucifer discovers your condition," Nathaniel said, taking my hand and leading me into the next room. There were three guards on the floor.

"Or before anyone discovers the string of unconscious bodies we left in our wake," J.B. said. "Next time you get the bright idea to put yourself under Lucifer's power, just slap yourself three times and then forget about it."

"He would have locked me up no matter what," I said. "I was just trying to streamline the process. Besides, in a way it was better. If I had stood there arguing with Lucifer, my water would have broken right in front of him. And if that happened, then he would have whisked me away from the rest of you and put so much security on me you would have never found me."

"I would have found you," Nathaniel said.

There was no arrogance in his tone, just a statement of fact. He would find me no matter what. He would fight for me. I don't know why it had taken me so long to see this and understand it, and finally, to value it. To value him. I wanted to tell him, but there wasn't time now. There wasn't time for anything except escape.

Nathaniel expertly guided us through the warren of passages in this part of Lucifer's mansion. We saw surprisingly few people, and those servants we did see were dispatched very quickly.

"Where are we going?" I asked.

"There is a back entrance for servants," Nathaniel said. "I lived here for a time. I should be able to find it again."

"And once we're outside, then what?" Jude asked.

"I am hoping to make a portal to transport us away,"

Nathaniel said. "There are many magical restrictions on portals within Lucifer's home, less so on the grounds. But it is imperative that we get outside before he discovers you have escaped. Once he finds out, he will lock down the entire area, and we will be unable to even walk to the edge of his property."

"Are you saying Lucifer could freeze us in place? Keep us from moving around?" Jack asked.

"That is precisely what I am saying," Nathaniel said. "This is his home, and a magical creature can always draw more power from the place where they are rooted."

"It helps that he's one of the strongest immortals in the universe, too," J.B. said.

"Yes, that as well," Nathaniel said.

We were moving along pretty steadily when a contraction hit me so hard I had to stop in the middle of a hallway, gripping my stomach with both hands. I'd been vaguely aware of fluid running down my legs, and now there was a great gush of it. All of the men except Nathaniel turned their heads away in embarrassment. Beezle, who was perched on Samiel's shoulder, had his claws over his eyes.

"It's just blood," I said to them. "You don't seem to have a problem with it when you're hacking apart bad guys."

"I'm the mascot. I don't hack apart bad guys," Beezle said. "I'm delicate. I could be scarred by this."

"Says the gargoyle whose favorite movie is about a shark that eats a bunch of people," I said.

"A shark is one thing. This is *Carrie*," Beezle said.

I wasn't embarrassed about the blood, but it was getting a lot more difficult to walk, never mind run.

Nathaniel picked me up in his arms, cradling me like a child. I started to protest—his shirt, my weight—but he shook his head at me.

"You weigh nothing to me," he said. "And a shirt can be replaced. You cannot."

He began to run then. We both sensed that time was short, and our luck had held out for a surprising amount of time already.

Just as we burst through the door that opened onto a long driveway, I felt an unearthly rumble under our feet. I was almost choked with the anger that I felt coming from Lucifer. Nathaniel felt it, too. His breath drew inward sharply.

"He knows," Nathaniel said.

He handed me to J.B., who looked a little more uncomfortable holding me than Nathaniel had. I heard Nathaniel muttering the words to open a portal.

"You can put me down," I said to J.B., who appeared to be straining manfully. J.B. was part faerie, but his strength wasn't anything close to that of a fallen angel's. In fact, of everyone present, J.B. was the weakest—excepting the 100 percent human Jack, of course.

"Nope, I've got you," J.B. said.

"You're going to give yourself a hernia," I said.

"Never mind a hernia. He's going to have a heart attack," Beezle said.

Samiel, who could probably lift a train off the ground using only his biceps, reached for me, and J.B. passed me over, conceding defeat. Beezle flew off Samiel's shoulder.

"I'd better not add to the strain," Beezle said.

"It sounds like you're trying to insult me," I said. "But really you're just implying that you're a fat gargoyle."

"I'm not fat," Beezle said. "I'm adorably round."

Jude sniffed the air. "They're coming for us. You'd better get that portal open, Nathaniel."

"It is too late," Nathaniel snapped. His face was strained.

"Lucifer is closing down the borders. We can't get out this way."

"No," I said, my heart pounding in panic.

I realized that it had never occurred to me that we might not escape, that we might not slip out of Lucifer's net. The lot of us had faced long odds before. I had faced the longest odds of all in the Maze, and yet I'd always survived. To be so close and yet know that Lucifer would win, that Lucifer would take my child from me after everything I'd done to prevent that very thing . . . It was unacceptable.

"Put me down, Samiel," I said, and he obligingly placed my feet on the ground. I held on to his arm to steady myself and he walked me to Nathaniel's side. I took Nathaniel's hand. "We're going to get out of here."

"How?" he said, and his jewel-bright eyes were bleak. "Lucifer has exerted his will. We cannot make a portal. The net is closing around us."

"I have the power of Lucifer inside me," I said. "And you are Puck's son. And Samiel, too, is a child of Lucifer's line. You said that a creature draws strength from his roots, right? Well, as much as we all hate to admit it, we come from that root—the line of Lucifer and Puck and Alerian and Daharan. If he can draw on that power, then so can we."

His fingers gripped mine harder, like he was grasping on to the rope that kept him from falling into the pit.

"To do this, to overcome Lucifer's strength, you will have to touch the shadow inside you, and so will I. We cannot do this with half measures," Nathaniel said.

"I know," I said, and the darkness opened up its eyes and smiled.

15

WHAT SHOULD WE DO? SAMIEL SIGNED. I'M NOT AS
*powerful as you two. And I don't use my magic as much. I
mostly use my fists.*

There was another surge of emotion that was not mine,
and I felt the sinking sensation that always accompanied
Lucifer's approach.

"Just send as much power as you can through me," I
said.

"No," Nathaniel said. "I will be the conduit. The surge
might harm the baby."

"Fine," I said. "We don't have time to argue."

As if to illustrate the point, several foot soldiers came
streaming out the servants' entrance and entered into a
pitched battle with J.B. and Jude, who immediately transformed into a wolf. Jack staggered back away from the
swinging swords, flying magic and gnashing teeth.

"Stay out of the fray," I ordered Jack as Nathaniel positioned himself in the center of Samiel and myself.

"You don't have to tell me twice," Jack said. Beezle landed on his shoulder. The blogger looked startled to see my gargoyle there.

"I'll keep an eye on him," Beezle said, squeezing Jack's shoulder. His beak wrinkled in disgust. "What have you been doing, running a marathon? You smell like a sweaty gym sock."

"Madeline," Nathaniel said, drawing my attention back to him and Samiel.

I nodded, took a deep breath and opened up my power fully. It crashed out of me and into Nathaniel, the shadow seeking his. Our magic felt like a huge and miraculous thing as it mingled together, strong enough for us to overcome Lucifer's spell, perhaps strong enough to overcome Lucifer himself. It was a dangerous feeling, and I realized the combining of power was going to my head. Nathaniel's expression told me that he felt the same madness, the same pull of darkness.

It was a struggle to focus on what we were trying to do, to look for the seam, the opening in Lucifer's magic that had to be there. There had to be an escape hatch, a way for us to break through and break out. But it was hard to think of it with the shadow rising inside us.

Suddenly there was a burst like sunlight, a pure and undiluted stream of magic, the reflection of Samiel's heart. The light curled around the darkness and into it, lit up all those black places, sent the unnatural things scuttling away. His magic was so clear and beautiful that it brought tears to my eyes, and when I looked at Nathaniel I saw that he was crying, too.

Samiel's power illuminated ours. It didn't smother it or

try to crush the darkness. And as it did, I felt the light inside me, the light that had been blanketed by the shadow for so long. It was the heart of the sun, the heart of an angel, and it burned free and true for the first time since Gabriel had died.

The shadow shrank away under that light, which burst forth from all three of us, shining like a star. Lucifer's servants staggered back, away from the light, covering their eyes.

And a portal opened in front of us. A wind whipped up before it, a sharp breeze that quickly turned into a gale, pulling us toward the opening.

"Where does it go?" I shouted to Nathaniel. "I didn't give it any kind of direction."

He shook his head. "I don't know, but anywhere is better than here."

He tugged me to the portal. I turned back to make sure everyone else was coming along, but they were already there. Nathaniel stepped through, pulling Samiel and me after him. I hoped everyone else would get through all right.

The portal roared with wind and pressure, and the stress of the passage made me scream in pain. Nathaniel kept a tight grip on my hand. The baby pushed inside me, and suddenly I felt like *I* had to push.

Of course, he would want to break out of his little prison just this second. While I was in a portal having my head squashed.

Nathaniel and I emerged from the portal less than gracefully. He pulled me into his arms and opened his wings at the very last second so that we didn't crash to the ground. Samiel did the same, and we all floated down to wait for the others.

First Beezle came through with Jack Dabrowski, who

promptly threw up as soon as he exited the portal. Beezle flew away from him and landed on my shoulder.

"Humans are disgusting," he said.

"You've never seen yourself eating chili," I said.

J.B. came next, followed by Jude.

Nathaniel turned to close the portal once our head count was complete. For the second time I saw him struggling to complete a task that should have been very easy for him.

"What is it?" I asked.

"There's something else in the portal," Nathaniel said, his eyes wide. "I can't close it."

A ghostly hand as large as my head emerged from the portal. It looked like a special effect from a movie, a huge groping appendage.

"It's Lucifer," I said, and that was when my body finally laid down the hammer. I fell to the ground, the contractions so close and painful that I couldn't think about anything else.

"Close that portal!" Beezle shouted. He fluttered to the ground next to me, putting his little clawed hand in mine. I squeezed his fingers so hard as the contractions came that he pulled away from me. "Ow! Jeez, what are you trying to do, break my hand?"

Nathaniel and Samiel were facing the portal, straining together to close it. Jude changed back into a man and came to kneel at my side.

"Put some clothes on," I said weakly.

"You should see yourself right now," Jude said, taking my other hand. "And even though I am naked, I say this in a completely nonsexual, nonthreatening way—you have to take your pants off."

"Yeah, the kid is going to come out at that end," Beezle

said. "You don't want him to strangle on your Eeyore pajamas."

"My pajamas are ruined," I said, glancing down at myself. I was covered in blood and birthing fluid and dirt from rolling on the ground.

Another contraction came, and I rolled to my back. J.B. had joined Nathaniel and Samiel to help try to push Lucifer's magic into the portal. I felt something huge approaching, and realized that Lucifer himself was following the grasping, ghostly hand.

"He's coming!" I shouted. "You have to close it and seal it, now!"

I pushed some energy out and into Nathaniel, and it was just enough to help snap the portal shut. Nathaniel and J.B. hurriedly poured their power into an incantation to seal the portal so Lucifer couldn't reopen it from inside. He would have to go out again, make a new portal to our location, and then try to come through. Assuming he was able to figure out where we were. I didn't even know where we were. It looked like a forest clearing. We might not even be on Earth. I could hardly think anymore. My stomach felt like it was going to split open and I had to push. Only pushing would make the pain stop.

As soon as the portal was closed, Nathaniel was with me, talking, murmuring encouragement, helping me take off the unnecessary garments and get into the proper position for the birth. He kneeled before me, ready to catch the baby when he emerged.

J.B. moved behind me and put my head in his lap. My hair was wet with sweat and I could hardly breathe. Samiel sat opposite Jude, holding my hand, totally unaffected by my death grip on his fingers. He looked worried, and I tried not to let it worry me. He was a guy and the whole birth thing probably seemed strange and frightening to him.

It was strange and frightening to me, too, but I would never admit it. I was a woman and I wasn't supposed to be afraid of this.

I suddenly realized I didn't know where Jack was. I looked around and saw him holding a smartphone up, filming the whole thing.

"You had a phone this whole time?" I shrieked.

He looked at me over the top of the screen. "Of course. Lucifer trashed my camera but I've always got some kind of backup. I filmed that whole battle on the lawn at his house. It's going to be awesome when it goes live on the net."

"Do you not remember that I wanted a phone when we were trying to get out of the basement?" I said.

"Oh, yeah," Jack said. "I don't know. I was kind of out of it and you didn't seem to be making a lot of sense. You were talking about pajama pants, not phones."

"And if video of this birth ends up online—" I began, but I didn't even need to finish. Nathaniel looked at the phone and it caught fire in Jack's hands. He dropped it to the ground with a howl.

"Dammit! How much of my equipment are you people going to destroy?"

"All of it until you stop taking pictures of Madeline," Nathaniel said. "Sooner or later the lesson will sink in."

Beezle landed on Nathaniel's shoulder, glanced where Nathaniel was looking, then immediately clapped his hands over his eyes.

"Well, the good news is that it looks like a human head and not a freaky spider-thing," Beezle said, his eyes still covered. "The bad news is that it looks like it's stuck."

"It is not stuck," Nathaniel said calmly. "Madeline, you just need to push. Once the shoulders are through, the rest of the baby will come easily."

"Who died and made you the obstetrician?" Beezle said. "Have you done this before? It looks like she's losing a lot of blood."

"It is perfectly normal," Nathaniel said.

"How do you know?" Beezle said.

"Beezle, you're not helping," I panted.

"Don't worry about him," J.B. said, stroking his fingers through my wet hair. "He's acting like a nervous grandpa."

"Who are you calling a grandpa?" Beezle said.

"Yes, who are you calling a grandpa? That is my right alone," a silky voice said.

I looked toward the voice, and there stood Lucifer, flanked by Alerian and Puck. They were just on the edge of the clearing.

"Did you think you would be able to stop me with this feeble attempt at escape?" he said.

I'd never seen him so angry, but it was that terrifying kind of still anger, the kind that doesn't seem obvious until the person suddenly snaps and lunges at you with a knife.

"Go away," I said weakly. "You can't have him. He's mine."

"No," Lucifer said. "He is mine. As are you. Mine to manipulate, mine to control, mine to keep forever."

He started toward our little cluster of people, then stopped abruptly, fury rising on his face. J.B.'s head was just above mine, and I saw him smile with satisfaction.

"I put a circle around us," he said. "This is my kingdom, and it should have a little more oomph than your regular ordinary spell circle."

"Ah, I thought the trees looked familiar. This is the woods around Amarantha's castle," I said. "Apparently my brain directed us somewhere safe."

"How would you know what the trees looked like?" Beezle said, his eyes still covered. "You burned down half the forest."

"How many times do I need to say it was an accident?" I said.

Lucifer pounded his fist on the invisible wall of the circle. "You cannot stay in there forever. You belong to me, and so does your child. And when you emerge I will claim what is mine."

"I belong to no one but myself," I said. "And my baby is mine, mine and Gabriel's."

I had a moment to wonder why on earth Puck and Alerian were with Lucifer; then I suddenly felt it. It was happening. It was happening right now.

"He's coming!" I shouted to Nathaniel, and I gave a tremendous push, pouring all of my remaining energy into giving birth to my son.

It seemed like the world narrowed to this one action, just me and Nathaniel and the baby between us, and then the pressure abruptly ceased, and he was free.

Nathaniel wiped the baby's face with a handkerchief he pulled from his pocket, and my son gave a loud, angry cry.

"Let me see him," I said, trying to sit up. "I want to see him."

Beezle peeked out from between his fingers. "He looks like an alien."

Nathaniel held the baby up so I could see him—a perfectly normal-looking human baby, his skin mottled purple and red from the birth. As I watched, tiny little white wings unfolded from his back.

I burst into tears and reached for him.

"I need to cut the umbilical cord," Nathaniel said, and used his magic to do so.

A moment later my son was in my arms, his angry little face being cleaned with my tears. My wings unfolded from my back and closed around us, keeping us safe inside. My son and me. My son.

"He's mad that it's so cold out here," Jude said.

Nathaniel quickly unbuttoned his shirt and handed it to me to wrap the baby in.

"Shh," I said. "Shh, it's all right."

He quieted immediately, blinking up at me with eyes the color of the sky in deepest space. His hair was as black as mine and he had a full head of it, wild and thick.

"He can't really see you," J.B. said. "But he knows your voice."

I stared at the baby in wonder, at the tiny perfection of his little eyelashes and lips, at his so-small fingers and toes.

"He's perfect," I said.

Beezle fluttered over to my shoulder, peering down at the baby. "I still say he looks like an alien. He looks just like you did when you were born."

"Then he will be beautiful," J.B. said, and kissed the top of my head.

The ever-practical Nathaniel had been cleaning me up and fashioning a kind of skirt out of his coat for me to wear while we were all cooing over the baby. J.B. helped me to my feet, and Nathaniel wrapped the cloth around my waist. I wobbled a little as I stood.

Nathaniel and J.B. flanked me, both of them helping me stay on my feet, and Jude and Samiel joined the line. Beezle had clung to my shoulder throughout. Now we all faced the furious Lucifer and his brothers.

Puck winked at me. Normally this would make me want to blast him in the face with nightfire, but I was feeling so at peace at the moment that I couldn't work up the energy to be mad. The birth of my child and the revelation that I didn't need to use the shadow to exercise my power had gone a long way toward improving my feelings about the world.

Of course, we were basically trapped inside a circle inside J.B.'s forest, and Lucifer waited outside for us to get tired or go crazy. Obviously this situation was not sustainable.

"What are you going to call him?" Beezle said.

"I have no idea," I said. "I guess I thought I would have more time to think about it."

I didn't say that I'd always secretly been worried that he would be a monster, like so many of Lucifer's children, and that it had seemed like bad luck to think of names for something that might have to be destroyed or locked up. It seemed like a miracle that given this child's bloodlines he was completely normal—or as normal as a kid with wings could be.

Lucifer seemed to grow in size as we watched. I remember he had done this once before, to try to stare me down when I'd been insubordinate. Puck seemed vaguely amused by Lucifer's display. Alerian appeared bored.

I felt the waves of frustration and anger coming from Lucifer, and then it seemed like there was more pressure in the air than there had been before.

"He's trying to break the circle," I said, holding my baby a little closer. After the initial bout of crying, he had settled down, and now seemed to be looking around in curiosity with his unfocused eyes.

"The circle should hold," J.B. said. "He's not in his

kingdom. He's in mine. This is my ground, and my power comes from here."

"But we can't stay here forever," Jude said.

"No, you cannot stay there forever," Lucifer repeated, and he pressed his will against the circle again.

J.B. seemed awfully confident that the protection would hold, but I wasn't sure. Lucifer was a lot stronger than J.B., even if this was J.B.'s home ground. And Lucifer was very determined.

"Nathaniel," I said, but he had anticipated me.

The portal opened in front of us, and through it I could see the panting, happy faces of Lock and Barrel.

"See ya," I said to Lucifer with a salute, and stepped into the portal with my baby snuggled close to me and Beezle on my shoulder.

My grandfather's roar of rage followed me into the portal.

My son began to cry as soon as we entered. I couldn't blame him. It felt horrible to pass through a portal when you were an adult. I couldn't imagine what it felt like for a little baby, so recently snug and warm inside his mom and now exposed to a world that was loud and cold and *hurt*.

A moment later I was in my own living room, with the dogs clustering around me. I sat down on the floor, exhausted, relieved to be home and safe. Lucifer could not get me here. The power of the domicile was absolute over a creature like him.

Lock and Barrel stuck their wet noses into the bundle in my arms, sniffing the baby. He stopped crying as soon as the dogs approached, and I heard him make a little coo.

The horror of everything I'd been through—how close I'd come to losing my son forever—hit me then. When Nathaniel emerged from the portal, he found me weeping on the floor, holding my baby tight to me. Beezle sat on my shoulder, patting the side of my head. He flew away with a sigh of relief when Nathaniel arrived.

"Maybe you can get her to calm down," he said.

He knelt down beside me, put his lips in my hair and his arms around me. "You are safe. You are safe. Lucifer can't get him here."

The others climbed out of the portal. They all dispersed to perform various tasks—Jude to dress, Samiel to cook, J.B. to walk to the front window and glance worriedly out. Jack stood with hands in his pockets, looking awkward.

J.B. went still as he lifted the curtain aside. "There's a giant squid in the middle of the street."

I laughed. It was a wet, surprised laugh, coming so close on the heels of my tears. "Beezle told you there was a squid."

"And fire," J.B. said, wrinkling his nose. "I can't believe anyone on this block wants to keep living here. I wouldn't be able to eat if I knew that thing was outside my front door."

"Imagine how I feel," Beezle said. "Calamari is one of my favorite foods, and I may never be able to stomach it again."

"I'm not worried," J.B. said. "I'm sure you'll find something else to stuff yourself with."

"Let's get you into the shower," Nathaniel said.

He helped me up and into the bathroom, throwing away the jacket that was wrapped around my waist. He held out his arms for the baby so I could take off my shirt.

I shrank back, holding my son to my chest. I didn't want to let him go, not even for a second.

"I won't let anything happen to him," Nathaniel said gently. "I will care for him as if he were my own."

"What if Lucifer comes?" I whispered. "He'll figure out where I am soon enough."

"Yes," Nathaniel said. That was one of the things I liked about Nathaniel. He didn't try to sugarcoat. "But he is not here now. I am. And you need to clean yourself. While you do this, I will wash the baby."

"He needs special stuff," I said helplessly. "Like baby shampoo and whatever. I don't have any of that."

"Madeline," he said, and his voice was full of infinite patience. "I know how to do magic."

"Right," I said. I still didn't want to let my baby go. He was mine.

"Madeline," he said again, and he held his hands out. "I was the first person to hold him. Trust me."

I did trust him. Because you couldn't love without trust. And finally, after everything we had been through together, after he had protected me from harm over and over, I did trust him. I loved him.

But again, the circumstances didn't seem right to tell him. I handed Nathaniel my son, and knew he would take care of him.

I took off my pajama shirt, shoved it in the trash bin (I seemed to be throwing away a lot of clothing lately) and climbed in the shower. I turned the water up as hot as I could make it and scrubbed all over until I felt really clean. My legs looked even worse than I'd thought. Birth is a messy thing.

My belly felt strangely empty. I poked the formerly taut bump and everything there kind of jiggled around.

"Oh, that's sexy," I said.

I turned off the water and climbed out of the shower, wrapping up in a bathrobe and putting a towel around my head. Nathaniel was nowhere to be seen.

When I entered the hallway I could hear a lot of ruckus coming from the kitchen. I padded toward the noise in my bare feet.

Nathaniel was washing the baby in the kitchen sink. Beezle was sitting on his shoulder, giving him instructions, which Nathaniel ignored. Jude and Samiel were making goofy faces at my son, and J.B. was watching all of it with an indulgent smile on his face.

"Nothing like a baby to turn perfectly rational adults into a bunch of goofballs," J.B. said. "He is pretty cute, though. He looks just like you."

I looked critically at my offspring, a tiny being cradled so gently in Nathaniel's huge hands. "I can't tell. He just looks little and wrinkly to me right now."

"Gargoyle, make yourself useful and hand me that towel," Nathaniel said, indicating a small baby towel with a blue elephant on it that was on the counter beside J.B.

"Where did we get that?" I asked. I knew for sure that I had not bought any baby stuff.

"I got it," Beezle said. "Or rather, Samiel and I did."

"When did you have time to go baby shopping with all the crises going on around here?"

Beezle shrugged as he handed the towel to Nathaniel. "We did it a while ago."

Samiel nodded. *We didn't think you would have time, so we got towels and diapers and pajamas and all that stuff.*

"Don't cry again," Beezle said. "I just didn't want the kid to spend the first week of his life wrapped in a dish-cloth, which is what would have happened if we had left you in charge."

I wiped at my eyes, which had grown suspiciously watery. "You're probably right. Although I don't even know how to put the diaper on him, so I'm not sure they'll do me much good."

Nathaniel very gently laid the baby on the counter. He covered him all over with baby lotion, expertly wrapped him up in a diaper, put him in a cute little footie sleeper that had lions printed on it, and topped off his head with a matching hat. His little baby wings tucked neatly inside the sleeper. No one would ever know they were there. Then Nathaniel presented my child to me, all perfect and clean and sweet-smelling, and said, "You should feed him."

"With what?" I asked blankly as I snuggled my little bundle to my shoulder.

"With those," Beezle said, pointing at my chest.

"Oh," I said. I had no idea how that would work. It didn't feel like there was any milk in there.

"You'll figure it out," J.B. said, correctly interpreting my expression.

"Oookay," I said, and went into the bedroom to try to figure it out. Luckily the kid knew what to do, and after a bit he pulled away, so I figured he had gotten what he needed out of me.

I carefully placed him in the very center of the bed with no blankets around him—I had read enough of the pregnancy book to know that babies shouldn't be surrounded with blankets because they could suffocate—and got dressed in some comfy sweats and thick socks. Then I lay down on the bed beside him, listening to him breathe. His eyes were closed and he was making little suckling motions with his lips.

I kissed his soft little cheek, and wished that Gabriel were here to see him. Gabriel would have been the world's most amazing dad.

Of course, I reflected, Nathaniel seemed like he would be

a pretty good stepfather. He already knew how to do the diaper-fu, which was more than I could say. I wondered how long I could pass off diaper duty by claiming incompetence.

I put my head down on the mattress, just watching my son's chest rise and fall with his quiet little breaths. I must have fallen asleep, because the next thing I knew the baby was screaming, the house was shaking, and there was noise like thunder. Lightning flashed outside the bedroom window.

Either there was an earthquake in Chicago, or the apocalypse had arrived.

Nathaniel appeared in the doorway. "Lucifer is outside. As you may guess, he is not very happy."

16

I SCOOPED MY SON UP AND FOLLOWED NATHANIEL into the living room. All the men had washed and changed into clean clothes, and there were the remains of several take-out pizzas on the table. Beezle was perched on the mantel, reading the pregnancy book I'd never finished. The dogs were on the floor, sleeping.

My stomach rumbled at the sight of the pizza. "Did you save any for me?"

"Pizza isn't good for the baby," Beezle announced.

"The baby isn't going to be eating the pizza," I said.

"Oh, yes, he is," Beezle said. "Whatever you eat, he eats. And I don't think pepperoni is good flavoring for milk."

"You, of all people, will not be monitoring my food intake for nutritive value," I said. "Your body probably hasn't seen anything resembling a vitamin in decades."

Samiel, Jude, J.B. and Jack stood in the front picture

window, looking out. I handed the baby to Nathaniel so I could go see what they were all gawping at.

The floor trembled, and I stumbled into Samiel, who caught me and set me upright.

He's trying really hard to take down the house, Samiel signed, pointing outside.

My grandfather stood in the center of the street, again flanked by Alerian and Puck. They seemed to be combining their powers to break the protective spells Nathaniel and I had put around the house.

The squid had disappeared. I doubted the city had found a way to transport it in the short time we'd been home, so it was very likely one of the brothers had zapped it into oblivion.

Lucifer looked up at the window, as if he sensed my presence there. I gasped and stepped back. He wasn't the handsome angel anymore, more beautiful than the sun. His face was twisted and dark, and his eyes burned red. Obsidian horns had sprouted from his head, and his beautiful feathered wings were the leathery appendages of a bat. This was the devil that so many had feared. This was the true Prince of Darkness, and he would not be thwarted by me.

"They can't break the protection of the domicile," I said. "Can they?"

"I don't think so," Beezle said. "I've been thinking about this for a while. The shifter was able to because, I think, he was not a fully formed creature. But Lucifer and Puck and Alerian—their personalities and their powers have been well established for eons. The magic that protects a home would recognize them and keep them out. However, they can try to break the spells you two put around the house."

"And if they do, what then?" I said, stepping away from the window.

"Only the power of the home will stand between you and them," Beezle said. "And I imagine they can find a way to make us pretty miserable with just one thin layer of protection between us and Lucifer's rage."

"You seem very calm about all this," I said.

He looked up from the pregnancy book. "Either I'm in a food coma or I just know you. Sooner or later you'll come up with a solution. It will probably involve fire and destruction, but you'll find a way to chase him off like you have everything else that's ever come after you."

I took the baby back from Nathaniel, shaking my head. "Everything else was nothing compared to Lucifer. I've never managed to beat Lucifer or his brothers at any game."

"This isn't a game," Beezle reminded me.

"They've treated it as such," I said. "They've twisted and manipulated and put me in untenable positions over and over again. And why are they teaming up all of a sudden? I thought they hated each other."

Beezle shrugged. "Maybe they don't. Not really. Not when it comes down to it. They are brothers."

"Brothers who've gone to war time and again," I said. "And *where* is Daharan in all this?"

Nathaniel and Beezle exchanged a familiar look. I raised my hand to stop them from saying anything.

"I'm sorry I mentioned his name. Don't start," I said.

The baby hadn't stopped crying since the house started shaking. I rubbed his back, shushing him, and after a few moments he calmed down.

"Have you named him yet?" Nathaniel asked, putting his arm protectively around my shoulder.

I shook my head. "Nothing seems to sound right to me."

"You could name him for his father," Nathaniel said. He was obviously trying to distract me from the nightmare outside.

"He's not a junior," I said, going along with it. "He's his own little self."

"How about Nicholas?" Beezle said.

I wrinkled my nose. "Nope."

"Scott? Michael? Jonquil?"

"Hey," J.B. said.

"I wouldn't do that to my kid. Sorry, J.B.," I said.

"Don't be. There's a reason why I go by my initials," he said.

"Yeah, and your initials don't even stand for Jonquil whatever," Beezle said. "Because before we knew your real name and Maddy was annoyed with you, she called you 'Jacob Benjamin.'"

"If your name was Jonquil, you'd have another name, too," J.B. said. "Besides, it's not like Jacob Benjamin is a random choice. It was my father's name for me. And it is my legal human name."

The house continued to be battered by the storm outside, the physical manifestation of Lucifer's anger.

"You know, I don't really get it," I said, and I was surprised at the calm in my voice. Lucifer was trying to shake my house to the ground in order to kidnap my child and I wasn't feeling nearly as panicked about this as I thought I would. "Why is he so bound and determined to have my baby? It sort of made sense when I was his last link to Evangeline. But now he's got the kid he and Evangeline conceived in the land of the dead."

"But that kid is a weird freaky monster," Beezle said. "He can hardly present a child like that as his right hand

and heir in front of the court of the Grigori. Angels are very vain creatures."

"So what you're saying is that even though Lucifer has paid a lot of lip service to loving all of his children the same, he really loves the photogenic ones more?" I asked.

Nathaniel shook his head. "I do not think it has anything to do with Lucifer's vanity—at least, not in the way that the gargoyle proposes. His pride has been hurt by your refusal to give in, to allow yourself to be manipulated. You escaped from his home in front of his court and his guests. He cannot allow that slight to pass."

"And he also wants my child," I said.

"And he also wants your child," Nathaniel acknowledged. "As for why he wants this particular child so badly— well, we have all known that Lucifer can see the future."

My fingers tightened on the baby, just for a moment. "You think he's got some kind of special fate? Don't say that. Don't tell me that just by being born he's been condemned to carry out some sacred mission. I grew up knowing that, hearing that it was so important to be an Agent, that without me the souls of the dead would wander the planet without a purpose. And I hated it. I hated knowing I would never be free, that I would always be shackled to that one destiny."

"You broke free of your destiny," J.B. reminded me. "And made Sokolov and the Agency very angry in the process."

"Yes, but how could I have known that would happen? Nobody had ever escaped the Agency before."

"Nobody ever escaped the Maze before, either," J.B. said. "You're special, Maddy. And it stands to reason that your child will be, too. Lucifer has claimed that he can't see the future perfectly, but he saw it well enough to know that if you and Gabriel married, there would be a child. Your baby will do *something* in the future, for good or ill, that Lucifer wants to control. If you stack that on top of his fanatical need to keep his family close and his wounded pride at your actions, you get this."

He gestured out the window. I didn't need to approach the glass this time to see what was going on. Lucifer's soul, his essence, whatever you wanted to call it, was rising out of his physical body and becoming a huge demonic manifestation in front of the house. First the tips of his horns passed the window, then his burning red eyes, then his twisted mouth and bared teeth.

I sincerely hoped that my neighbors had run away or were buttoned up tight in their basements. Collateral damage seemed like a very strong possibility at this point.

Suddenly a tremendous sound came from the roof. I looked at Nathaniel in alarm.

"He's trying to break through the roof," I said.

"If there's a hole in the house, he might be able to construe that as an invitation and get around the protection of the domicile," Beezle said, putting up his little hands in a defensive gesture when I glared at him. "I'm not sure. I'm just saying."

"I'm not dealing with a hole in the roof on top of everything else," I said, handing the baby to Nathaniel. The snake tattoo on my palm suddenly burned bright, like a glowing coal, and I cried out. "That's it. I'm going outside to talk to him."

"I do not think that is a wise idea," Nathaniel said, handing the baby to Samiel. "But if you insist—as I imagine you will—I am going with you."

"In the state Lucifer is in, he might kill you just because you're in front of him," I said. "No, you stay inside."

"Madeline," Nathaniel said. "Why will you not understand? You do not have to do everything alone. We are stronger together. And I would not be the man who loves you if I allowed you to face such danger while I hid inside."

I did understand. I did. But the feelings I had for Nathaniel were new and complicated and still kind of hard to look at, and I didn't want to lose him just as I was starting to figure things out. The image of Gabriel, run through with my father's sword, falling in the snow with blood pooling around him—that image would never leave me. I didn't want to see Nathaniel vaporized by Lucifer, and told him so.

"I do not think Lucifer will be able to do such a thing," Nathaniel said. "My father is out there. He may have no love for me. He may have been willing to sacrifice me for his own ends. But I do not believe he will allow Lucifer to kill me in a fit of rage. Puck, I think, still hopes I will come around to his way of thinking. It would be more beneficial to him to keep me alive."

"That won't help if Lucifer blasts you before Puck realizes what's going on," I said.

"Puck can catch the starlight in his teeth," Nathaniel said. "He is a creature who has not even remotely shown the depth of his power. If Lucifer tried to blast me, as you say, then Puck would be able to stop him if he so desired."

"There's a lot of 'ifs' in there," I said.

"Madeline, it is this simple. If you go, I go. You will not be able to stop me, and if necessary, the others will aid me in holding you here." He looked at Jack, Jude, J.B. and Samiel, who all nodded in agreement.

"I knew that sooner or later all you men would gang up

on me," I said. "I should have thought about this earlier and got some nice, supportive girlfriends."

"And what would you have talked about with these mythical women?" Beezle asked. "Your macramé hobby?"

"Fine," I said to Nathaniel. "Let's go."

J.B. and Jude immediately fell in behind him.

"I'm not missing this," J.B. said firmly. "And Lucifer can't kill me without dealing with repercussions from all of Faerie. Puck is the High King of Faerie, so I think that any safety that applies to Nathaniel from that quarter would also apply to me."

"I'm not letting you go outside to face him on your own," Jude growled. "I watched one person I love fall at his hands. I won't let it happen again."

I looked at the three of them, and thought of everything we had all been through. We had started this journey together, and it was only right that we should finish it that way.

Because I was going to finish it. If I stepped outside that door, I wanted it to be the end of my association with Lucifer forever. I was no longer willing to deal with a temporary accord or a brief call of truce. I did not want to be Lucifer's plaything for the rest of my life. Nor did I want my son to face the constant threat of his loving great-grandfather's attention.

I turned to Samiel, who had the baby nestled in one arm. My son had fallen asleep, his tiny chest rising and falling with his soft breath. Beezle had dropped the pregnancy book and flown over to sit on Samiel's shoulder. They both stared down at his little face in fascination. The Retrievers had woken up and had their heads on Samiel's knees. Both of them also stared at the baby, occasionally snuffling at his head.

"You keep him safe," I said to Beezle.

"Like I would let anything happen to him," Beezle said, waving me away. "Now, go. Be a heroine and all that."

Jack held his hands up. "I don't need to be a close-up witness to this. I'll stay here and take notes through the window."

"Gee, thanks," I said. He probably would take notes through the window. And then he would publish them as breaking news on his blog, along with his personal account of his time in Lucifer's prison. I still thought he was cruising for a run-in with something big and bad and intolerant of having its news released on the Internet, but Jack seemed to have rebounded from his ordeals pretty quickly.

I started down the stairs, still in my comfy sweats. I didn't exactly look powerful and intimidating. I didn't have makeup on or a perfectly coiffed hairstyle. I didn't even have the sword that I had kept so close to me for so long. It seemed like the sword, which was tied to Lucifer, would probably choose the master who forged it over the person who had carried it for a few months.

No, I didn't look like much. And maybe to the average person neither did the ragged band behind me. But all of us had defied expectation in one way or another, over and over again. That had to count for something.

"What are you planning on doing when you get outside?" Nathaniel asked.

"I didn't have so much of a plan as a general idea," I said.

"Which means she hasn't got a clue and she's just going to roll with whatever happens," J.B. said from behind Nathaniel. "You should know better by now."

"Yes, I should," said Nathaniel.

"You don't have to sound so agreeable when you insult me," I said, but I wasn't really annoyed.

As we got closer to the end of the stairs my fear was rising. I wasn't really sure what I would do at all. I had said "talk" to Lucifer, but he obviously wasn't in a talking mood. The roof-pounding continued, and plaster was falling down from the ceiling.

Part of my mind was still upstairs with the baby, even though I knew Beezle and Samiel would defend him with their lives. It was hard to overcome that immediate instinct to be the one to protect him, to believe that only I could properly keep him safe.

But it had to end. Ever since I'd discovered I was Azazel's daughter, my life had become a gradually escalating series of horrible events, each one worse than the last. I paused at the bottom of the stairs. Once I went outside, I'd be committed.

I might also be dead, and my child would grow up an orphan, a toy in Lucifer's court.

"No," I said out loud.

Nathaniel gave me a puzzled look.

"I won't let Lucifer take my baby away, whether he kills me or not," I said.

That thought gave me courage, and I pushed open the door. We crowded into the foyer, peering through the glass to the nightmare outside.

Lucifer's body still stood between his two stalwart brothers, but there was a black shadow that rose from his open mouth and up over the house. This was the part of him that was currently pounding out his fury on my roof.

The other two didn't appear to be doing much of anything except presenting a united front with Lucifer. I had to wonder again why either of them was working with a brother they claimed to despise, and why Daharan wasn't there—on my side or Lucifer's.

I took a deep breath, and suddenly I was hyperventilating. I was about to do something beyond frightening, something so terrifying that I could lose my life, my child, my love and my friends all in one fell swoop.

Nathaniel put his hand on my back and drew me close. He didn't say anything, only breathed slow and even, waiting for my breath to fall in rhythm with his. And eventually, it did. The connection between us opened wider, and our power mingled, giving both of us strength.

"You see?" he murmured against my hair. "We are stronger together. We can face him. We can defeat him."

I nodded, and I pushed open the door.

It was frigid outside, colder than winter, and I shivered all over as soon as the howling wind touched me. Rain lashed at my house. Thunder rumbled, a constant growl of menace above. Lightning struck the lawn several times as I watched.

Puck noticed us cautiously moving out onto the porch. He lazily tugged at Lucifer's arm, his eyes bright with speculation. I'm sure he wondered just what the hell I thought I would do. I was thinking the same thing.

"Lucifer!" I called. My voice seemed to disappear into the roar of the wind, but he must have heard me.

The shadow shrank down and reentered Lucifer almost immediately. The wind and rain disappeared, though his demonic visage did not.

"Madeline," Lucifer said, and his voice was a terrible thing that vibrated over my nerves and through my bloodstream. I truly understood for the first time that he was a monster. His heart, though born of the sun, was black as a moonless night. Whatever humanity Evangeline saw and loved in him was an illusion.

"Lucifer," I said again. "Now that the formalities are

out of the way, you can move along and stop trying to wreck my house. My property value has dropped to nothing since I met you as it is."

Puck sniggered with laughter, covering his mouth with his hand. Lucifer glared at him, and Puck immediately went back to serious soldier mode, although his eyes still danced, as always.

"Madeline," Lucifer said, rolling my name around in his mouth like a fine delicacy. "You still have yet to understand. All that you are, all the power within you, comes from me. You cannot defy me."

He lifted his hand toward me and I felt something twist inside me, like he'd somehow grabbed my heart and my lungs and was crushing them in his grip. I staggered and fell against Nathaniel. The pain was searing, ten thousand times worse than the childbirth I had so recently endured.

Nathaniel shot at Lucifer with a bolt of nightfire and Lucifer batted it away casually, like a man waving at a fly. He held out his other hand toward Nathaniel, to hurt him, too, but Puck stayed him.

"He is not yours," was all he said.

"The boy attacked me," Lucifer said.

"He is not yours to discipline," Puck said, and Lucifer nodded.

It was interesting that Nathaniel had been right about that. Puck wouldn't allow Lucifer to hurt his son. He might be willing to do it himself, but Lucifer had to keep his hands off. Interesting, but I wasn't really in a state to contemplate it. It felt like everything inside me was being twisted into a giant knot. I gasped for air.

"What are you doing to her?" J.B. demanded.

"Taking back what is mine," Lucifer said.

My throat felt like it was full, like something inside me

was backing up and trying to come out. Every cell in my body seemed to strain toward Lucifer. All my limbs tingled, that horrible pins-and-needles feeling amplified.

Nathaniel gently rested me on the ground, then stood, stepping in front of me so that all I could see were his boots. I could feel his fury, the shadow inside him rising up. He seemed to grow larger, as Lucifer had done. The air was suffused with his power, so thick with magic you could choke on it.

"Let her go," he said to Lucifer.

Lucifer's attention was not distracted from me for a moment. The pressure inside my body never wavered. It was almost as if poison were being drawn from my blood, but it wasn't poison that was leaving.

It was my magic.

My magic was born of the sun, born of Lucifer himself, and as both his many-greats-granddaughter and his Hound of the Hunt, my power was inextricably bound to this source. And now the source was taking that power back into himself, to show me that he could, that I was not so special after all.

"Let her go," Nathaniel repeated.

I didn't know what he was going to do, but I could tell that his anger would make it something foolish. J.B. knelt at my side, holding my hand.

"What can I do?" he asked.

"Stop Nathaniel," I choked out. "Don't let Lucifer kill him."

"I won't kill him," Lucifer said. "That is my brother's responsibility. Puck, control your boy."

I couldn't see Lucifer's face at all, only J.B.'s worried green eyes. But my grandfather did not sound like he was troubled in the least by Nathaniel's anger, or like he was exerted at all from the effort of drawing my magic out of me. In fact, he sounded bored.

There was a sudden sound of fire sizzling in the grass, and then the streaks of light that accompany flying magic. I tried to sit up to see what was going on.

"Puck and Nathaniel are having it out," J.B. said.

A shadow crossed over us as the two of them rose into the air. I could just see Nathaniel's twisted face and Puck's amused one as they traded magical blows. Then one of Nathaniel's spells hit Puck square in the chest, and the elemental spirit suddenly did not look so amused.

I wanted to speak, to cry out, but the magic that had lived so long in my body was filling my mouth, spilling out into the air like a thin stream of smoke.

Lucifer opened his own mouth and drew that stream inside. I could feel the power leaving me, making him stronger. Jude growled and stepped in front of me. I saw that he had turned into a wolf, and was crouched, ready to strike.

I couldn't stop him, couldn't save him. He leapt for Lucifer's throat.

Alerian shifted in front of Lucifer, blocked Jude's attack. The wolf landed on the ground. There was a long streak of blood along his flank where Alerian had struck with a shiny silver knife he'd produced seemingly out of nowhere.

Jude lunged for Alerian now, tearing into my great-uncle's leg with his teeth. The flesh there tore away from the bone but Alerian did not cry out or make a noise in any way. Instead, he methodically swung the knife at Jude, cutting here, cutting there. Blood splashed over the street.

J.B. squeezed my hand tight as the last of Lucifer's magic exited my body. The stream of power sputtered to a halt, and I coughed, rolling to one side, away from Lucifer.

My throat felt dry and swollen, like I'd been breathing smoky air. But the rest of me felt light, like an unimaginable burden had finally been lifted from me. And it had.

Lucifer chuckled, and it was not a pleasant sound. "Now do you see, Madeline? All that made you special and unique came from me. You cannot defend your child from the weakest goblin now. You will never be able to keep him from me."

I pushed to my feet. J.B. helped me up, the two of us face-to-face for a moment. The battle between Puck and Nathaniel still raged above us. Alerian and Jude tore into each other behind me. But I took one moment, and looked into J.B.'s eyes, and smiled.

"I'm glad that you're my friend," I said, and kissed his cheek.

He gave me a look, his eyes full of understanding. "I guess this means my chance has come and gone, huh?"

"I still love you. But not that way," I said.

He sighed. "I'm sure I'll be able to convince some fairy courtier to have rebound sex with me."

I laughed, and turned to face Lucifer, who looked surprised that I wasn't weeping on the ground.

"Thank you," I said, and I really meant it. I glanced at the palm of my hand. The tattoo that had been imprinted there by Lucifer's sword was gone.

Now the Prince of Darkness looked bewildered, and the expression was so comical on that Milton's devil-face that I laughed out loud again. I felt giddy, and a little reckless.

"Thank you, really," I said. "Thank you for finally, finally, *finally* releasing me from you. Thank you for taking the burden of your bloodline away from me. Thank you for basically disowning me. This is one of the happiest moments of my life."

Lucifer's eyes had narrowed as I spoke, and I could see the realization dawning that his master plan had somehow backfired.

"Oh," I said, and held out my hands before me. "Your magic wasn't the only magic inside me, by the way. I am Azazel's daughter, you know."

And I let my nightfire fly.

17

HE WASN'T EXPECTING IT; OTHERWISE HE WOULD HAVE easily been able to block my shot. But the nightfire blast hit him full force in the chest, and it took him off his feet. Alerian and Puck both paused in their battles, obviously shocked to see Lucifer on the ground.

Which allowed Nathaniel and Jude to take advantage. A moment later, Alerian was flat on his back with a growling wolf standing on top of him. Puck was on the ground sitting on his butt with a confused look on his face. Nathaniel floated down to land beside me. He watched his fallen father with steel in his eyes.

"I'm not bound to you anymore," I said to Lucifer. The shock of my blast had shaken away the magic he'd used to maintain his demon face, and he'd returned to looking angelic as usual. "You cannot force me to do your bidding. You cannot draw on the blood tie or on the power of the Hound of the Hunt. I don't have to perform any more of your crappy errands or be any kind of ambassador anywhere. I am free."

"I still have dominion over you and every other mewling human on this Earth," Lucifer snarled.

"No, you do not."

It was the very thing I was going to say, but somebody else took the words out of my mouth.

The voice had come from behind me, and as I turned and looked I saw Daharan was there, and it seemed like his entire body was lit by dragon fire. His voice was measured and controlled as always, but his expression was so suffused with anger that I had to turn my face away. Daharan was frightening like that. It made me remember that he was a dragon at heart, and one should not take a dragon lightly.

Lucifer and Puck visibly shrank back—not a lot, but enough that you would notice if you were watching them closely. I had never seen either of them cower before anyone.

Jude was still growling away on Alerian's chest. If his victim had not been a billions-of-years-old immortal, then Jude probably would have slashed his throat open by now. But Jude knew as well as I did the physical consequences of killing something so old. When I'd taken out Titania, I'd actually sent her to another galaxy far away, so that when the magical energy that had built up inside her for thousands of years exploded outward, it wouldn't flatten the entire city of Chicago and its neighboring suburbs. Alerian was significantly older and more powerful than Titania, so his death would probably take out the center of the continent and then cause the rest of it to fall into the sea.

Daharan stalked toward his three brothers. When he reached Jude he tapped the wolf on the shoulder. Jude twisted around and looked up. When he saw Daharan he stepped off Alerian, who stood up with careful deliberation and then joined the other two, who were watching Daharan warily.

The eldest brother faced off against the other three, and even though there was a disparity in numbers, it was clear who had the advantage.

I didn't want to break the spell of his dominion over the other three, but I had to know.

"Daharan," I said, and I was surprised by how small my voice sounded. "Where have you been?"

"I am sorry, Madeline," he said, but he never looked at me. He kept his eyes locked on Lucifer, Alerian and Puck, like he was a snake charmer keeping three reptiles at bay. "None of this would have happened were I present. However, these three ensured that I would not be."

My eyes went from Lucifer to Puck to Alerian. "It's a conspiracy? Really? They're all working together? I thought they all hated one another."

"A convenient fiction that has allowed them to work in secret for many months, each of them putting their individual pieces in place," Daharan said.

"But they did not reckon for your involvement," Nathaniel observed.

"Correct," Daharan said. "And they knew that my willingness to remain silent would last only up to a point. I have been attempting to draw all the threads together for some time, and then to dissuade these three from enacting their plan, long before you knew me. But matters were greatly accelerated after Puck sent you to that dead world and manipulated you into killing the Cimice to release your shadow. Even then I tried to block them, to protect you, to protect humanity. When it seemed that their pieces were finally falling into place for their ultimate plan, I moved to stop them once and for all. And they betrayed me."

I understood immediately that this was almost worse than anything else these three had done. Despite all of their wrongdoing, Daharan had always tried to keep their family matters in the family. He had kept things hidden even from me, believing it better to take care of the matter quietly unless he was forced to otherwise. For the three brothers to reward Daharan's loyalty with betrayal—well, let's just say that it wouldn't sit well with a being of Daharan's character.

"How did they betray you?" J.B. asked.

"They imprisoned me. It took all three of them to do it, but they lured me from your home with promises of negotiation, and then trapped me in what they thought was an unbreakable prison," Daharan said. I couldn't see his eyes, as his back was to me, but for a moment I thought that there was a red light that flared on the faces of the other three.

"It *was* an unbreakable prison," Puck muttered, sounding pouty. "I spent a lot of time crafting that spell. I entwined it with the essence of your magic so you wouldn't be able to break out. I don't understand how it would fail."

"Obviously I should have done it myself rather than leave the matter to your incompetence," Lucifer hissed. "You were too busy pretending to be king of Faerie and lording your superiority over Oberon to give the matter the proper amount of attention."

"Like you would have had time to invest in Daharan's cage when you were playing house with Evangeline," Puck retorted.

"I was not 'playing house.' I was attempting to make

the commitment of a lifetime when she was brutally murdered," Lucifer said.

"Everyone knows Maddy didn't really kill her. My niece has a lot of bad qualities, but cold-blooded murder isn't one of them," Puck said dismissively. "You probably killed Evangeline yourself. It was the only way you'd ever be free of her. She stuck to you like static cling, and it was just as unattractive."

"Evangeline was loyal," Lucifer said.

"She was sickening, was what she was," Puck said. "And you would have gotten annoyed with her in a few months and then had her publicly executed under some pretense. Probably for bearing you another freak show of a son. Your kids just don't turn out right, do they? Not like mine."

He gave a smug, satisfied smile then, looking at Nathaniel, who frowned at this confusing paternal pride so soon after Puck had tried to blast him into oblivion.

Lucifer leapt on Puck then, punching him in the face. His brother came back swinging with ferocity, and soon the two of them were rolling on the ground, trading blows.

We all stared in silent shock at the spectacle of two of the oldest and most powerful creatures in the universe having a school-yard fight in the middle of a Chicago street.

"Enough," Daharan said. He had turned toward the other two, and I could see the calm and resolute anger still on his face.

Puck and Lucifer stopped rolling around. They scrambled to their feet, looking chastened.

I looked from Puck to Lucifer to Alerian to Daharan, and realized something I'd never realized before. Yes, they were magical and powerful and older than most galaxies. But they were nothing but children, and I did not have to fear them, and neither did anyone else. This was probably what everyone else was thinking, too, and that was affirmed a moment later when J.B. spoke.

"I'd say you both lost a lot of ground on the intimidation front," he said.

"Be careful," Puck said. "You are still my subject."

"No, he is not," Daharan said. "Henceforth, you are no longer the High King of Faerie. Nor are you master of the Grigori."

Lucifer looked shocked. "You cannot take that right from me, or from Puck."

"Lucifer," Daharan said. "You have not yet asked how I managed to break free from the unbreakable prison fashioned for me."

"I'll bite," Puck said. Despite his obvious fear of Daharan, his natural playful manner reasserted itself. He spoke in a singsong tone. "How did you break out of the prison, Daharan?"

Daharan smiled, and it was not the warm and gentle smile that protected me. It was a thing of cold and fury, and also of satisfaction.

"Our mother is awake."

Now even Alerian, always as calm as the still surface of a lake, turned pale. Puck looked like he might throw up.

"You lie," Lucifer said.

"You know that I cannot lie to you," Daharan said. "Our mother is awake, and she is not happy with the three of you."

I knew very little about the parents of these four. Daharan had once told me they were very ancient and elemental, and that they spent most of their time asleep. He'd also implied that it was better that I knew as little as possible about them, and I'd hoped that they would never wake up and decide to interfere in our lives.

"Is she coming here?" Puck asked. His lips were white.

Daharan shook his head. "She wishes you to come to her. Immediately."

Lucifer looked from me to Daharan. "This is all part of your own plan to keep Madeline and her child out of my clutches."

"If it is, then our mother certainly approves of my intentions over yours," Daharan said. "She can see the future with more clarity than any of us."

"What were their plans?" I asked curiously.

"Oh, the usual," Puck said breezily, although he still looked like he was on the verge of being sick. "Total dominion over the Earth, split three ways. No more hiding in the shadows or manipulating from afar. The three of us, worshiped and feared as gods."

"Knocking down whoever got in your way, I suppose. And you thought I would just let you do that?" I asked.

"We knew that you wouldn't let us do that," Puck said. "That was why we needed you to turn into Bad Maddy, because then you might come over to the fun side. Failing that, Lucifer would have Junior as a tool to get you to do what we wanted."

"So my son was just a means to an end for you?" I said.

"No," Daharan said before Lucifer could speak. "Your son is very important to the future of this planet. He has a destiny that will affect the course of humanity. Lucifer wanted that destiny in his hands, so he could pull the strings."

I didn't want to hear that my baby had a destiny, or that he was important to humanity's future. I wanted him to just be my own, my own little angel, the last tangible symbol of the love I had for Gabriel.

Much of this must have shown on my face, because Daharan said gently, "His destiny is a long way off. You still have time to be his mother, and for him to be your son."

He turned again to Lucifer. "And before I return you to the loving bosom of our mother, I want to ensure that you understand that Madeline and her son are no longer subject to your influence. They are protected by me always, and are no longer of your line."

"You cannot do that," Lucifer said. The color returned to his face in an instant as his anger rose.

"He already took care of that part himself," I put in. "He took away all the magic that came from his bloodline."

"From you, yes," Daharan said. "Not from your baby. Please bring the child to me."

Lucifer reached toward his brother. Daharan stared at Lucifer's hand until the Prince of Darkness dropped it at his side, clenched in a useless fist.

"Daharan, you cannot," Lucifer said. "Do not take him from me. He is mine. He belongs to my blood."

"You forfeited your rights by your actions," Daharan said.

He turned toward me. I was frozen in place, shaking my head from side to side.

"I'm not bringing him outside," I said. "He's safe inside, safe from *him*. Lucifer can't break down the door and take him. If I bring my baby outside, he'll snatch him up and run away and there won't be a thing I can do to stop it."

"I will stop it," Daharan said. "Madeline, you must trust me. I have never meant you or your child harm."

I looked up at Nathaniel. He shook his head. "It is too risky. He may be working with the other three. This may be a performance all for your benefit, to ease you into thinking the child would be safe if you brought him outside."

Daharan nodded, almost as if he were acknowledging the wisdom of Nathaniel's words. "I understand why you would think such a thing. But I assure you, with all of my heart, that I mean only to protect the child."

"Then go inside and do whatever you need to do," J.B. said. "Why should Maddy have to bring him outside?"

"Because Lucifer needs to see what will happen, and to understand that the child is lost to him forever. I do not believe you wish to invite him into your home, as the invitation will never be able to be rescinded," Daharan said.

I nodded. There was a reason I'd never invited Lucifer inside—once he came in, I'd never be able to get rid of him. Although Puck had gotten in, because of the jewel that I'd been tricked into taking. And as I realized this, I looked at Puck in puzzlement. If Puck could get in, and he and Lucifer were working on the same side, then why hadn't he just materialized in my living room and snatched the baby away?

Unless Puck didn't really give a damn about Lucifer's ambitions, and was still working some separate plan of his own.

He noticed me looking at him, and winked. I swear that Puck can read minds. Or at least my mind.

Now was the moment of truth. Nathaniel and Beezle had told me not to trust Daharan, that just because he'd never revealed an agenda didn't mean he didn't have one. And I had always insisted that Daharan was exactly what he claimed to be, and that they needed to stop being so suspicious.

"I don't like this," J.B. said, and Jude whined in agreement.

"You know how I feel," Nathaniel said. "And I know you have always kept your own counsel with regard to Daharan."

He spoke as if Daharan were not right there, listening to every word.

"Regardless of what you choose, I will defend your child with my life," Nathaniel said. "And you. Always."

Tears pricked at my eyes, and I wiped them away impatiently. "I know. And you know that if there's a chance that the baby will be free from Lucifer forever, then I have to take it."

He closed his eyes, like he'd known I was going to say that.

I felt almost no confidence in this decision. I trusted Daharan, but I wasn't certain he'd be able to fend off a truly determined Lucifer. Could I really risk my baby? Could I take this gamble?

Daharan's eyes, though fierce with fire, told me that I could. The first time I'd met him I'd felt like I was coming home. I'd never had a father, not really. Not someone who would stand between me and the world, and keep me safe and warm in a way I'd never been.

He would keep my baby the same way. He would stand between my child and the world. He would protect him from those who would harm him.

"Beezle!" I called. I knew that no matter how fascinated he was with the baby, he wouldn't be able to resist watching the show outside. My gargoyle is just about the nosiest thing going.

As expected, he immediately emerged from the front window of the house and landed on my shoulder.

"The kid's crying," he announced. "Samiel and I don't have the right parts to make him stop."

"Bring Adam out to me," I said.

"Adam, huh?" Beezle said. "What made you decide that?"

I shrugged. "I don't know. It just seemed right all of a sudden."

Puck snorted with laughter and we all looked at him. "Am I the only one who appreciates the irony here? You're trying to keep the baby away from Lucifer and you name him after the guy in his most famous story."

"He has a point," Beezle said.

"His name is Adam," I repeated. "And please ask Samiel to bring him outside."

Beezle gave me a sideways look. "Are you sure about this? Weren't we all distressed a half hour ago because we thought these three clowns were going to break a hole in the roof and take him away? It seems like bringing him outside plays right into their hands."

"Daharan says it is necessary," I said.

"'Daharan says,'" Beezle said flatly. "And where has Daharan been all this time?"

"I'll give you the recap later," I said. "Just bring Adam to me."

"I want to make sure my objections are on the record," Beezle said. "I don't trust Daharan."

He flew toward the house, grumbling to himself. It bugged me, the way that he had pretended Daharan wasn't there just like Nathaniel had.

"It does not injure my feelings," Daharan said to me, responding to the worried look I'd given him. "Beezle and Nathaniel are only attempting to protect those they love."

I half turned toward the house, watching for Samiel's appearance. A few moments later I saw him behind the glass of the front door, cradling the baby and looking uncertain.

Just as he was about to open the door, Lucifer and Alerian both lunged for Daharan at the same time. Daharan opened his palm and the two of them slammed into an invisible wall, falling to the ground. Puck began laughing hysterically.

"You're not really on their side at all, are you?" I asked him.

"Hell, no," he said. "I'm on my own side."

"I knew you would betray us," Lucifer snarled. "You're as changeable as the air itself. But the consequences will belong to all of us, so your attitude is of no matter."

Puck shook his head, still amused. "I was always our mother's favorite. Well, after Daharan. He is the firstborn and all that. Still, she never could stay angry with me for very long."

Lucifer's face twisted, and I could see the thoughts moving behind his eyes. He would get blamed for this, and Puck would walk free. Alerian said nothing. His expression never changed, although he seemed resigned to the fact that Daharan had won this round.

"And don't think he's on your side, either," Puck said, jerking his thumb toward Alerian. "Did you really think he was going to let you lead the supernatural army he was assembling here? All that business with the mayor and the caging of magical creatures—that was his idea. He was working his own angle, too."

Lucifer looked at Alerian, whose eyes did not flicker. "You would lead them against me."

Alerian nodded once. "Of course. Just as you, too, had your own plans in all of this, separate from ours."

"None of us are really reliable," Puck said, looking at me. "Well, except for the white knight, here. Daharan always does what he's supposed to do."

Samiel poked his head out the door, looking unsure. I waved him out, signing that it was okay.

Still, he hesitated. I walked up to the porch so he would see that it was really me, and that I wasn't under any kind of duress. Beezle was perched on his shoulder, looking grumpy. Adam was screaming, a red-faced bundle in Samiel's arms. I reached out for my baby.

"It's okay," I said, making sure Samiel was looking at me so he could read my lips. "Daharan is going to do something to protect him from Lucifer."

He snuggled Adam a little tighter, like he didn't want to let the baby go.

"Samiel," I said. "I am his mother. And I trust Daharan."

He finally released Adam into my arms, and my son quieted immediately. I kissed his forehead under the cute little cap that kept his head warm, and hoped like hell I wasn't making the biggest mistake of my life.

I walked back to the street, Samiel and Beezle following. Every person who had influenced my life for good or ill in the last several months was there, except Gabriel. And Gabriel's spirit lived on in our son.

Lucifer looked desperate as I approached, his skin drawn tight and bloodless over the carved bones of his face. "Madeline, don't do this. You could be a queen in my kingdom, the heir to all that I possess. Your son is far more important than you understand. Don't let Daharan take that away."

"I am not taking away his importance, only your ability to influence him. Or harm him," Daharan said.

He held his hands out for Adam, and I had to decide. I trusted him. I passed him my little bundle.

Adam's unfocused eyes searched for Daharan's face. He made a little cooing noise, and Daharan smiled down at him.

"No," Lucifer said again. "Please."

"You've never taken my wishes into account," I said, my voice cold. "Why should I consider yours?"

Daharan lifted Adam close to his face and closed his eyes as he placed his lips on the baby's forehead. The air filled with light and heat, a glow that grew from the point of contact to surround the two of them in a shining aura. Whatever Daharan was doing, I could feel that it was a good thing.

Beezle's mouth had dropped open. "Whoa."

"Whoa what?" I asked.

"You were right about Daharan. It's probably a first in the history of the world," Beezle said.

"I've been right about a few things before," I said.

"Your record is nothing compared to mine," Beezle said.

"What is he doing, anyway?" I asked, not wanting to be drawn into yet another pointless argument. Pointless because Beezle never conceded anything, so it was just a waste of energy. Maybe I was getting more mature now that I was a mother.

"He's infusing your son with his grace," Lucifer said, answering before Beezle could. I had never seen him so angry and defeated. "This is what Michael did to protect the children of myself and Evangeline so many centuries ago. He removed all trace of my magic, and replaced it with his own. I could not find the children or influence them because they would no longer answer the call of my blood. Until you. Until you acknowledged my blood inside you."

My heart surged in hope and happiness. "So we're both free of you, then?"

"Yes," Lucifer said. "You have gotten what you always wanted."

"And because Daharan is putting his grace into Maddy's child, he'll watch over him; isn't that right?" Beezle said.

"Yes," Puck said, looking amused at Lucifer's bitterness.

"Your Adam will be protected by Daharan always. So the three of us would essentially be picking a fight with Daharan if we tried to threaten or manipulate you as we have done in the past."

"We're free," I said. The word echoed in my head. *Free, free, free.*

The glow in the air receded. Adam kicked his little legs from side to side as Daharan kissed his cheek and then handed him back to me. Daharan seemed larger somehow, more dragon-like, but still not scary to me. I'd never really been frightened of him. I'd always known, in my heart, that Daharan would be good to me.

"I will watch over you, and him, always," he said. "Now I must take these three wayward children home."

Lucifer appeared sullen. Alerian was calm and collected, as always. And Puck's eyes danced with delight, almost as if he looked forward to the coming conflict.

"You needn't worry about the supernatural camp," Daharan said. "I have been to see the mayor and wielded my influence. His decree is being reversed as we speak, and everyone who was arrested is being returned to their homes."

"Thanks," I said. At least I didn't have that crisis to deal with. Of course, changing people's attitudes toward what was different from them was another problem. Maybe Jack could finally be useful on that front and spread some good propaganda for the preternatural among us.

"And now, Madeline, I bid you farewell," Daharan said. "Do not fear for the future of your child."

"Thank you," I said again, and before our eyes he transformed into the dragon I'd first met.

He scooped up his three brothers in his claws, and disappeared into the sky.

18

"WELL, THAT WAS AN UNUSUAL ENDING TO THINGS," Beezle said later. "You weren't required to destroy a single piece of property."

J.B. and Jack had returned to their homes. Jude and Samiel were downstairs in the spare apartment, moving Samiel's things from Chloe's place. My heart still hurt when I thought of Chloe, and the horrible way she'd been killed. It got me thinking that a lot of bad things had happened in this house, and maybe it was time for a change.

"Maybe we should buy a new house," I said to Nathaniel. He was sitting in a chair by the fire, the baby in his lap, his eyes drowsy. I was across from them, watching. My heart had never been so full of love.

Beezle snorted. "First of all, you have no money."

"I have this house. I could sell it."

"Yeah, I wonder what the resale value is on a hundred-year-old house that's been the site of two murders and assorted supernatural phenomena?" he said. "What you would get for this place wouldn't pay for a brick on a new condo."

"I have money," Nathaniel said quietly.

"What was that?" Beezle said, his hand at his ear.

"I have money," he repeated. "Lots of money, as a matter of fact. My father is wealthy and so am I."

Beezle looked outraged. "And you let Maddy act like a poor mouse all this time?"

"Nathaniel's always paid his fair share," I said. "He even paid me rent when he lived in the downstairs apartment. But I didn't know you were rich."

He shifted in his seat, looking embarrassed. "I thought you would not like it if you knew. Your pride might have kept you from accepting my help if necessary."

"It probably would have," I admitted. "But if you're going to be Adam's dad, then I guess we'd better talk about these things."

"*Am* I going to be his father?" he asked carefully, his eyes bright now, and no longer drowsy.

I took a deep breath. It was now or never. Beezle flew out of the room, muttering something about not wanting to get caught between two clueless people.

"Yes," I said. "Because I love you. I want you to stay. I want you to stay with me, with us, to be a family. Maybe we won't have a white picket fence and all that, but it will be ours. And Lucifer can't harm us anymore. I can finally think of the future for the first time in my life."

He closed his eyes for a moment, then looked at me again. "I have waited a long time to hear you say those words. You have made me very happy, Madeline."

Nathaniel rose, and crossed to me, and placed the baby in my arms. Then he bent to kiss me, and there was heat and promise there that had never been before. He had been so careful of me since I'd returned from that other planet, since he thought I had died there. In many ways he'd been a very chaste lover, but now he was telling me that was going to change, and soon.

He pulled away, resting his forehead against mine. "You need not worry that I will press my affections just now. The gargoyle has informed me that it is not healthy for a woman to engage in relations so soon after childbirth."

I choked, torn between laughter and annoyance. "I don't know which is worse—that Beezle knows about such a thing or that he discussed it with you."

"He apparently has been reading a child-care book. He has many 'helpful' things to tell us," Nathaniel said, and smiled.

My cell phone began to ring, and Nathaniel went to fetch it from the dining room table.

"It's J.B.," I said as I clicked it open. "What's up?"

"Sokolov was fired," J.B. said. "Thought you would want to know."

"How did that happen?" I asked. It seemed too good to be true. Everything was falling into place.

"Upper management got wind of that plan he had to get rid of you. He was working with one of Lucifer's kids, that one that you told me to ask about," J.B. said.

"Zaniel," I said.

"Well, I guess somebody decided that was the last straw. Apparently he's been off the reservation for a while, using up Agency resources in an attempt to take you down. The board decided that they had enough, so he's out."

"It sure is nice not to have to worry about being attacked from all sides for a change," I said. "I might even get a full night's sleep for the first time in six months."

"I won't," J.B. said. "Puck is gone, so there's a huge power vacuum in Faerie. There's going to be a lot more infighting and a lot less posturing there for a while."

"I'm sorry," I said, and meant it.

"You're just lucky that Lucifer took you out of the running as heir to his kingdom. He's got a lot of kids, and I bet it's going to get messy over there. In the court of the Grigori, too," he added.

I hadn't thought about that. I could, I suppose, technically be still linked to the Grigori by my ties to Azazel. But it wasn't my problem, really. Plenty of others would vie for the head of court, and I didn't want any part of that mess.

"I just thought you'd want to know that you don't have anything else to worry about from this quarter," he said. "And I hope that you invite me to the wedding."

"I love you," I said, laughing.

"And I will always love you," he said, although he meant it a little differently than me. Then he hung up before I could say anything else.

Nathaniel was watching me with a frown on his face. "I feel like I should be jealous, but I am not."

"You don't have anything to be jealous of," I said. "J.B. and I—well, I guess you could say we were never meant to be. There was a time, I suppose, a window where if he'd only told me about his feelings, he could have had a chance."

"But once Gabriel arrived, there was no one else," Nathaniel said.

"Yes," I said. "But now Gabriel is gone, and there is you. And there is no one for me but you."

Nathaniel knelt at my side, and kissed me again. Adam wiggled in my lap between us.

"Maddy," Beezle said, his voice breathless.

I broke away from Nathaniel at the urgency in Beezle's voice.

"What is it?"

"The shapeshifter," Beezle said. "He's standing in the middle of the backyard. And so is Sokolov. And he's asking to see Jude."

"Sokolov?" I asked. "The shapeshifter? I thought Alerian was his master, that it was all part of the big Lucifer/Puck/Alerian scam. What does this have to do with Jude?"

Beezle shook his head. "I guess the shapeshifter wasn't connected to that mess. And I don't know what it's got to do with Jude, but he and Samiel are going outside now."

Nathaniel and I hurried after Beezle and down the back stairs. I stopped when we reached the back porch. Samiel stood there, watching Jude face off against Sokolov. The shapeshifter stood to one side, wearing the face of someone I'd never seen before.

"What's happening?" I asked Samiel.

Remember how Daharan said that Jude's problems came from his past? I guess that guy isn't really Sokolov.

"No, he isn't," Beezle said, and his voice was full of wonder. "I never looked at him properly before, all the way down. I should have seen. I should have known."

"Who is it?" I asked impatiently.

"Michael," he said.

"Michael?" I said, looking at Sokolov's fat little body and bald head. "Michael the archangel? All this time?"

No wonder Michael had seemed familiar to me when we had met. It wasn't that his power had given birth to the Agency. It was because I'd seen him before, and had not known.

"Yes," Sokolov said, and then he was not Sokolov. He

was tall and golden and beautiful, and his eyes were made of flame. "All this time."

"J.B. just told me you were fired from the Agency," I said. "What were you doing there in the first place?"

"What do you think?" Michael snarled. "Keeping an eye on you, as I was told to do. Trapped in a human body, hiding my power. And the board has finally released me. They have always been suspicious of my connection with Lucifer. And once they discovered my other activities they let me go. All my centuries of devotion have been for naught."

"The board? You mean, the board is . . ." I pointed my finger toward the sky.

"Yes," Michael said. "They told me to watch you, to ensure you did not become a threat to humans. And I did what I was supposed to do."

"You were *supposed* to torture J.B.? To set the Retrievers on me? To act like a petulant child at every turn?" I asked, feeling anger rising inside me. Adam made a little noise in my arms.

"You would act thus if you were more powerful than the sun and forced to submit to humans," Michael said. "But all of my actions were approved and condoned by the board. All of them, except two. Working with Lucifer's son, and working against Judas's pack."

Jude stared at him. "You killed my friends. My family. Why?"

Michael's eyes narrowed, and it seemed the flame in them rose higher. "You were responsible for the death of the one we loved best."

Jude growled. "You know very well that was not my fault. Lucifer tricked me."

"It is by your actions that it occurred," Michael said.

"And I have been watching you for many centuries, waiting for an opportunity to hurt you most. When I discovered Alerian's creature, I knew I had found a way."

I shook my head, pulling Adam close to me. Nathaniel hovered protectively at my side, keeping an eye on the shapeshifter in case he decided to attack. But the shifter just stood there like a broken robot, its face blank.

"So everything that happened—the attacks on this house, the killing of Evangeline—that was all part of your plan to get back at me?" No wonder the shifter had been able to work its magic inside the house. Only Agents could cross the line of a domicile and use their power freely. Michael's power had started the line of Agents in the first place.

"And Judas," Michael said. "Do not forget that. It would hurt him if you were hurt, as it would hurt Lucifer to discover you killed his fiancée."

"I hate to tell you this, but Lucifer never believed that farce in the first place," I said. "He just wanted an excuse to lock me up and take my baby, and you gave him what he wanted."

"And yet somehow you are standing here," Michael said. "Despite all of my attempts and all of my machinations, you have managed to escape me over and over, and Lucifer's heart is never harmed, and neither is Judas's."

"You won't have to worry about Lucifer or his heart for a while," I said. "He's been called back to his mother, and I think there's going to be a power void in the Grigori for a while. Oh, and Lucifer's brother Daharan is watching over me and my kid, so don't think that messing with us will affect the Morningstar anymore."

"I no longer care about you," Michael said. "I only want to kill this traitor, so that I can finally rest after all these years."

"I told you, Lucifer tricked me," Jude said. "I loved him as much as you did. You have no idea how I've suffered all these years, knowing I was responsible for his fate."

"I do not care for your sufferings," Michael said. "I only want it to be over."

He lunged for Jude, his fingers twisting into claws, reaching for Jude's throat. I thought Jude would change into a wolf and tear out Michael's throat, but instead he defended himself as a human, with fists and teeth and the knife that he always kept in his boot.

For a moment I wondered why, because Jude would have a very clear advantage as a wolf. Then I realized that his guilt motivated him to do this, to give Michael a chance to kill him.

I wanted to shout at him, but I was afraid I would distract him and then Michael would move in for the kill.

In the dark it was hard to make out one from the other as limbs punched and kicked and blood splattered. There was just enough light to tell that the fighting was savage and bloodthirsty. Jude wasn't going to just give in, and Michael was motivated by the contemplation of vengeance for more than two thousand years.

Suddenly it was over. I couldn't really see how it happened, but Michael was on his back and Jude was at his throat with the knife. Jude's face was visible in the glare of the streetlamp from the alley, and I saw him hesitate.

"It would be a mercy," Michael said, and I realized something then. He'd been cast out by the board. He was no longer welcome home. He was just like Lucifer.

"I don't see why I should be merciful to you," Jude said, and he stood.

Michael rose to his feet, his white angel's wings covered in blood. He was no longer powerful, no longer the first of the host. He was fallen. He looked at all of us, and I could see the flame in his eyes was dimming.

He said not another word, but took to the air, and disappeared in the night.

"He will go to the Grigori," Nathaniel said.

"Fine with me," I said. "They can have him."

Jude's face was impassive, half in shadow and half in light. "It is over, then. I must find Wade and tell him that the threat to the pack is gone."

"I understand," I said. "Go."

He turned into a wolf and leapt over the fence, racing away. I think he needed not only to see Wade, but to run fast and free for as long as possible. He needed to outrun the grief in his heart.

Beezle sighed. "At least there isn't another dead body to get rid of."

I wondered whether Nathaniel kept tossing the bodies in the same place, and whether the police were going to start to wonder if there was a serial killer in our neighborhood. Then I realized that with all the other stuff that happened in our neighborhood, a serial killer was probably the least of their worries.

"What about the shapeshifter?" I asked Beezle. Adam was starting to fuss in my arms.

The shifter had stood perfectly still throughout the battle between Michael and Jude. He was still posed like a statue at the edge of the yard. I wanted to approach him, but not while I was holding Adam.

"I'll take him," Nathaniel said, lifting the baby away from me.

"I'll go with you," Beezle said, knowing what I was thinking.

"And what will you do if he attacks?" I asked skeptically.

"Slay him with my wit," Beezle said. "Besides, I think he's broken. He hasn't moved at all."

I cautiously approached the shifter. The shifter's eyes registered my presence, but that was all.

This was the thing that had broken through the defenses of my house. It had taken my guise and committed more than one murder. And yet I felt sorry for it. The shifter had no will of its own. Its will came from his master, and now his master was gone.

"Did Alerian make you?" I asked.

"Yes," it said. "And forgot me, for many years. Then Michael found me, and gave me purpose again."

The shifter was too powerful a weapon to anyone who found and controlled it. I couldn't let it leave, and I didn't have the stomach to master it myself.

"Give me your hand," I said to it.

It put its palm in mine, willingly, trustingly. I sent a little questing thread of magic from me into its body, looking for the place where his magic was born. I found it where his heart should have been, and instead there was a changing cloud, a little ball of power that could become whatever its master wished it to be.

I sent my magic inside that cloud, untangling the knots that held the shifter together. The air filled with little droplets of silver water, like the shifting surface of Alerian's eyes. The water floated up and dissolved as little by little the shifter disappeared.

After a few moments, it was all over.

"Well," Beezle said. "Yet another unexpected ending. You've hardly set anything on fire for days. Are you feeling all right? Do you want to burn the shed down just to get it out of your system?"

I laughed and walked toward the house. Nathaniel and Samiel had returned inside with Adam. "I think we should buy a new place. Too many bad things have happened here. And maybe we'll be able to keep the address away from Jack Dabrowski this time."

"I doubt it," Beezle said. "But we can have a new house if you want to."

"I want to," I said as we climbed the stairs back up to my apartment. Nathaniel passed Adam back to me, and I smiled down at him.

"You know what I want?" Beezle asked.

"What?"

"Chinese takeout."

"Pork dumplings?" I said, picking up the phone.

"Pork dumplings!" he said, raising his fist in the air.

I looked down into the face of my child, my beautiful Adam, and was grateful. Grateful for him, and grateful for the man who had fathered him as well as the one who would be his father. I was grateful. We were safe. We were home.

I picked up the phone, and placed the order.

FROM
CHRISTINA HENRY

BLACK HEART
A BLACK WINGS NOVEL

Former Agent of death Madeline Black is caught in a turf war between a group of fae and a disturbingly familiar foe—and discovers she cannot escape the twisted plots of her grandfather Lucifer no matter where she runs...

PRAISE FOR THE BLACK WINGS NOVELS

"Great snarky dialogue, continuous action, excellent world-building and innovative twists on urban fantasy conventions are par for the course in Henry's series."
—*RT Book Reviews*

"Prepare yourself for plenty of snark, plenty of action and plenty of fun from this endearing and exciting series."
—*My Bookish Ways*

christinahenry.net
facebook.com/authorChristinaHenry
facebook.com/AceRocBooks
penguin.com

M1504T0614